A Prophet who loved Her

L E K E   A P E N A

Library of Congress Control Number:		2020915616
ISBN:	Hardcover	978-1-6641-1234-6
	Softcover	978-1-6641-1233-9
	eBook	978-1-6641-1232-2

Print information available on the last page.

Rev. date: 08/19/2020

To order additional copies of this book, contact:
Xlibris
UK TFN: 0800 0148620 (Toll Free inside the UK)
UK Local: 02036 956328 (+44 20 3695 6328 from outside the UK)
www.Xlibrispublishing.co.uk
Orders@Xlibrispublishing.co.uk
787729

For Isabella, Daddy's girl. Always.

PROLOGUE

June 1990

After everything they had been through together, after the promises he had made to her, Elijah could not believe what he was about to do to the woman he loved. He'd had a choice to make, and the decision he had come to still took him by surprise.

He was going to break up with Esther Nubari.

For good.

If not for the drawn-out war between his heart and his head, fighting like two warriors in the arena of his conscience, he would have broken up with Esther three weeks ago. Instead, he had left the decision until today. The day they were due to fly to Chicago.

Terminal five was teeming with activity. Elijah sat on a metal waiting chair. Around him, holidaymakers were dragging their suitcases, clutching the handles tight as if their whole lives were inside. Many of them wore sunglasses, Hawaiian shirts and denim shorts, ready for their summer breaks. Some of them had brought their energetic offspring, who were running around the terminal's wide-open space, all smiles and eyes bright with innocent happiness.

With a sense of longing, Elijah watched these children in their carefree bubble. *How easy life is when you're so young.* At twenty-two, he could feel adulthood standing in front of him like a looming giant, intimidating in its size and significance.

Sighing to himself, Elijah buried his head in his hands. Even now, he was thinking about the last time he had made love to Esther. He recalled, with a pained smile, how he had lain on top of her that night, gliding in and out of her, deriving pleasure as well giving it. For an hour, maybe longer, his soul, his mind, had concentrated only on the warmth of her rich, caramel-coloured body. That would be the last time he would enter her, and the thought made his diaphragm clench.

Up until three weeks ago, Elijah would never have comprehended what he was about to do. His relationship with Esther had made sense. He would graduate from university and begin a new life with her, a beautiful girl he knew he loved, who had survived Brixton with him. She had big dreams to sing in front of millions, like Whitney Houston. And he would be by her side as they conquered the world together.

That is what he had promised her.

But promises can sometimes be like writing on the pavement in chalk, eventually the rain comes and washes the words away.

His guilt was taking pleasure in tormenting him. The memory of what he had said to Esther when they sat beside the pool in

Brockwell Lido, covered by a ghostly fog, engulfed his mind. Even as he shut his eyes, he could not rid himself of the memory, or erase the words he had said or extinguish the false hope he had allowed to grow and burn within her.

But what had changed his mind? It was his father. As much as Elijah loved Esther, he could not ignore what his father had said. He now had a great purpose, a calling from God. And it was a calling bigger than his love for Esther.

A beeping noise came from Elijah's Motorola pager, and he pulled it out from the right pocket of his jeans. Esther had paged him.

Look up potato head. I can see you

Elijah looked up. Esther was standing some feet away from him, glorious in all her curvaceous Nigerian beauty with her dangling gold hoop earrings and her curly afro, big and bold like her personality. Elijah moaned quietly to himself. *Why does she have to look so damn fit today?* Esther sauntered towards him, dragging her suitcase behind her. Elijah had to summon all his discipline not to let her hips sway the decision he had made.

Esther came to a halt in front of him, and he caught a whiff of the coconut oil she always used to nourish her voluminous hair. Would this be the last time he would breathe that familiar scent?

"I'm impressed babe; you got here before me. You're the only Nigerian who comes on time in the whole of south London, you know that?" Esther said. Her playful tone made Elijah's chest contract in pain. After a quick embrace, she stepped back and studied him with her eyebrows raised. "Where's your suitcase? Have you checked in already?"

Elijah took a deep breath. There was no going back on his choice now.

"Esther, I'm so sorry," Elijah said, his voice on the brink of shattering into a million fragments, like a glass balancing on the edge of a sink. "I can't come with you to Chicago anymore … I'm going to be a pastor."

For Esther, Heathrow Airport was more than just an airport; it was a gateway to a new life and a fresh start.

Dragging her suitcase, she could feel the rush of excitement propelling her forward as if a jet pack were strapped onto her, thrusting her upwards to the stars. No longer would her life be confined to the streets of Lambeth or tethered to the scrutiny and disapproval of her parents.

Walking through Heathrow Airport's busy Terminal Five, Esther's gaze caught on a family standing by one of the check-in desks – a father, a mother and a daughter – who were laughing together, like a perfect, conservative family that had stepped out from the pages of a Christian pamphlet. As Esther looked at them with a deep sense of resentment and a tingle of longing, which irritated her, her memory went back to the last conversation she had with her parents. It was probably the final conversation she would have with them for a long time – possibly forever.

Her mother had gone into a state of inconsolable grief, collapsed onto her knees, her hands clasped together as she begged her daughter to stay in Brixton.

"Please, Esther, please don't go," her mother wailed. Her pleading had made Esther briefly reconsider her decision to start a new life in Chicago. But it was her father who had cemented it again.

"Go then," her father said, standing in their box-sized living room at the family's tiny flat in Loughborough Estate. His tone was frosty and detached, his dark-skinned face emotionless as he looked at her. Esther stood by the front door with both her suitcase and her body halfway out. She was ready to release herself entirely from her father's grip.

Through gritted teeth, he added, "Don't come grovelling back to us. Understand this, Esther, if you open that door and leave this house, you are no longer my daughter."

Esther met his blank stare with a fire burning in her eyes. "I don't give a fuck. I hate you." With those final words, Esther stepped out of the flat, not bothering to look at her father one last time as she slammed the door shut behind her.

But all of that was the closing paragraph in that chapter of her life. It was time to start a new chapter with Elijah.

Esther came to a halt and scanned the busy terminal, trying to see if she could spot Elijah among the holidaymakers and airport staff. A smile crossed her face as she saw him sitting on one of the blue waiting chairs a few feet away from her, his head buried in his hands. *Is he tired already?*

Esther took out her small Motorola pager from her jeans. She smiled cheekily to herself as she typed her message:

Look up potato head. I can see you

Once Esther pressed send, she waited for a minute, anticipating Elijah's reaction. Chuckling to herself, she watched as he took out his pager, checked his screen and cocked his head up in her direction. A sort of uncertain half-smile formed across Elijah's face, as if he were not sure whether smiling back at her was the appropriate response. *But why wouldn't it be?* As Esther walked towards him, she sensed something unusual in his demeanour. When he stood up to greet her, it seemed as if the very act of getting up from the bench caused him great pain. Having known Elijah for a decade now, she could tell something was wrong.

"I'm impressed babe; you got here before me. You're the only Nigerian who comes on time in the whole of south London, you know that?" Esther said, attempting to cheer him up.

Elijah's hug felt stiff and reluctant. Esther pulled back and examined him. Dressed in baggy denim jeans, a white t-shirt and a blue bomber jacket, Elijah did not look like someone who was about to travel. He did not even have any luggage with him.

"Where's your suitcase? You checked-in already?" Esther asked.

She saw the pain wash over Elijah's face as he cast his eyes downwards. Even before he spoke, Esther knew what he was going to say.

"Esther, I'm so sorry," Elijah said, in a voice so shaky his words seemed to limp from his mouth. "I can't come with you to Chicago … I'm going to be a pastor."

Although she had heard what Elijah said, the meaning of the words did not register immediately, but once her mind swallowed their significance, she suddenly felt as if someone had spun her around fast. Without thinking, she uselessly said, "What?"

"I'm going to be a pastor. I've been called to the ministry," Elijah said, his voice still wobbling. "I have to stay in Brixton."

Esther's initial shock had now been overtaken by rising anger, coming from deep within her chest. Her breathing became heavy. "And you're telling me this now?" She could feel her hands trembling on the handle of her suitcase and felt as if she had lost the ability to control them.

"I was thinking about it for the last three weeks, but I decided today," Elijah said, his voice now threatening to break completely. "I've been so uncertain about it, but I can't ignore my calling."

Everything around Esther seemed to go silent. A kind of dread, thick and terrible, engulfed her. Her heart began to beat quicker against her chest, and she thought, at that moment, that she would collapse. They had made love three days ago. He had kissed her and whispered in her ear that he loved her. Now he was doing this to her, breaking her heart, after everything they been through.

Elijah tried to touch her hand, but she flung the gesture away as if it would burn her.

"Don't touch me."

"Esther, listen—"

But Esther did not care what else Elijah had to say. A head-spinning mixture of pain, anger and confusion consumed her. How could Elijah, the only boy who had accepted her for everything that she was, betray her? No, she couldn't do this. All she wanted to do now was get on that plane and leave London. Leave it behind forever.

"Esther, I still love you. I can take it back if—"

"If what? I change? I become a proper Christian girl? Live my whole fucking life pretending to be something I'm not for you? No Elijah, I'm not doing that again."

Elijah's lips parted, but no words materialised. Instead, he stood on the spot, wearing the expression of someone struggling to comprehend what was happening. Esther's anger towards him swelled. He wasn't even brave enough to be confident in his own choices.

"No, don't fucking bother," Esther said, feeling the burning tears now running down her face without her permission. "I don't need my parents, and I don't need you. I am strong on my own. How could you break your promise to me?"

"Esther, please—"

But it was too late for Elijah and too late to save their relationship. Esther turned away from him and walked towards the security gate, clearing the tears in her eyes with the sleeves of her denim jacket as she clutched to her suitcase. From behind her, she heard Elijah call her name but forced herself to block his voice from seeping into her heart and making her turn back to him.

At the gate, Esther showed the check-in officer her British passport. As the woman took it from her, opened it and examined its contents, Esther could hear Elijah coming closer, still calling after her.

"Esther, wait. I'm sorry."

The check-in officer handed Esther's passport back and beckoned for her to walk through the security gate. Just as Esther was about to make her way through, she felt Elijah put his hand on her shoulder, but she shrugged it off. This time she turned to face him, bitter and enraged.

"Have a good life, Prophet."

With those final words, Esther stormed through the gate. She did not look back at the old life she was leaving behind. Her life in London had brought her too much pain and disappointment, right to the very end. Maybe, by starting all over again in Chicago, she would finally find the peace and sense of purpose that London had never given her.

18 YEARS LATER

CHAPTER 1

June 2008

Draped in expensive Nigerian attire, Elijah sat on the far right of the back seat in the black Mercedes limousine.

Beside him was his mother, Dinah Oduwole. Seated beside her was his younger brother by two years, Jairus Oduwole, and opposite Elijah sat his junior sister, Mary Akinyemi. All four of them remained silent as the limousine drove through Peckham High Street on a humid Sunday afternoon.

A few yards behind the limousine, two large white horses trotted down the road, pulling a matching white carriage. An elmwood coffin, carrying the body of Elijah's late father, Pastor Emmanuel Oduwole, lay inside.

In both Yoruba and Christian tradition, death is a celebration of a life lived rather than a life lost. Death does not mean the end of life but the start of a new one. Still, a week ago, when Jairus had broken the news that his father had passed away, he knew it would be woven into the fabric of his soul for as long as he lived.

His father had been the lighthouse in Elijah's life, guiding him whenever he felt lost or uncertain, and his absence left a void. But Elijah took solace in the belief that his father was with the Lord now.

For as long as Elijah could remember, his father had served the Lord with an unwavering fervour that was renowned across Lambeth. Such dedication to serving Christ would be rewarded in the afterlife. But today, in the realm of the living, they would celebrate his father's accomplishments.

And it was going to be a big celebration, the type of party only Nigerians could pull off. Elijah had made sure of that.

The influence his father had cultivated across the African and Caribbean community in Lambeth, from Brixton to Clapham and beyond, meant that the funeral was never going to be an understated affair. Elijah had spent every day, every hour and every second God had given him to plan the lavish funeral with meticulous precision. It had been funded mainly by the Oduwole family, but there were also significant contributions from the five hundred regular members of the Pentecostal Church of Christ in Peckham. Pastor Emmanuel Oduwole was loved by many.

The limousine began to slow down on Commercial Way as it approached the destination a few metres away. Elijah turned towards the window and peered through the glass. Founded in the seventies by his father and his father's younger brother, who had died many years ago, the Pentecostal Church of Christ in

Peckham was one of the biggest churches in Lambeth – solid and impressive – rising above all the buildings in its vicinity.

Looking at the church now, a memory suddenly played in Elijah's mind. Around the age of sixteen, he had sat by his father one evening and asked him about its origins. His father had explained that the building took severe damage in the Second World War during The Blitz, but the walls had never crumbled because it was God's will that the Oduwole family would use it one day to spread the Lord's message.

As a result, the church had a distinctly weathered appearance, as if it had been in Peckham for centuries. Large gothic windows stood out amongst the light-brown brickwork, and the sun bathed the umber coloured tiled roofs with a glorious light as though heaven were genuinely shining down on it. The church had impressed Elijah as a young boy, and today, as it did every Sunday and every other day he visited, it still impressed him as a forty-year-old man.

"Everyone feeling okay?" Jairus asked, straightening the sleeves of his snow-white, long-sleeved kaftan.

"We are fine," their mother replied, in a soft yet firm voice, still heavy with a Yoruba accent despite having lived in London for well over three decades. Elijah watched his mother studying her adult children for a moment, staring at each of them with her dark eyes. As she did, he noticed that the light-brown skin beneath her eyelids had become puffy and saggy with the weight of age. "Your father would be so proud of you all today."

Elijah rested his right hand on his mother's shoulder. "Thank you, Mother." He then looked at Mary and smiled at her. Mary returned the smile and reached out her left hand to hold Elijah's for a moment. His sister was radiant in her white and gold *iro* and her *buba* decorated with yellow, flower-shaped designs. Her costume was completed with a gold-coloured *gele* around her head.

Jairus had already opened the door of the limousine on his side, and he turned to Elijah with a look of irritation. "We're here. Let us go inside."

Together, the Oduwole family stepped out of the car. Elijah straightened the sleeves of his white kaftan, identical to that of his younger brother. The only difference was that Elijah wore a gold *agbada* that hung over his shoulders and reached down to the bottom of his knees.

Elijah took his mother's hand and they walked towards the entrance of the church with Jairus and Mary following behind them. As they did, Elijah could not help but smile to himself. The Oduwoles looked and carried themselves like a royal family. In a way, they were royalty – a respected family that had preached the teachings of Christianity from the sandy and broken roads of Osogbo all the way to the concrete streets of Lambeth.

With his father's passing, it fell to Elijah to uphold the legacy of the Oduwole family as God's advocates. As he entered the church and met the mostly brown faces of the four-hundred-strong congregation, Elijah felt a wave of pride and purpose wash over him.

The torch of his father's and grandfather's legacy was in his hands now, and he intended to keep it burning fiercely. He had sacrificed so much to reach this point in his life.

This was his calling.

"In Isaiah 57:2, it is said that 'those who walk uprightly enter into peace; they find rest as they lie in death.'"

Elijah stood at a podium in the front of the church hall with a microphone next to his lips. Hundreds of faces stared back at him, eyes burning with respect and recognition. It was in these moments, preaching the scripture, that Elijah understood the great responsibility he held as an ordained pastor.

"My father was a man who walked righteously with God for all of his life. He lived every day as a loving Christian. This love extended to his family." At this, Elijah paused to look at his mother sitting in the front row and nodded at her before he continued.

"It extended to his community. It extended to every soul that crossed his path. He walked uprightly in all that he did, and Jesus was always the centre of his life. While I mourn my father's passing, I'm happy knowing that in death, he has found peace with the Lord. In the end, is it not peace that we all seek? Praise the Lord."

As if the Holy Spirit had sent an electric shock through the church hall, the bodies of everyone in the congregation jolted to life. People bellowed "Hallelujah!" and "Amen!" from the depths of their lungs. Their voices reverberated off the walls in one thunderous roar.

For Elijah, it was not the outpouring of love and gratitude from the crowd that made him swell with emotion, causing tears to trickle down his cheeks. It was the moment he caught his mother beaming at him, tears sliding down her puffy, light-brown cheeks as she joined in the rapturous applause, lit up with what could only be pride for her eldest son.

After the church service had finished, the funeral transitioned into an open-casket service so people could pay their final respects to the great Pastor Emmanuel Oduwole.

Elijah and Jairus stood together by their father's casket, greeting the many people –business leaders, young students and even politicians – from Lambeth and other parts of London that had known and respected their father. After the funeral, their father's body would be flown back to Nigeria and finally laid to rest alongside his younger brother and their grandfather at the Pentecostal Church of Christ in Osogbo.

By late afternoon, the entire funeral liturgy had come to an end. Those who wanted to pay last respects had done so and left. Some of the congregation remained in the church's main hall, either engaging in conversation, switching between Yoruba and English, or devouring plates of jollof rice and meat that had been prepared by Elijah's mother and other female members of the church. As soon as the casket was closed and taken out of the church, the party could begin. Afro-juju music, which had been Elijah's father's favourite music genre, would play from the rented sound system, and cases of Supermalt and Guinness were lined up, ready to be gulped down in droves by the men and women.

Standing side by side, Elijah and Jairus stood in front of the open casket, looking upon their father's lifeless yet peaceful face. It felt melancholic but oddly comforting to Elijah that this was the last time he would lay eyes on his father.

"Do you remember that proverb father said to us when we came to see him at the hospital?" Jairus asked, without looking up. "The final time we'd see him alive." Although he was standing right next to Elijah, his voice seemed far away.

With a tired smile, Elijah turned to face Jairus and put his right hand on his younger brother's shoulder. "It's been a very long week, Jairus. You're going to have to remind me. Father told us many proverbs."

"It's been a long week for everyone, big brother. But what he said was *'where you fall, you should know that it is God who pushed you'*."

"Oh, that one. What about it?"

"I've been thinking a lot lately. Why do you think he told us that?"

Elijah heard his brother's question but did not answer him immediately. Instead, he turned away from Jairus's face, back to his father. He did not look dead but more like he had been drugged into a deep sleep, laid out with his arms folded across his chest in his favourite white *agbada* and plain green *fila* on his head. His father had never had a flamboyant fashion sense; he had led a reserved and conservative life.

"Maybe, in his wisdom, father was telling us not to be afraid of the challenges we will face now that he's gone," Elijah finally said, still staring at his father's body. "Whenever we fall, it's nothing God has not prepared us for."

Elijah felt that his brother wanted to say something to him but then seemed to decide against it. This was unusual, since Jairus had a habit of always needing to express his opinion – a trait that led to many arguments between the two of them over the years.

"I'm going to tell mother that we are ready to move father's casket into the car," Jairus said after a few minutes of reflective silence between them. "The sooner we can have father's body in Osogbo, the better."

Elijah nodded. "Okay. Thanks, Jairus."

No sooner had his brother hurried away, Elijah's eight-year-old nephew, Joshua, dressed in a purple *dashiki* outfit, ran towards him. Joshua was his younger sister's only child. Although Dinah Oduwole had wanted more grandchildren from her daughter, Mary did not share the same enthusiasm, and Elijah could not blame her. Joshua seemed to have been born with an unlimited supply of mischief in his veins – enough for five kids. He flung himself onto Elijah's right leg and hugged it tightly.

"Good afternoon, Uncle, "Joshua said, beaming up at Elijah.

"Hello, Joshua," Elijah replied, bending down so he could face his nephew. "Where are your mummy and daddy?"

"Joshua, I told you not to run in the church. Do you want me to pull your ears, O?"

Elijah stood up and saw Kunle Akinyemi, his sister's husband, walking towards him. As always, Kunle had the look of a man that stress followed like a shadow. With each step, his brown *agbada* fell to one side, forcing him to keep pulling it back into position. Reaching them, he gave his son a hard tap on the back of his head, which triggered a long-buried memory within Elijah of his father doing the same to him when he was a young boy.

"*Oya*, go and find your mum," Kunle said to Joshua. Ignoring his father's earlier warning not to run in the church, Joshua darted off in another direction. Kunle rubbed his forehead and sighed heavily.

"Children, what a wonderful gift from God," Elijah said, smiling despite the pain that pricked at him as he said it. "Sorry I haven't come to visit you and Mary in a while."

"No need to apologise. Mary has been giving me *wahala* about the funeral all week, so I can only imagine what you've been going through. Sorry, *oga*." Sighing with exhaustion, Kune removed his *fila* and wiped the sweat on his brow before placing it back on his head. "Anyway, there is a woman outside who wants to see you."

"A woman? Did you ask her name?"

Kunle closed his eyes, put his hands on his forehead and shook his head. "I didn't even ask. My head is somewhere else today."

"Don't worry. Thanks for letting me know. I'll go see who she is." Just as Elijah began to turn away, he looked back at Kune and smirked. "Oh, and why is your *agbada* so big?"

"I don't know, ask your sister," Kunle moaned. "We've been married for ten years; you would think she knows my size by now. Honestly."

Elijah chuckled, said goodbye to his brother-in-law and then proceeded to make his way through the church hall towards the front entrance. As he went past, members of the church nodded towards him in acknowledgement or made passing remarks praising his service. Elijah must have thanked dozens of people before finally reaching the entrance of the church. He pushed open the red wooden doors and stepped outside.

When he saw her, it was like someone had thrown a speeding leather ball to his chest without warning.

He could barely catch his breath.

Wearing a long, tight navy skirt with an orange and yellow shirt, Esther Nubari stood in front of him.

Whatever words that were supposed to come from Elijah's mouth were lost in his throat.

Esther's lips slowly formed into a shy half-smile.

"Hello, Elijah. It's been a long time."

CHAPTER 2

June 2008

Eighteen years. Has it really been that long?

Elijah was shocked to find that so much time had passed since he had last seen Esther. Looking at her earlier today from the steps of his church, the intervening years had seemed to collapse on each other like clothes in a laundry basket.

When Esther had taken that plane to Chicago, Elijah forced the romantic love he felt for her to retreat into the remotest corners of his mind. There, he allowed his love for her to bleed out like a wounded animal and die. For years, Elijah did not hear from or see Esther. He made no effort to find out how she was doing in America or if she was even still living there. It would have been too painful. But that all changed when Esther's voice unexpectedly found him again.

It was around 1994. He had been driving to work, listening to Choice FM – an unwritten ritual of his morning commute.

DJ 279, the radio station's most popular presenter at the time, championed a lot of indie hip hop music from America. That morning, he had announced, with much excitement, that he would be playing an R&B song that was gaining popularity in the US. The song had been recorded by a female artist who grew up in Brixton. As soon as he heard the voice singing over the silky, slow R&B tempo, a jolt rushed through his body.

Her voice had changed, not so dramatically that Elijah could not recognise it, but she had developed a noticeable American inflection, which mixed with her British accent. This union of tones created a distinct but curious singing voice, like combining two flavours of ice cream that gave you an unexpected but not unpleasant taste.

Esther's booming soprano sailed confidently across the track. Elijah's ears caught the rhythm quickly – it was the type of song that was designed to be catchy, so it stayed with you long after you had listened to it. Smiling inwardly, Elijah remembered one of the reasons he had fallen in love with Esther. From the first time he had heard her sing at his church when they were young, Esther's voice had the power to grip him and hold his attention. As he listened to her sing from the radio, this had not changed.

The song was called 'Choices'. When Elijah had researched it later, he discovered that it had entered the US Billboard Hot 100 chart at fifty and climbed to number three. It had beaten songs from established artists at the time like Boyz II Men and Brandy; music journalists were comparing her favourably to Sade. 'Choices' stayed in the top ten for an impressive five weeks.

But while Esther's first single had been popular in the US, it didn't garner much attention in the UK, and for some reason, an album never materialised. After four more songs, she stopped releasing new material and seemed to disappear along with all the fanfare around her.

Seeing Esther in the flesh today felt like seeing her again for the first time. Everything about her appearance left Elijah tongue-tied.

True to her nature, Esther seemed to have defied the ageing process. Although she had developed a frown line and barely visible creases around her lips, her caramel-brown complexion had lost little of its youthful glow. Underneath a red bandanna, she still had her kinky afro hair in all its full glory. Impressively, her figure seemed fuller and more curvaceous than Elijah remembered. It was as if the intervening years had kept moulding and shaping her body, like a sculpture that was maintained to add to its beauty.

Their conversation outside the church had been brief. In a wordless state of shock, Elijah had not fully registered what Esther said to him. She appeared nervous when she told Elijah that she was searching for her father and asked Elijah if he had seen him. Elijah could only answer that he had not. In fact, he had not seen Esther's father in nearly as many years as he had not seen her.

After hearing his answer, Esther had simply nodded her head. She then remarked, with a reluctant tone now that Elijah thought about it, that it was nice to see him again. Before

Elijah could respond, Esther quickly mumbled something about needing to leave in a hurry. She gave Elijah a faint smile then turned on her heels and walked away from the church without so much as a glance back.

Eighteen years. Has it really been that long?

"How much rice do you want? Elijah? Elijah?"

Immersed in his thoughts about Esther, Elijah had utterly forgotten his environment, and Tiwa's voice pulled him back into the present moment. Elijah blinked rapidly, the memories of Esther vanishing from his mind. Tiwa was standing beside his chair at the dining room table with a pot of jollof rice in her hand.

"Are you okay? Thinking about work again?" his wife asked, her Nigerian accent peeking through her voice. She slowly began to fill his plate with a wooden spoon.

"Oh no, I'm not thinking about the office on a Sunday evening," Elijah said, observing how much of the dark orange rice his wife was putting on his plate. "I was actually thinking about how beautiful you looked in that dress today at the funeral."

Tiwa's lips formed into a half-smile. "Thank you. Is that enough?"

"Yes, thanks."

Without one look at Elijah's face, Tiwa stopped filling his plate and walked around the glass dining table, placing the pot of jollof rice in the middle, to take her seat at the opposite end.

"How is the preparation going for your mother's birthday? It's in a few weeks, right?" Tiwa asked.

Elijah swallowed a mouthful before he answered, "That's right, and it's going well. Now that my father's funeral is done, Mary, Jairus and I can focus on preparing the church for the big party. I suspect more than half of Peckham's Nigerian population will be there, so we'll probably need enough jollof rice to feed Lagos."

Tiwa responded with a weak smile she always gave him these days, which disappointed him, and nodded her head. "Let me know if you need help with the cooking."

"Of course. You know my mother loves the way you make *egusi* soup."

Elijah was hoping Tiwa would at least give him a proper smile for his compliment. Instead, she continued eating in silence.

Feeling lost as to what else he could say to bring out some warmth in his wife, Elijah returned to eating and let his gaze wander around his living room. In addition to carrying out God's will as a senior pastor, Elijah worked as Finance Director at a large IT company in Canary Wharf. He found his corporate job, a position he had been in for seven years, tiresome and emotionally unfulfilling. But his considerable salary overshadowed any grievances he had. Tiwa was a French teacher at a school in Peckham, which paid a modest salary, but their combined income enabled them to afford a mortgage on a newly built three-bedroom flat in Streatham Hill, close to

Brixton – which was becoming increasingly more gentrified and different from the Brixton Elijah grew up in.

Although it had been challenging to find a suitable, well-priced flat in the area, Elijah did not want to leave this part of south London. Tiwa, on the other hand, had been reluctant, understandably not sharing his sense of belonging. She had grown up in Nigeria and heard about the notoriety that was associated with Brixton from relatives living in London. But for Elijah, Brixton would always be home, no matter its reputation.

Elijah scooped a spoonful of jollof rice into his mouth and took in the entirety of the flat. It was an undeniably comfortable place to live – as modern and slick as you would expect from a new build. The smooth walls had been given a Venetian plaster finish, and it was open plan, with plenty of space. Tiwa's favourite part about it was the marble kitchen, which looked like it had been torn straight from the pages of an Ikea catalogue.

Yet despite the polish of Elijah's surroundings, it could not make up for the growing lifelessness currently engulfing his marriage. If anything, it just emphasised it even more.

Another fifteen minutes of eating passed in silence before Elijah felt his belly was full. It was time to change into his evening robes and begin his one hour of Bible study and prayer. "The rice was delicious, Tiwa," Elijah said, standing from his seat as he patted his stomach. "I'm already getting tired, so I'm heading to the bedroom. You want me to wash the dishes? I don't mind."

Tiwa stood up from her chair and started stacking the two plates and the cooking pot on top of each other as if she were building a small tower. "No, that's alright. I'll do it. I'll come and join you when I've finished." She turned to face Elijah and gave him a reassuring smile he knew was forced.

With no further words, Tiwa continued tidying up the dining table. Elijah turned away from her to make his way to the bedroom but then decided against it. He pivoted on his heel and looked at his wife.

Tiwa was standing in the kitchen by the sink. As if she were a piece of artwork to be admired, Elijah watched his wife washing the plates. Six years his junior, Tiwa was a short woman with a full figure and dark-black hair, which she currently wore in long, thick braids. Her blouse gently lifted as she craned forward to pick up a plate, exposing her light-brown waist. Elijah felt a strong pull towards her, as intense as the feeling he'd had when he first laid eyes on her.

Elijah strode towards Tiwa, savouring the sight of her. When he reached her side, Tiwa was so engrossed in washing that she jerked as he wrapped his arms around her waist. He leaned into her, appreciating the fullness of her backside against him.

"You really did look good in that dress today," Elijah whispered in her ear, slotting his hands in between her wet fingers.

Tiwa began trembling and then broke into a fit of tears. Surprised, Elijah removed his fingers from her hand and retreated. "I'm sorry, Elijah," Tiwa said quietly, in between sniffles. "I'm just not...It was hard seeing all those children today at the funeral."

Elijah stepped forward again and went to wrap his hands around her, but he did not want to feel the pain of rejection from his wife again so stood back.

"I understand, *ife mi*. I am here. Always."

Elijah sat up in the king-size bed. His King James Bible was opened in his left hand as he held a pen with his right, and a notepad, scribbled with his observations on scripture, lay beside him. The bedroom was not in complete darkness; a shaft of moonlight pierced through the window, bouncing off the walls and illuminating the room with a blue hue. On the other side of the bed, Tiwa was in a deep sleep, her stillness occasionally broken by a soft groan before she tossed and turned and returned to her rest.

Tomorrow evening, after he finished work at his corporate job, Elijah would be hosting a lecture on marriage counselling at the church as part of his final sermon on marriage. After that, there would be a meeting with the church's executive board members which consisted entirely of his immediate family. Elijah breathed a heavy sigh. Even though he would be facing his own relations, he was not looking forward to the meeting.

As Elijah continued reading Ephesians, adjusting his glasses as he scanned the biblical text, he came across a verse that made him stop reading:

Husbands love your wives, as Christ loved the church and gave himself up for her.

This was his favourite verse in the whole of *Ephesians*. In fact, he had loved it so much that he had paraphrased it when he read his wedding vows to Tiwa.

"I will love you as Christ loved the church and give myself up for you."

After another forty minutes of studying scripture and scribbling notes, Elijah closed his Bible and his notebook and placed them on the bedside table. He turned around, looking at his sleeping wife. Tiwa was breathing quietly now as she lay on her stomach, her head angled towards him. Her eyes were shut, but her mouth was slightly parted.

Elijah gently kissed Tiwa's forehead before turning away from her and resting his head on his pillow. As he drifted into sleep, his mind travelled to thoughts of Esther.

Elijah still could not believe she had come into his life again, after all these years. He regretted that he had not spoken more to her, but just seeing her, with her curvaceous figure and that striking aura seemingly still intact, had made him feel oddly refreshed, like stepping out of a hot shower. What a strange coincidence that on the day of his own father's funeral, Esther would be searching for hers.

Eighteen years. Has it really been that long?

With that final thought, Elijah eased himself into a peaceful sleep.

CHAPTER 3

June 2008

Esther gently touched Ayesha's soft, pink lips with her right index finger. For a few seconds, she rubbed the tip of it around them in slow motions, feeling the wetness at their edge. Delicately, as if Ayesha's face were so fragile it could bruise with too much force, Esther ran her finger down her lover's chin and her neck, stopping at Ayesha's exposed breasts, which were the colour of coffee beans. Esther licked her finger then started playing with Ayesha's erect nipple, twirling her wet fingers around its base.

"Alright, alright, calm down," Ayesha said. She grabbed Esther's index finger and wrapped her lips around it, exposing the gap in her front teeth, which Esther always found so irresistibly sexy. Ayesha sucked on Esther's finger for a moment before promptly taking it out. "Sex time is over, babe. I have a plane to catch in four hours."

Esther and Ayesha were both lying naked on a mahogany four-poster bed in Ayesha's flat in south London. The air was heavy with the scent of sex and unleashed pleasure. Although Esther had reached orgasm – even after all these years Ayesha had not lost her innate understanding of where and how to touch her – she felt like they could still go on pleasuring each other well into the night. Unfortunately, there could be no more orgasms for either of them; Ayesha had a flight to catch.

"You still know how to use that tongue of yours," Esther said as she stood from the bed. She stretched her arms and then bent down to pick up her bra and underwear from the Persian rug on the floor.

"And you, girl, have still got an ass to die for," Ayesha said, slipping on a pair of jeans. With the panicked movements of someone who knows they are on borrowed time, Ayesha scurried over to her walk-in wardrobe, which took up almost a quarter of the flat. "We're living proof that forty is the new twenty-five," she added, throwing vests, bras and socks into her open suitcase lying beside the bed. "We may be thicker, but thicker is always better. Am I right?"

Esther chuckled as she put on a grey t-shirt that reached her knees. She walked over to Ayesha and put her hands around her waist, just as Ayesha finished pulling a white t-shirt over her head. "It's a shame you're leaving. We could have got into a lot of trouble while I'm here in London. Just like when we were unruly south London teenage girls. Remember?"

Ayesha turned around and pecked Esther on her lips. "Speak for yourself, I'm still unruly, babe. But I wouldn't miss a four-week Caribbean cruise for anything." She bit her lip and winked at Esther. "Not even for another taste of you."

"I can't argue with that," Esther said. She watched as Ayesha paced across the room, grabbing whatever looked useful and tossing it in her suitcase. "And thanks again for letting me stay at your flat for the next couple of weeks. You've rescued me from the hassle of finding a hotel in Brixton or Streatham. When did south London become so damn expensive?"

"Ha, Brixton is full of yuppies now. Them lot have driven prices up." Ayesha shook her head. "And no problem, babe. What are long-term, old shag buddies for?"

As Ayesha continued scurrying across the flat with the frenzy of a decapitated chicken, Esther strolled towards the kitchen to pour herself a glass of red wine. She took out an expensive bottle of Chateau Grand-Puy-Lacoste from the built-in fridge and grabbed a wine glass from the rack under the cabinets.

Esther had to give Ayesha credit – it was an impressive two-bedroom flat. The decor reminded her of a swanky television set from the sixties. It had a bohemian sensibility to it with various abstract paintings on the blue walls, a purple glass table in the living area, a stack of vinyl records by the window and a thirty-two-inch, retro-style TV.

A few months ago, Ayesha had won a hefty divorce settlement from her ex-husband, who was the CEO of one of the biggest public relations agencies in Europe. True to her impetuous nature, Ayesha immediately bought a two-bedroom flat in Pullman Court, a grade II listed residential estate in Streatham Hill, and booked a four-week holiday to Jamaica, which included a Caribbean cruise. As luck would have it, when Esther had called Ayesha to find out if she could stay with her while she was in London, Ayesha was more than willing to let Esther have the whole flat to herself. Now Ayesha was about to go off and enjoy her new life as a newly-single and newly-minted woman.

"This is delicious; you want me to pour you some?" Esther asked, taking a sip of the velvety wine.

"I love the way you say *'delicious'* in that American accent," Ayesha said, as she forcibly pushed down a pair of heels into her suitcase, which looked like it might burst open at any moment. "But I don't drink before I fly. Once I start drinking, it's a slippery slope, as you know, babe."

"Wow, look how mature and boring you've become. Married life really did take its toll on you."

Ayesha chuckled and then sat on top of her suitcase to stop it from flying open. "Well, I'm not married anymore." She gave Esther a devious grin. "So, any warm leads on your missing daddy?"

Esther sighed and took another sip of her wine before responding. "No, not really. I mean, I'm not entirely sure where to start. This afternoon I went over to my old church in Peckham. It was a spur-of-the-moment thing really, and I met…" Her voice trailed away as she recalled Elijah's face, frozen in shock, his mouth hanging as his eyes fell on her.

"Who did you meet?"

Esther smiled, despite herself, and bit her lip. "I met Elijah."

Ayesha stared back at her with a puzzled expression. "Who's Elijah?"

"You don't remember Elijah?" Esther looked at Ayesha as if she had just taken a hit to the head. "My ex-boyfriend from almost two decades ago? Went Dick Sheppard with us? The prick who broke up with me at the airport?"

Ayesha still had the same perplexed look on her face and shook her head.

"Did all those years living in a fancy flat in Mayfair make you bury the dark memories of growing up in Brixton?" Esther joked.

"Oh, that's not fair, babe. You can't expect me to remember every man and woman you've shagged. I have trouble keeping up with my own body count."

"God, you're too much sometimes," Esther said, shaking her head as she laughed. "He had a potato head at school. He always used to quote Bible verses. We used to call him Prophet. Come on, Ayesha. I dated him for four years."

Ayesha's face suddenly lit up with recognition, as if a switch had been flicked on in her brain. "Ohhhhh, him. Bible boy. To this day, I still don't understand how an openly bisexual and gorgeous woman like yourself dated a religious bore like him for so long."

"He might have been a pastor's son, but he did some very naughty things when we dated. I always told you he was very open-minded for a Christian," Esther said, now thinking about the groups of people she had seen leaving the church. "I think he'll take over Peckham Pentecostal now that his dad has passed away from what I was told by someone who had gone to the funeral. It's what he wanted." There was a time when admitting this would have summoned a sharp pain in Esther's stomach, but now the truth about Elijah no longer held any power over her.

Ayesha scoffed. "All I know is that bloody Nigerian bastard broke up with you at Heathrow airport on the day you were both meant to begin in a new life in Chicago. Please tell me you kicked him in his balls or something?"

"No, I'm not going to make a fool of myself. I didn't do anything, really. I asked him if he had seen my father, he said he hadn't, and then I sort of ran away like a frightened puppy, which is kind of pathetic now I think about it."

"I can't believe it," Ayesha said, checking the time on her gold Rolex. "You have a sassy mouth, second only to yours truly, and you didn't give him a piece of your mind for what he did to you? It doesn't matter if it was all the way back in the nineties, his balls deserved some overdue pain from your foot, babe."

Esther let out a loud laugh, swinging her glass of wine with more force than she intended, so a little of its contents splashed on the tiled marble floor. If she was being honest with herself, it had been an awkward yet oddly welcoming surprise to see Elijah. For a long time, anger and resentment had whirled inside her whenever she thought of him. There were nights when she had first started living in Chicago where she would cry herself to sleep, thinking about how Elijah had ended their relationship. But after eighteen years of living stateside, with enough wild stories to write a New York bestseller, any residual bitterness Esther felt towards Elijah was crushed underneath all of that.

Still, the memory of Elijah staring at her from the concrete steps of his church earlier today overtook her mind. Age had been a good friend to him. Of course, she missed the afro of his youth, which had clearly long departed. But his baldness did compensate somewhat by emphasising his facial features, which had naturally become more masculine and defined with life experience. The beard around his mouth, not too much and not too little, and the fact he now wore glasses made him look distinguished, more sure-footed than when Esther had dated him.

Age really is a generous friend to those blessed with melanin.

By 11 p.m., Ayesha had left to start her four-week getaway under the Caribbean sun. Esther now had the flat all to herself, but it felt strangely cold and barren, as if the comforting warmth of the home was fuelled by Ayesha's big personality.

Rather than put the television on and reacquaint herself with *EastEnders* or get even tipsier than she already was on Ayesha's expensive wine, Esther decided to reread the letter her mother had sent her from Ogoni. The letter was addressed to her mother as it had been the final correspondence she received from Kelechi Nubari, Esther's now missing father.

Esther rested her head against the armrest of the purple, three-cushion couch. She took the letter out from its envelope and unfolded it. Even though she had read it numerous times, she felt like there was something still hidden in its contents, a cryptic message that may reveal the whereabouts of her father – a man she hadn't seen or spoken to in eighteen years. Letting out a soft sigh, Esther began to read:

December 2007

> *To my beloved Zina, the second piece of my soul and keyholder to my heart, I hope this letter has reached you in good health and strong spirits.*

> *Firstly, I pray you have been receiving the money I send over. It is not as much as it used to be, but I am no longer teaching at the primary school I told you about in my previous letter. I will explain why in a separate note, as I am deeply ashamed of what I did.*

> *Since returning to London, not a day has come and gone where I haven't dreamed of holding you for long, hot nights under the silver moonlight, caressing your nightshade skin and losing myself to your body and spirit. Distance truly does make the heart grow fonder.*

> *My sweetheart, I hope you can forgive me now for leaving you and fleeing Nigeria. One day I will*

explain it all in person. I had become a spectre of death hovering above you, crippled by my fear of being hung and left to die like my brothers; like my friend, Ken Saro-Wiwa. Every day I think of the brothers that I have lost fighting this conflict with Abache's despicable Nigerian government.

I hope you can find some comfort in knowing that I am doing fine again, but it has not been easy, my beloved. The devil's temptations succeeded in turning me into a wreck. I lost everything I worked hard to build returning to this country for a second time. But, to God's glory and grace, I am now in the company of good people. I have met a brilliant man who has lifted me from the darkness. I believe God has placed this man in my life to help bring more international support to the plight of the Ogoni people.

My dearest, I pray that I will soon be reunited with you, and we can rebuild our home in Kegbara-Dere.

I miss you so deeply, at times I can hardly bear it. But God is good, and He will deliver. For all that has happened and will happen, I will never lose faith in Him.

You will forever be in my prayers, my love.

Kelechi

After Esther finished reading the letter, she put it back in its envelope and placed it on the table. She reached her hands behind her head and looked up at the white ceiling, letting her mind wander.

When she had first read the letter, she could hardly believe it was written by her father. It wasn't the quality of the prose that surprised her – she knew her father had been an English teacher in Nigeria before she was born. What surprised her was how much love her father could express. The man she grew up with did not seem capable of expressing, let alone feeling, any love at all.

Esther sat up on the couch and ran her fingers through her messy afro. Even after reading the letter for the umpteenth time, it had not provided any breadcrumbs that might pinpoint her to her father's whereabouts in Britain. He mentioned that he had been teaching at a primary school but did not provide any details. Nor had her father bothered to reveal the name of the *"brilliant man"* who had *"lifted him from darkness"*, whatever that meant. Her father's final letter to her mother said so much and yet so little. This aggravated Esther. The search for her father was going to be more complicated than she initially realised.

Midnight came quicker than expected, and Esther felt the long day weighing down on her body and mind. She stood up from the couch, stretched and yawned. She picked the envelope up from the table and walked towards the bed, the prospect of sleep more inviting with each step she took.

Rereading the letter might not have given her any indication of her father's whereabouts, but it did provide an idea of where to start looking next. For the most part, her father's letter was puzzling to her; it was like the middle chapter of a book. But to piece together the story of his return to Britain after fleeing Nigeria, she needed to go back to the beginning.

So tomorrow, Esther would pay a visit to her childhood home in Brixton. It was not a place she was particularly excited to return to, but sometimes, to understand the present, you have to return to the past, no matter how unpleasant the memories.

CHAPTER 4

January 1980

When the dark-skinned girl with a short, curly afro and big cheeks walked into the classroom, something inside Esther rang like an alarm clock going off. Whenever she rested her eyes on this mysterious girl, Esther felt like she was soaring through the sky. It was the type of attraction that made her heart beat a little faster, and the feeling confused and excited her. But she had not yet summoned the courage to speak to her.

The classroom buzzed with a multicultural mix of eleven- and twelve-year-old students chattering to their friends or chasing each other around the room. A white boy with spotty skin and a mop of brown hair ran past Esther's desk and knocked down her school bag as a black boy chased after him, laughing with excitement. Esther barely took notice of this, her concentration fixated on the girl as she sat down at the single wooden desk one row away. The dark-skinned girl's blonde-haired friend, who had followed her into the classroom, sat at the desk beside her.

As if sensing Esther's eyes following her, the dark-skinned girl turned her head away from her friend and looked at Esther. Her eyes were dark and dreamy like a midnight sky dotted with stars.

Feeling oddly shy, Esther smiled at the girl, who smiled back, revealing a gap in her two front teeth. Without warning, the thought of kissing this dark-skinned girl's pink lips made Esther tense, as if she were about to leap off a plane, hoping that she could trust the parachute to work. Why did she want to taste the lips of another girl? Esther could not understand where this desire had come from. Had it always been there, but only now decided to make itself known?

"Alright, that is enough now. Please take a seat."

Mr Freeman, the religious studies teacher, had entered the classroom wearing a white shirt and a dark-brown blazer, which was too big for his slim stature.

Having moved to Brixton with her mother and father a month ago, Esther had been attending Dick Sheppard School in Tulse Hill for a week. Mr Freeman was the first teacher she had been introduced to, and he reminded her of Shaggy from the Scooby-Doo cartoons she watched every Sunday morning before attending church with her parents.

"I don't want to repeat myself, please," Mr Freeman said, failing to raise his voice above the chorus of energetic twelve-year-olds running around the classroom. Mr Freeman ran his hands through his untidy, straw-brown hair and picked up a thick book from the desk in front of the class. He slammed it down with a bang that reached every student's ear, stopping them mid-sentence and, in many cases, mid-mischief.

"Everyone take a seat, now. I am not going to repeat myself."

Unfortunately, Mr Freeman did, in fact, repeat himself several more times before the students took their seats.

Esther stole one last look at the dark-skinned girl. She seemed to be sharing a secret joke with her friend and Esther desperately wished she had chosen a desk that was closer to where the girl sat. With a pang of regret, Esther looked away and picked her school bag up from the floor. She took out her schoolbook and her rubber pencil case to appear as though she wanted to learn about religion, when the truth was that she couldn't care less. Her life at home was deeply rooted in Christianity, shrouding every part of it like a thick, suffocating smog.

Mr Freeman began to do the register. Once Esther answered her name, she found herself losing concentration, so she turned her head to the right to look at the dark-skinned girl again. There must have been a telepathic connection between them because the girl turned to her at the same time and smiled. Esther felt a jolt rush through her body.

The dark-skinned girl opened her mouth, but she did not speak. Instead, she mouthed her name – Ayesha – and then pointed her finger at Esther, indicating that Esther should mouth her name back.

"Excuse me. Excuse me."

Preoccupied with responding, Esther didn't notice Mr Freeman standing in front of her desk. She only realised when the other students in the classroom started snickering. Esther turned her head upwards to see the visibly impatient Mr Freeman looking down at her with a scowl slapped across his thin, scarcely bearded face.

"Esther, is it?"

Before Esther could even respond to the question, Mr Freeman had already continued speaking. She wondered why he had bothered to ask her to confirm her name.

"Well Esther, since you clearly like speaking even when you're not supposed to, I think you'll be the first person I'll ask. Do you believe in God?"

"Yes sir, I do," Esther replied, hearing the other kids' hushed laughter.

"That's very interesting," Mr Freeman said, sounding genuinely intrigued. "And what religion do you follow?"

"Christianity because that's what my parents follow, sir," Esther said reluctantly and in a matter-of-fact tone. She did not feel comfortable exposing her personal life, especially since Ayesha and the other students in the classroom were listening.

Mr Freeman nodded at Esther and remained silent for a moment. "Now that's very interesting," he said again, in the same tone, as if he knew something the students didn't,. "There are quite a few religions, and Christianity is one of the most, if not *the* most, popular. Is anybody else here a Christian like Esther?"

All the students seemed disinterested and, as Esther suspected, probably reluctant to talk about their religion in case the other students made fun of them in the playground. All except one black boy. Sitting two rows away from her, at the front of the class, this boy raised his arm before Mr Freeman had finished his sentence. He began waving his right arm and bouncing on the plastic chair as if he were sitting on pins.

"What's your name?" Mr Freeman asked as he turned away from Esther to face the boy, who had now put his arm down and turned around on his chair to face the class. Esther recognised the boy's face, but her memory couldn't quite pinpoint where she had seen him, only that it was somewhere she had been a few times.

"My name is Elijah, sir," the boy said with a confident voice and a British accent which, Esther assumed, meant he was born here. There had not been many in her previous school, and Esther was surprised and glad to be surrounded by so many other black kids.

"You're a Christian?" Mr Freeman asked.

"Yes, sir, I am a Christian, and my dad is a pastor," Elijah replied. For some reason, and she didn't understand why she felt this way, Esther found it annoying that this Elijah boy had emphasised the last part of his answer. Was everyone in the classroom supposed to be impressed by this? Elijah continued, "He has his own big church in Peckham, sir."

As soon as Elijah had said that, Esther studied him. Now she remembered why she knew his face. He was the son of the pastor who preached at the church she was forced to attend every Sunday. Esther had not immediately recognised Elijah since he wore a freshly ironed shirt and black trousers and had neatly combed hair at church, which made him appear a little older than his age. But today, in his grey and black school uniform, he looked much younger. He had a dark complexion, not as dark as Esther's father's, but nowhere near the same tone as her own light-brown skin. For some reason, his head reminded her of a potato, only with small, black eyes, pink lips and a short afro growing on top.

"Thank you for sharing that with us, Elijah. As a pastor's son, you must know a lot about Christianity?" Mr Freeman said, walking towards Elijah.

"Yes, sir," Elijah replied, barely concealing the pride in his voice. "I read the Bible every day with my dad and my mum."

"That's very good to hear, Elijah," said Mr Freeman. "Do you know about any other religions? Islam? Buddhism? Judaism?"

Esther watched Elijah give Mr Freeman a bemused look, and he made a funny face as if he were annoyed by the teacher's line of questioning. Esther wasn't sure why, but she smiled when Elijah scrunched his face like that. He was kind of cute when he was annoyed.

"I don't need to know about other religions," Elijah said, a defensiveness in his tone. "Christianity is the only religion people should follow. My dad tells me, and everyone listens to my dad."

Mr Freeman regarded Elijah's response for a moment. Then he turned to face Esther, who was not expecting the teacher to address her again. "Esther, do you agree? Is Christianity the only religion people should follow?"

At that moment, Esther felt like throwing a pen at Mr Freeman's forehead. Why was he putting her on the spot? She wanted no part of this debate. Religion confused and deeply bored her. Yet before she could even reply, Elijah had answered for her.

"She goes to my dad's church. So, she has to agree with me."

Esther glared at Elijah. "What!? I don't have to agree with you, potato head."

The quiet concentration that Mr Freeman had worked so hard to establish instantly shattered, like a stone smashing into a glass window. The class erupted into laughter. Esther turned around and saw Ayesha laughing along with her friend. She looked at Esther with a grin on her face. Esther smiled back.

"Alright, everyone. Quiet down, quiet down. Please," Mr Freeman said, trying to restore order, and the laughter began to subside.

Esther looked at Elijah. He did not look like the tall, confident boy from a few minutes ago, who was proud his father was the pastor. Instead, he had hunched his shoulders and stared down at his textbook. Suddenly, Esther regretted calling him a potato head. Of course, he should not have spoken for her, but maybe she did not need to embarrass him like that either.

Deciding that Elijah was not worth her attention anyway, Esther spent the remainder of the class stealing short glances at Ayesha, who returned the favour. After this lesson was over,

Esther knew she had to find a way to speak to Ayesha. The thought of it made her heartbeat quicken and her fingers tingle.

Initially, Esther had been scared about coming to live in Brixton after hearing so many unpleasant stories about the area. But she was starting to feel like she was exactly where she belonged.

CHAPTER 5

June 2008

Twenty minutes ago, Elijah had been standing in front of the podium at the Pentecostal Church of Christ in Peckham, preaching the gospel to a forty-strong congregation on a warm Monday evening

Elijah did not have a natural inclination for public speaking. Yet every time he preached the Bible in front of an audience, the experience invigorated his entire being and empowered him. By contrast, when he had to present quarterly financial reports to the white bosses at his corporate job, he always felt uncomfortable.

Something changed within him when he preached the gospel. As soon as he opened his mouth to start a sermon, looking upon the expectant faces of the congregation, his whole body seemed to become charged by a current. It animated him, like an electronic toy springing to life when you turned on the switch. All his feelings of nervousness and uncertainty vanished as though they had never manifested in the first place. He peppered scriptures with entertaining anecdotes and words of wisdom, flowing from him like a waterfall. His words washed over the congregation, refreshing their bodies, massaging their minds, and cleansing their souls. And Elijah would smile to himself as he felt the power of the Holy Spirit do its great work through him.

But his sermon was over. Now, Elijah was standing in front of his family members. Their purpose was to hold him accountable for any decisions he made regarding the church while also managing the day-to-day functions of the parish. The confidence and certainty he felt when he was preaching had vanished, replaced by a weariness on his mind and shoulders. Before him, the executive board members of the church sat in chairs that formed a semi-circle around Elijah.

When Elijah's father had become too ill to govern the church effectively, Elijah became the de facto leader in his absence. Feeling that the church had become outdated and conservative under his father's governance, Elijah had retired all the original executive board members, barring his mother. Now, in addition to Dinah Oduwole, who was the chairwoman and Jairus, who was second-in-command as the head pastor and treasurer, Elijah had appointed the rest of his family into roles within the executive board. Mary was the Head of Evangelism, and her husband, Kunle was the Youth Leader and Head of Communications and Marketing. Even Tiwa acted as the church's secretary.

Elijah had thought that having his family close to him and providing support as he led the church would make it easier for him to modernise it. Over the months, he had learned that this was not going to be the case at all.

Much to Elijah's relief, the meeting with the executive board had started on a pleasant note. Discussion focused on the party that was being organised for Elijah's mother's seventieth birthday. But once the topic shifted towards the church's planned program over the next few months, egos began to sit in on the meeting as well. Now Jairus, not for the first time, was engaging Elijah in a war of words.

"What you are proposing is completely unacceptable," Jairus said, standing from his chair in a defiant challenge. "*Iya,* are you hearing this?" Jairus turned to their mother, the look in his eyes a plead for empathy. Elijah's mother made a soft humming sound and stared at Elijah, her dark eyes piercing into him.

Elijah understood the unspoken meaning behind his mother's gaze and sighed. He would need to do more convincing. "Jairus, I understand your concerns," Elijah said, talking directly to his brother, who had sat down but was still shaking his head. "But a strong church reacts to what is happening within its community. Right now, a lot of young black people in Lambeth are involved in drugs and violent crime. As a church, we have done nothing so far to address this, and we've seen the numbers of young people attending our youth service steadily fall."

Jairus sucked his teeth and waved his right hand in disapproval. "That is not what I disagree with you on, Elijah. I don't even disagree with you inviting an ex-criminal to speak at our youth service, but one who is…homosexual? Too far." The unmistakable tone of disgust in Jairus's voice was as clear to Elijah's ears as the cars blowing their horns outside in the traffic.

Perhaps realising how he sounded, Jairus softened his tone. "I'm not against inviting homosexual and bisexual people into our congregation. We are all children of God. Of course we can be healed of our transgressions and taught to resist the temptations of the flesh. But giving these people a platform in the church will not only alienate the older members, it is also completely against scripture."

"These people?" Mary said, widening her eyes.

Jairus ignored his sister's words and scoffed.

"Elijah, I understand where you're coming from," Kunle said. "But are you sure this is the right way for the church to tackle this issue?"

"Although I don't like the way Jairus has communicated his opinion," Mary interjected, pausing briefly to give Jairus a quick side glare before she continued, "I actually agree with my husband, which doesn't happen often." Mary smiled at Kunle, and her husband's mouth dropped open in an exaggerated manner. Mary went on, "Black youth in Lambeth are going through a lot right now, especially with all these stabbings. However, as a church, we must be careful not to send out a message that would confuse them and anger their conservative parents. Our church has always had its roots in Nigerian culture and bringing in a homosexual to preach is a risky move."

Before Elijah could respond, Jairus was on his feet again, his Nigerian accent becoming more pronounced as he spoke more aggressively. "Even all this talk of losing young people in the church. Is it really a concern? The median age of our church is forty, and many of these people are working professionals who provide the church with very generous tithes. The church is not losing any money, even if the number of young people attending our church is decreasing. Financially, the church is in a strong position as our late father always ensured." Jairus narrowed his eyes at Elijah when he mentioned their father.

Elijah closed his eyes and adjusted his glasses before speaking. "Yes, financially, the church is doing well, and we are retaining our older members. But the younger people, those aged thirty and under, who I have personally spoken to, feel our church is behind the times. We need to be doing more to really address the issues of the youth, and God has given me someone who can understand them and speak their language." Elijah looked directly at Jairus. "And he is one of God's people. His sexuality is not important. And I expect that what we have discussed today will not be shared outside this meeting."

Perhaps out of some husbandly instinct, Elijah turned to Tiwa, expecting her verbal support. Instead, his wife simply stared at the door of the meeting room, her facial expression as blank as a sheet of paper. Elijah felt like prompting his wife for her opinion if only to hear her speak but decided against it.

Jairus spoke up again. This time there was a mocking tone in his voice. "If you spent more time being the senior pastor of this church, instead of working at a fancy office most of the week, you would see that what you are proposing is absurd. It goes against what this church our father built stands for and what the Bible teaches."

A frisson of anger trickled along Elijah's spine at his younger brother's jibe, but he did not let this feeling push him into retaliation. It was not lost on Elijah, or anyone else on the executive board, that Jairus harboured resentment over their father making him the leader of the church. A few years ago, Elijah and Jairus had taken a vocational course in Nigeria to become qualified pastors. Both wanted to prove to themselves and their father that they were committed to ministry After the course was over, they returned to England, and Elijah chose to become a bi-vocational pastor. This meant having a job in the secular world alongside his pastoral duties. But Jairus had eschewed the secular world entirely. Instead, he chose to immerse himself in Biblical scripture, learning Hebrew and obtaining a master's degree in Christian Theology, supported financially by church tithes and the profits from various community activities. Elijah knew that Jairus felt his total commitment to ministry made him better qualified to lead their father's church than he was.

After a few minutes' more back-and-forth debating, Dinah Oduwole, who had, by default, become the matriarch of the family, cleared her throat and the room fell silent. As she spoke, she closed her eyes. "Elijah," she said, a tenderness in her heavily accented voice, "You are like your father. Looking ahead. O, there is an old African proverb that says, 'If the rhythm of the drumbeat changes, the dance step must adapt.' I agree with you that the church must address the issues of its community but not at the expense of God's teachings and our reputation."

Her eyes snapped open and stared at Elijah, never shifting from his face as she spoke. "But remember, my eldest son, to trust in the Lord with all your heart, and do not lean on your own understanding. In all your ways acknowledge Him, and He will make your path straight."

Elijah bowed towards his mother, giving her due respect as was custom in Yoruba culture. "I understand completely, Mother," Elijah said, glancing at Jairus quickly before addressing the whole room. "I ask you all to please put your faith in me and trust me. And please, let what we have discussed today remain only with us. I want harmony in this church. That is what my father always maintained. Harmony."

Wearing black jeans, a grey turtleneck sweater and a cross around his neck, Elijah meandered through the market on Electric Avenue. To Elijah's mind, Brixton Market had become a microcosm of his British childhood. As soon as he had turned ten years old, his mother would send him on a weekly errand by himself to go and buy yam and *garri*, and, if he had been a good boy that week, he could buy a small treat for himself too. Throughout his youth, he relished the constant sound of reggae music, the aroma of Caribbean food and the sight of dreadlocked men bopping on the streets with their boomboxes.

By the time Elijah was in his teens, the market had become his favourite place in Brixton. This had not changed now that he was an adult, despite the facelift this part of London had undergone over the years.

It was almost 7 p.m. and the market traders were closing shop. Asian butchers were pushing trolleys filled with rubbish to empty into the bins. Black and white traders, who sold bright African-patterned clothing, bags and other accessories, were dismantling their stalls and tents. Everyone else was noisily filtering out of the market and into the cacophony of human life swarming on Brixton Road. None of this bothered Elijah since he hadn't come to Electric Avenue to buy anything but instead came to clear his mind after the meeting had finished.

Before coming to Brixton, Elijah had driven his wife to Camberwell, where she attended a Christian women's support group every Monday night. He would go to pick her up at around 9.30 p.m., when it finished. Now he had time to let his mind wander as he digested the day's events and thought about what the coming weeks could potentially bring.

As Elijah walked through the market, he passed shopkeepers and stall owners who gave him a knowing nod or a smile, and sometimes even a wave. Some of them had worked at Brixton market for decades; they had sold fish to Elijah when he was ten and still sold fish to him now. Several of the black traders were regular attendees at the church. Elijah was often stopped in the street by a regular churchgoer who would ask for his advice or request a personal prayer. Being a senior pastor meant that you were always in demand. Fortunately, on an evening where Elijah's mind was troubled by the executive board meeting, no one approached him.

Turning onto Atlantic Road, he spotted her almost immediately. Esther was on the other side, standing by a fruit stall underneath the blue rail bridge. Elijah instinctively registered how attractive Esther looked in her ripped denim jeans, black leather jacket, and her red bandanna. Her gold hoop earrings dangled as she turned her head, a puzzled expression on her face. Elijah smiled to himself as he remembered that she'd always had a fondness for big earrings. He adjusted his glasses and put his right hand over his head to tidy his hair, only to be reminded that he hadn't had a full head of hair for almost five years. It was a realisation that irrationally annoyed him now, though it hadn't before.

As he watched Esther standing across the road, a mischievous idea occurred to him. Elijah crossed the street and walked towards Esther, but came from behind to surprise her.

"Well I didn't expect to see you in Brixton Market this evening," Elijah said, appearing beside her.

Unfortunately for Elijah, his attempt to surprise Esther didn't quite have the intended effect. She spun on her heel, her right-hand swinging in the air and knocking Elijah's glasses from his face as he stumbled back in shock. As he knelt to collect his glasses from the pavement, he could hear Esther's American-accented voice.

"Oh my God. Elijah? I'm so sorry. You made me jump."

Doing his best to conceal how stupid he felt, Elijah smiled at Esther as he stood up and put his glasses back on. Now that he was near her, he could smell the cocoa butter on her twisty afro hair.

"No, it's alright, I'm fine. I wanted to surprise you. My punishment for not acting my age."

To Elijah's equal surprise and pleasure, Esther laughed lightly and smiled back at him. It had been so long since he had heard her laugh and seen her smile, and a wave of warmth coursed through his body, a feeling he usually experienced when he drank hot chocolate on a cold winter morning.

"You were in such a hurry when I saw you on Sunday that we didn't get much of a chance to catch up. Are you living in Brixton again?"

"No, I'm here on a short visit actually, and yeah, sorry for being rude that day, I did have to rush." Esther let out another light chuckle. "I'm apologising to you too much."

Elijah grinned. As she spoke, he now noticed how thick her American accent had become compared to when he had heard her singing on the radio. "It's honestly nice to see you again. You look great."

"Thanks. You look good too. The glasses are a nice touch."

"I knew that was coming. I am surprised you didn't say anything about my baldness."

"Thought about it, to be honest, but I wasn't sure how sensitive you are about it. You used to love that afro. It must have been painful when it grew tired of you."

They both laughed, and Elijah didn't take his eyes off Esther as they shared the joke, noticing her teeth and her pink lips. There was a short moment of silence after their amusement subsided, and they looked at each other as if they were the only two people in the market. Elijah broke the silence, not sure what would happen if he had let it continue any longer.

"You asked me on Sunday if I'd seen your father. You haven't spoken to him?"

Esther shook her head. "I haven't spoken or seen my father in almost eighteen years. The last time I saw him was the day me and you were supposed to…" Esther's last sentence trailed off, and she cleared her throat. Much to Elijah's relief, it seemed she could also sense the awkwardness creeping in, and she quickly shut the door on it. "Anyway, I'm in London for a few weeks to try and figure out where he is."

"Oh, I see. So, I'm guessing you just came to Brixton Market to eat a Jamaican patty?"

"Well yeah, what else?" Esther chuckled softly. "But I was also going to head over to my parents' old flat."

"The one in Loughborough Estate?"

"That's right, and as you might have been able to tell from my confused expression earlier, I think I've gotten lost." Before Elijah could give her a look, she continued. "I know, I know, I'm ashamed of myself, living in Chicago all this time isn't an excuse. Blame it on very early middle age."

"Or you could blame it on the odd smell of marijuana in the air right now."

"I can't remember if you were always this cringy with your humour," Esther said with a smirk. She looked at her watch and then towards the darkening sky. "I really do need to find this place soon; I don't even know who lives there now and I'm pretty much going to knock on their door unannounced on a Monday evening. You must know how to get there?"

"Yes, I do; I've driven past there on a few occasions. I'd be happy to give you a lift. My car isn't too far."

"Well if you're offering to drive me there, I won't refuse. Asking directions with this accent makes me feel like a tourist."

Elijah smiled at Esther, and she returned the gesture. It had been a pleasant surprise to see her at his church last Sunday and then again today, but he hadn't expected the two of them to share such an easy rapport. It felt like they had just carried on from a time when they both felt good about each other, as if all that pain in the past had been an unofficial part of their lives that could be ignored. He realised this probably wasn't true, but it certainly felt that way right now.

"I'm just parked behind Brixton Station," Elijah said, pointing his finger towards the direction of the parking area. "It won't take long to drive there at all."

CHAPTER 6

March 1980

Esther stood outside Loughborough Estate, wiping her tears with the sleeve of her grey school jumper. It was a chilly morning, and the cold air lashed against her body like an invisible whip. She shivered a little and desperately wanted to go back to her flat and collect the coat she had forgotten, but her stubbornness firmly rooted her to her spot. Going back to the flat would mean that she would see her father's face again. Her right cheek still stung from the slap he had given her this morning following their heated argument. The very thought of seeing him made her shake more than the blistering cold.

The painful reminder of her father's black hand slamming against her face, threatened more tears to spill from her eyes. With shaky hands, she removed her school bag from her back, unzipped it and took out the Sony Walkman her mother had purchased for her birthday. This gift had become another bone in the mounting bones of contention between her and her father.

The Walkman was larger than the palm of her hand, but she enjoyed holding it as she walked to school. It had become like a teleportation device from an episode of Doctor Who. Through the music, it transported her to more profound and vibrant places in her mind while blocking out the noise of her harsh, concrete reality. Esther placed the silver headphones over her ears and pushed down a button to play the cassette.

Listening to Bill Withers' 'Lovely Day', one of her favourite soul songs from the late seventies, Esther ambled through Barrington Road. She passed the derelict council houses and boarded-up shops, which somehow looked even more lifeless on this bitter morning. After making a right towards Coldharbour Lane, Esther then headed straight towards the centre of Brixton. Even at eight in the morning, she could detect the scent of marijuana. She walked past a barbershop on the opposite side of the road. Its owner, a middle-aged Jamaican man named Benny, who had long white dreads that resembled the end of a string mop, was opening the shop. He noticed Esther and waved at her. Esther returned the gesture and continued her journey towards Brixton central.

Before Esther's father had moved her and her mother to Brixton, they lived in Newham, east London, for six years. It was the first place in Britain her family had chosen when they arrived from Nigeria when Esther was five. Brixton and Newham were not drastically different, but they were not the same either. Many African and Caribbean people resided in Newham, along with a large Asian community. Yet, to her, it had always felt like blacks and Asians lived in Newham but were not actually part of it, almost as if they were extras in a movie in which they had no active role. Newham was still very much a place dominated by white people.

Brixton, on the other hand, had a sizeable black community made up of West Indian residents, many of whom came from Jamaica. Having lived in Brixton for three months now, Esther noticed how West Indian people did not just live in Brixton – their very culture pumped through its streets. Reggae music, from Bob Marley to Dennis Brown, would blast from boomboxes that were carried on the shoulders of crochet-wearing Rastafarians. These reggae songs sailed through the air and landed gently in her ears. The fast-paced rhythm of Jamaican patois was an everyday sound, as familiar as police sirens and traffic.

As Esther took a turn into Brixton market, where traders were opening their food stalls, and the aroma of African and Caribbean produce bombarded her nose, a white police officer frowned at her as she walked past him. Police in Newham, and now Brixton, intimidated her all the time. One night, Esther had overheard her father talking to her mother about how the police were abusing the Sus law to harass black people on Britain's streets and arrest them. Even her father had been stopped by the police and aggressively searched on several occasions, but he had never been taken in. For a reason she couldn't quite understand, being allowed to breathe and walk on the streets of London as a black person seemed to annoy the police, as if black people had no right walking these streets in the first place.

Esther made it to the bus stop, which was a few yards away from the Ritzy cinema. Standing in front of the cinema were a group of activists holding placards with slogans about high unemployment and more jobs for black people. Brixton really felt like a living jungle sometimes, with its mix of inhabitants either trying to survive, cooperate or fight with each other, depending on the day.

At the bus stop, there were a few other Dick Sheppard students and a group of youths who attended Tulse Hill school, an all-boys school not far from Dick Sheppard. Esther recognised some of her fellow students, but she wasn't friendly enough with them to start a conversation. On principle, she never spoke to the Tulse Hill School boys even though they always eyed her up. There was a long-standing rivalry between them and the boys from Dick Sheppard.

Standing at the end of the bus stop was a boy with an afro, who was wearing the same grey school jumper as herself. Esther recognised the boy's head shape. He turned his head towards her. It was Elijah.

Before she could turn away, Elijah had noticed her. His lips formed into a kind of awkward half-smile. Esther didn't return the smile and looked away, focusing her attention on the end of the road to see if the 2B towards Crystal Palace was coming.

Ever since she had called Elijah a potato head at the start of the year, he had been trying to form a kind of friendship with her. At church, when Esther sang with the choir, Elijah would fix his dark eyes on her from his seat in the front row. She was not sure if Elijah fancied her or not, but she was not interested.

The double-decker Routemaster arrived, and Esther stood back to wait for the other students to get on the bus. Elijah hesitated and looked at her, but Esther gave him a blank stare. Thankfully, he understood that she was not open to talking to him, and he boarded the bus, with Esther following behind him.

Ten minutes later, the bus parked outside Dick Sheppard School's low-rise building, with its old framed windows, black railings and tall brown tower. The school was directly opposite Tulse Hill Estate and behind Brockwell Park, where many students would go to settle fights, smoke cigarettes or weed and snog each other behind the bushes. Esther checked the time on her blue watch and realised she still had at least twenty minutes before morning assembly. With time to spare, she decided she would relax in Brockwell Park for a while.

Esther leaned back against the trunk of the tree and took a deep drag of her cigarette, closing her eyes as she did. She exhaled slowly, letting the thin smoke effuse from her mouth, savouring the calming effect that eased her troubled mind. She opened her eyes and looked up at the brown leaves dangling from the thick branches of the tree, ready to fall at any moment. These days, Esther felt like everything she had been taught by her father and mother about God, heaven and hell were like these withered leaves. Finally, she could admit to herself that reading the Bible and going to church did nothing for her. But if she didn't believe in religion, then what did she believe in?

Still examining the leaves of the tree, Esther took another drag from her cigarette. After exhaling a puff of smoke, she turned her gaze away and almost jumped in shock to see Elijah standing in front of her. On his face was the same awkward half-smile he had given her at the bus stop.

"Aren't you too young to be smoking? You're only twelve" Elijah said, casting a glance at the cigarette in Esther's hand. "Christians shouldn't smoke, you know. Our bodies are the temple of God. It says so in 1 Corinthians."

"Is it?" Esther said with a mocking tone. "Well, I know how old I am. I don't need you to tell me. And why are you talking to me for?" Esther made sure her voice was as unfriendly as possible so Elijah would go away. She took another draw of her cigarette and deliberately blew smoke in Elijah's direction. For some inexplicable reason, she found it a little adorable that he winced. He waved the smoke away as if it were a swarm of irritating flies.

"Sorry, sorry. I didn't mean to tell you what to do...You just have a pretty face." Elijah's eyes widened as if in shock at what he had just said, and he shook his head. "I mean, you have a pretty voice. When I hear you sing at church, your voice is amazing. It would be sad to lose your voice because you smoke is all I am saying."

Esther was about to tell Elijah where he should take his opinions and shove them, but she held her tongue and regarded him for a moment. She and Elijah were one of the few Nigerians who attended Dick Sheppard, as most of the black students were from the West Indies. To avoid drawing attention or ridicule because she was from the "jungle", as Africa was referred to, Esther often said that she was from the Caribbean when asked about her country of origin. If people said that she had an African-sounding surname, she would just shrug her shoulders.

Elijah, on the other hand, not only told everyone he was Nigerian, but he wore his African heritage like an expensive suit to be admired. Many of the kids at school had mocked him for being so proudly African and a strict Christian. Still, the name-calling did not seem to dent Elijah's pride. His refusal to deny where he came from, and what he believed in, had eventually earned him a lot of grudging respect from the other kids. Despite feeling mildly irritated by him, even Esther had to admit that she was impressed by Elijah's unfailing confidence in who he was – a feeling which eluded her.

"Thanks," Esther said, surprised she wasn't as annoyed by Elijah's words as she would typically have been. She took a final draw of her cigarette, dropped it on the floor and crushed it with her foot.

"I want to be a famous soul singer one day like Aretha Franklin or Leslie Gore." Esther wasn't sure why she had so quickly told Elijah something that she hadn't told anyone else, not even her best friend, Ayesha.

Elijah looked at her with a puzzled expression. "I've never listened to soul music. My parents only listen to gospel music. Like Harcourt Whyte. Soul singers must be amazing if you want to be one when you grow up."

"Soul music is like gospel music, but it's different, right… can't really explain it. It can make you cry, laugh and dance all at the same time."

"Sounds cool. I'd like to listen to it."

Esther felt an unexpected fondness for Elijah as she smiled at him, which was probably the first time she had ever smiled at him. Ayesha and the other girls she hung out with at school did not share her love for soul music. They were either into pop music like Davie Bowie, ABBA and Michael Jackson or pretended to be interested in the reggae dubplates blasted at sound system clashes so they could impress boys. But Elijah seemed genuinely interested in learning about soul music. Maybe there was a lot more to him than his potato head.

Just as Esther was about to offer Elijah her headphones so he could listen to one of her cassettes, she looked over his shoulder. Two white boys were walking towards them with their hands in their pockets. Their unkind eyes were fixed on them.

Elijah realised something behind him had caught Esther's attention and turned around. The two boys, one who had ginger hair and freckles and the other, slightly overweight with floppy brown hair, came to a stop in front of Elijah and Esther. Both had grins across their faces.

"What do you want?" Esther said, making sure her voice sounded stern and defiant.

Bobby Granger, the ginger boy, and Harry Reading, the larger boy, were the type of kids who seemed to come to school with the sole purpose of terrorising their peers. Usually, they hung around with a larger group of boys, who were also white. In the classroom and on the playground at Dick Sheppard, black, Asian and white kids got along with each other, but that did not mean there wasn't any racial tension. Most people suspected that Harry and Bobby's group were closet supporters of the National Front; closet supporters because they couldn't be too overtly racist – there were too many tough and rough black kids at the school.

"I saw Ayesha give you some fags yesterday behind the swimming pool building," Bobby said, sizing up Elijah as he spoke.

Esther sighed, knowing exactly where the conversation was going. "So what?"

"So you got any then?" Harry said. He barged past Elijah with his broad shoulders to stand closer to Esther. His big-nosed face was so close to Esther's that she stepped back out of repulsion rather than intimidation.

"I ain't giving you any fags. So fuck off, alright? I like smelling the fresh air," Esther said. She waved her left hand in front of her nose to imitate that she could smell something awful and heard Elijah chuckle.

Harry's face went slightly red. "You've got a big mouth. I should wet you up. You black cunt."

Before Esther could land the slap on Harry's face, Elijah had already sprang into action. With a force that surprised Esther, Elijah pushed Harry squarely against the chest, and a startled Harry stumbled and fell backwards into his friend. Both boys comically tumbled to the ground, with their arms and legs becoming entangled as they rolled on the floor. Elijah and Esther burst into laughter, watching the boys struggle to detach their limbs from one another.

Finally managing to separate, Harry and Bobby stood up. Harry lurched forward towards Esther, his face the colour of raw beef but Elijah placed his hand on the huge boy's shoulder before he could attack her.

For a moment, they stared at each in intense silence. Esther bit her lip, feeling guilty that she was mildly excited a full-on fight was about to erupt. The staring contest between Elijah and Harry lasted a couple of seconds before Harry shoved Elijah's hands from his shoulders. Without another word from either of them, the two boys walked away.

"Oi, try not to fall on top of each other as you walk," Esther shouted.

Harry turned around with a look of pure malice etched across his face and made a move in Esther's direction, but Bobby grabbed him by the shoulder, beckoning him to keep walking. Harry scowled at Esther before storming out the park, with his friend, whose pride was just as wounded, following close behind.

Elijah and Esther stood quietly for a moment, both reeling from the adrenaline rush before Elijah broke the silence. "We're gonna be late for assembly. I've never been late before," he said, sounding a little panicked.

Esther looked at Elijah with wide eyes. The fearless boy who was ready for a fight moments ago seemed to have vanished.

"If we run, we'll make it," she said, picking up the school bag she had left by the tree trunk. She bumped Elijah lightly on the shoulder as they began to make their way to the park's exit.

"You know I didn't need you to stand up for me."

"I know. Sorry," Elijah said with a mischievous smile.

"Maybe next time we can tag team."

Elijah looked at her and frowned. "I don't think God would like that."

Esther shook her head and rolled her eyes, but she was not annoyed. "I'm gonna give you a nickname."

"Thought your nickname for me was potato head?"

"I only called you that because you were being annoying. And, let's be honest, you do have a bit of a potato head."

Elijah responded with a sound of disapproval, which made Esther laugh lightly.

"I'm gonna call you Prophet. You like that?"

Elijah grinned. "It's a big improvement over potato head."

Esther chuckled alongside him as they approached the school gates; her mood was in a much better place than it had been this morning.

CHAPTER 7

June 2008

"You drive a nice ride," Esther said with a playful tone.

She stared at the array of buttons and circular screens covering the car's dashboard. It was an impressive BMW 3 Series, but she wasn't wowed by it. Back in the early nineties, at the height of her stardom, Esther had been a regular passenger in the high-end motors that celebrity musicians flaunt their wealth on. "Definitely a big step up from what you were driving way back in the day. Just how much tithes are you collecting from the church, pastor?"

Elijah grinned. "I'm a part-time pastor. I work full-time as a finance director for an IT company in Canary Wharf."

"Ohhh, look at you. The boy from Brixton done good. How do you find it?"

"It's tolerable, and it pays the bills. Most importantly, it lets me impress beautiful women with a BMW." Elijah winked at Esther, and she smacked him lightly on the shoulder at his admittedly terrible but amusing joke.

"You're a celebrity in America, right?" Elijah asked.

Esther raised her eyebrows at him. "What makes you say that?"

A flash of mischievousness lit up Elijah's face. His full lips parted to form a smile, revealing his white teeth. Much to Esther's equal surprise and confusion, he began tapping the steering wheel in rhythm as he hummed a faintly recognisable tune. At first, Esther had no idea what Elijah was doing and wondered if this was another appalling attempt to make her laugh. He took in her bewildered expression and started singing.

"We are because of our choices, baby. We are just a patchwork of choices, baby."

With those song lyrics came a sudden realisation. Esther burst out laughing so hard that tears emerged from the corners of her eyes. "You would be great at a karaoke bar," she said, as Elijah stopped singing. "I'm surprised you remember that song. I sometimes forget how briefly popular I was in the nineties because of that one hit record."

"Hey, don't knock my karaoke skills. I can do a serious Bobby Brown, you know…Your single got a lot of airplay over here in London. Mainly on the black radio stations. I enjoyed the silky R&B sound to it." He turned to her and gave her a warm smile. "I was happy to hear you'd achieved what you set out to do in America. I read that you were recording your debut album, but you only ever put out four tracks. What happened?"

Esther sighed. Her short-lived career as an R&B music artist had given her some unforgettable experiences. But it had also sunk her into the lowest and most destructive phase of her life. It was not a subject she wanted to discuss at this present moment, especially when she was completely sober and sitting in the passenger seat of her ex-boyfriend's car.

"That's a long story, Elijah. Let's just say, sometimes, in pursuit of our dreams, we allow others to poison it for us."

Sensing that Elijah might probe further, Esther promptly changed the course of their conversation. "How long have you been married?" She had noticed the silver wedding band on his left finger.

Elijah looked taken aback at the question, as if she had spoken a foreign language, but he quickly regained composure. "Oh, two years, but I've been with my wife for four years. We live in Streatham Hill."

Much to her surprise, Esther suddenly felt an intense desire to see who Elijah's wife was, what she looked like and how she carried herself. Several questions flashed through her mind: were there any similarities between herself and his wife? Did she have beautiful hair? A darker complexion? Of course, entertaining such thoughts was childish, but Esther was not sure if her feelings had come from a place of curiosity, jealousy or both. She dismissed the unhelpful thoughts from her head as if they were naughty children bothering her.

"Kids?"

A look of pain gripped Elijah's facial features. It only appeared for a moment, but Esther had caught it. Elijah cast his eyes down, and his whole face seemed to drown in deep sorrow. "No kids," he said, in a matter of fact tone that was entirely different to his happy demeanour a moment ago. The subject was clearly an emotional one, and Esther was smart enough not to pry further.

As Elijah parked the car outside Loughborough Estate, Esther turned towards the window and looked through the glass. She almost turned back to ask Elijah if his BMW was secretly a time-machine, like the DeLorean from *Back to the Future*. It had hardly changed since the eighties, as if time had chosen to sidestep this part of London. The low and high-rise flats were still greyish white, square blocks with uninviting windows and an air of urban roughness that covered the buildings like cracked paint. The trees and bushes still sprouted across the estate – their vivid green providing much-needed colour among its bleak greyness.

A couple of boys in hoodies walked past Elijah's car. One of them peered into the driver's window. He had untidy cornrows and a black bandanna wrapped around his mouth. With an unfriendly stare, he looked Elijah up and down then continued walking with his entourage.

Esther and Elijah looked at each and shook their heads, both smiling. These kids didn't intimidate the two of them. They had been walking on these streets long before those boys were born. In those days, Brixton was far more of a boiling pot of aggression and danger than it was now.

After turning off the engine, Elijah turned to Esther, swinging his car keys on his finger. "Do you want me to come and follow you? In case you need back up. It's still a rough area," he said in a mocking tone.

"You've forgotten what we got up to around here when we were kids," she said, poking Elijah on the shoulder. "In all seriousness, you're free to come up with me. For old times' sake."

Elijah put his car keys in his pocket. "Okay, for old times' sake."

As Esther knocked twice on the familiar brown door of flat 15, she wasn't sure what to expect. She stepped back and stood next to Elijah, waiting nervously. A minute later, a female voice bellowed from inside.

"I'm gettin' the fuckin' door. Go to bloody bed, Jack. I won't fuckin' say it again, yeh."

Esther could hear the locks turning, and then the door swung open with surprising force. A short woman, wearing a pink Nike hoodie and grey sweatpants that were so big Esther was sure she could use them as a blanket, stood in the doorway with a scowl on her face. Her curly brown hair had been pulled back into a tight bun on top of her head and she wore square glasses, which looked too big for her pale face.

"Who the fuck eh you? Police?" the woman said with a throaty cockney accent. It was a type of accent Esther had not heard in a long time, and it made her want to smile, but she stopped herself, not wanting to offend this angry woman unintentionally.

"What's Simon fuckin' dun now?"

"No, we're not the cops, I mean police," Esther said quickly, remembering she was in London, and not Chicago. The woman didn't look like the type of person who cared for patience or having her evening interrupted. "Very sorry for disturbing you this evening. My name is Esther, and this gentleman beside me is Elijah."

"So, you're not a copper?" the woman said.

"No, I'm not a copper," Esther replied, smiling inwardly as she had not heard someone say the word "copper" for eighteen years.

"So, what ya doin' then, knockin' on my fuckin' door at seven-thirty in the evenin'?"

"I'm sorry, ma'am," Esther said, thinking she must have sounded like she was from Texas saying *"ma'am"* in her American accent. "I lived here with my family from 1979 till 1990. I'm looking for my father, but I don't have his number, so I wanted to find out if he still lived here."

The woman leaned forward, peering at Esther as if she were trying to locate something on Esther's face. She adjusted her glasses and then her expression lit up with shock. "Oh my fuckin' God, Esther?"

Her familiar tone came as a complete surprise to Esther. "We've met?" she said.

"Ah shit, ya don't recognise me, huh?"

Esther shook her head, staring closely at the woman's facial features while mentally rummaging through whatever memories her brain could muster in the moment that would help identify her.

"It's Stacy."

The name failed to trigger anything in Esther's mind, and she shook her head again.

"From St. Luke's Primary School? You know, the primary school up in Cannin' Town? We used to hang out together, and we was in Mr Pullman's class, but you buggered off in '79, I fink."

Images of her childhood living in east London suddenly came into vision, as if Stacy had opened a locked attic in her brain and found some old pictures. Much of her formative years growing up in Newham were blurry, but the vague recollection of a girl called Stacy from that period of her life began to take solid form: a little girl with ponytails and braces who she used to play hopscotch with on the playground. They had lived close to each other and would often walk home together after school.

"Oh yes, Stacy!" Esther said, smiling at Stacy now. It was surprising that Esther and Stacy were roughly the same age; Stacy looked like she was approaching sixty rather than forty. Time wasn't kind to everyone. "It's great to see you again. Wow, you're living in my family's old flat...Is that a coincidence?"

"Nah, me Grandad, God bless his soul, owned this flat since the sixties and he gave it to me dad to manage. It was me dad who rented the flat to your dad when you lot moved to Brixton. Me dad and your dad had worked on the East End docks together in the seventies."

All this fascinating information was new to Esther. She couldn't remember if her father had ever told her that he'd worked on the East End docks – he had only spoken to her when he wanted to shout at or discipline her. But she did remember when her father would come home late, wearing muddy overalls.

"Where're my fuckin' manners? Come on in, you lot," Stacy said, gesturing for Esther and Elijah to come through the doorway.

As Esther stepped into the flat, Elijah close behind her, she briefly felt like a teenage girl again. Most of her former home had received a much-need makeover: the walls in the narrow corridor were painted white instead of the awful yellow from Esther's time living here, and the floor was no longer a patchy, green carpet, but now laminated wood. As Esther walked past the living room, she briefly glanced inside to see a big television with a gaming console and an expensive-looking leather sofa. Despite the drastic change to its interior, the flat still felt familiar to Esther. The memories of growing up there hovered around her like trapped spirits.

Once Stacy led them into the kitchen, Esther stood close to Elijah, who was looking curiously around at the cramped space. As a child, Esther remembered her mother complaining to her father that she felt like she was cooking in a hut. Standing in the kitchen now as an adult, with barely any space to move, Esther finally understood what her mother had meant.

"Fancy a cuppa? I got PG Tips? Tetley's?"

"I'm fine. But thank you for offering," Elijah said with a half-smile. Esther felt a tingle in her chest. Even after all these years, Elijah's smile still made her feel at ease.

"Same. But thank you, Stacy," Esther said.

"No worries." Stacy regarded Esther for a moment, her beady eyes gazing at Esther from behind her giant glasses. "You've got a funny accent now. Ya sound like a Yankee."

Living in Chicago for years had diminished Esther's proper comprehension of thick British accents, especially one that was as working-class as Stacy's. It took a few seconds for her to understand what Stacy had just said to her. "Oh yeah, I've been living in Chicago for the past eighteen years. Hence, my 'funny accent.'"

At this point, Esther thought Stacy would apologise for the insensitive remark, but Stacy merely blinked at her. Sighing to herself, Esther continued, "I've come back to Brixton for a short while. As I mentioned to you outside, I'm looking for my father and—"

Stacy cut Esther off mid-sentence. "Ya daddy ain't 'ere."

"Oh," Esther said, taken aback by Stacy's bluntness.

"But me old man might know where he is. About three years ago or thereabouts, me old man met ya dad, and they got chattin'. Dunno what they chatted about but that's what me old man told me. He calls ya dad Ken. They're still good mates."

Ken? Esther had never heard her father go by any name other than Kelechi. It almost seemed like Stacy had more knowledge about her father than she did, and Esther tried to shake off the odd feeling of betrayal that came over her.

"Thank you for the information," Esther said, smiling at her old school friend. "I know this might be a bit forward of me, but would you mind giving me your father's phone number, so I can speak to him about when he last saw my father? It's crucial that I find him."

Stacy closed her eyes for a moment, as if she were in deep thought. "I could give ya me dad's number," she said, opening her eyes as she spoke slowly, "but I know me old man. He would love to see ya. You 'member him, right?"

From what small fragments Esther could piece together, she vaguely remembered Stacy's father. He was one of the rare white men who had been friendly to her family.

"I do remember your father. A nice man. I'd love to see him again."

CHAPTER 8

June 2008

Stacy's father, Charlie Robinson, lived in South Norwood, which would take around thirty minutes to drive to from Loughborough Estate. But it was getting late, and not only was Esther feeling a little tired, both physically and mentally, but Elijah needed to go and pick up his wife from Camberwell.

Before Esther left her childhood home, Stacy provided the telephone number and address of her father's house in South Norwood. Esther promised that she would give him a call tomorrow to arrange a date and time to visit. With a joy that Esther did not share, Stacy threw her heavy arms around her, enclosing Esther in a tight and suffocating embrace. Esther was sure she heard Elijah titter.

It was approaching 8.30 p.m. by the time Elijah had driven Esther back to her residence at Pullman Court. As he parked the car, Esther looked up at the brightly lit apartment windows, illuminating the white walls of the building like lanterns.

Pullman Court had a certain Golden-Age-Hollywood charm about it that felt incongruent with the rest of the mundane houses in Streatham.

"Thank you for driving me around today. You were a great chauffeur," Esther said with a wink and a wry smile. She rummaged through her right jeans pocket and fished out the flat keys.

"My pleasure," Elijah said, smiling back at her.

"Well, have a good evening. It was nice to see you again, Elijah."

As Esther placed her hand on the handle of the car door to let herself out, Elijah gently clasped her elbow. It sent a jolt through her.

"Fridays and Wednesdays are the days where I'm often free in the evenings. I'd be happy to drive you to South Norwood on Wednesday. Just saying, south London can be intimidating for a tourist like yourself," Elijah said, winking at her this time.

Esther tutted playfully. "Chicago makes south London look like Disneyland, trust me on that."

They both laughed, and their eyes met for longer than necessary before they both swiftly looked away.

"Well, it would be nice to have my very own chauffeur driving me around in his fancy BMW," Esther said, nodding at the steering wheel of the car. "And you have offered your services…"

"Actually, I don't see myself as your chauffeur. I'm more like a partner, helping you solve this mystery of your missing father. We're like a Nigerian Mulder and Scully."

"You're too much, you know that?" Esther said with a barely repressed laugh as she shook her head. "Fine, give me your cell number. I'll let you know what time to come and pick me up on Wednesday."

"Cell number?" Elijah said, with a smirk.

Esther rolled her eyes. "Don't even start…You know what I meant."

After Elijah had entered his mobile number into her iPhone, Esther stepped out the car and closed the front passenger door. She stood for a few seconds and watched the silver BMW drive down the street and take a left, vanishing from her view. A smile appeared on Esther's face as she made her way back to the flat, dangling the door keys on her finger.

At around six-thirty on Wednesday evening, Elijah picked Esther up from Pullman Court. Since he had no time to go home and change, Elijah was still in his office clothing. As Esther sat beside Elijah in his car, she examined him in his navy-blue pick-and-pick suit and grey tie. Men always looked more attractive in suits and Elijah was no different. Confidence and maturity were stitched into the fabric of a man's suit, concealing whether the man truly had either.

Elijah stopped at a red traffic light a few metres from Norbury station. According to him, South Norwood was less than twenty minutes away, but there was a lot of slow-moving rush-hour traffic. Elijah lifted the handbrake and turned towards Esther. "So are you renting the flat at Pullman Court then?"

Esther shook her head, her gold hoop earrings swaying as she did. "No, not renting. I'm actually staying there rent-free."

"How are you pulling that off?"

"The flat belongs to Ayesha Smith. Remember her?"

Judging from the expression on Elijah's face, Esther knew that he did indeed remember Ayesha. It was not surprising that Elijah had frowned at the mention of her name.

"Yes, how could I forget," Elijah said as he released the handbrake and drove the car forward now that traffic lights had turned green. "I've seen her around on a few occasions over the years but never spoke to her. How is she these days?"

"She's fine. She's the only person I've really kept in touch with."

Elijah nodded his head, but Esther could sense his slight unease. He was never particularly good at concealing when he was feeling uncomfortable, and his body language always gave him away.

"We're not in a romantic relationship. It's casual." As soon as Esther said this, she quickly regretted it. Elijah hadn't asked to know about the current nature of her relationship with Ayesha, so why had she felt the need to tell him?

"Hey, it's none of my business what you do with her," Elijah said. Esther caught a faint hint of insincerity in his voice, but he looked at her and gave her a smile that seemed genuine. "You know I don't judge you on that."

It was true. Elijah was one of the few people in her life who knew about her bisexuality and accepted it as part of who she was. But it had not always been like that. Her mind briefly jumped back to Elijah's disgusted expression as he confronted her in the school corridor when they had been young teenagers. The painful words he had said to her that day echoed in her mind. *'You're dirty, and you're sinful, and you're going to burn in hell.'* But Esther let the image fade away as quickly as it materialised. She did not want to dwell on it.

Being bisexual wasn't easy, especially when it came to her romantic life. Having been with female and male lovers over the years, Esther had come to accept that it was easier to reveal her bisexuality to other bisexual people, like Ayesha. Straight men and lesbians were a lot more judgemental.

With straight men, most could not comprehend how she could be attracted to both sexes, and, much to Esther's annoyance, they also assumed she would be interested in threesomes all the time. Straight men thought her bisexuality meant that she was some overtly sexual freak. And this gave them permission to realise their dirtiest sexual fantasies and desires through her, in a way they could not with straight women.

Lesbians were not so accommodating either. In the early nineties, when Esther was living in Miami for a few months to record her album, she had been sleeping with a lesbian club owner. Upon discovering that Esther was bisexual, the woman had called Esther "a slut that plays both sides." To lesbians, it was as if Esther was insulting the whole lesbian community by refusing to be exclusively attracted to women or making women her default preference. But what many lesbians failed to understand was that Esther was attracted to the person first, and their sex second. Besides, men and women had different love languages and Esther enjoyed and understood both.

"There's a lot of traffic," Elijah said, bringing Esther out of her thoughts. "So we'll probably get to South Norwood just after 7 p.m."

By 7.20 p.m., Elijah was parking his car on Station Road, opposite South Norwood clock tower. Esther stepped out of the car and inspected her surroundings. Like most south-east London districts, South Norwood featured a Tesco, several corner shops and an assortment of British pubs spread across the high street. Having spent so many years living on the other side of the pond, Esther had a newfound appreciation for the unique Britishness of a fish and chips shop or a local pub.

"Remind me where he lives again?" Elijah said as he came to stand beside Esther.

"He told me on the phone that he lives just five minutes away from the clock tower on Upper Grove. Let me check where it is." Esther took her iPhone out of her jeans pocket and opened the map app. To find the location of the street, all she had to do was enter the name of the road and it would calculate the quickest route. Current mobile technology made the pagers and flip phones she had used in the nineties look like relics from ancient history.

Once the smartphone had given her the route to 8 Upper Grove, Esther started walking towards the main high street, with Elijah following quietly by her side. Occasionally, she would glance at the digital map to ensure she was on the right route. In less than ten minutes, Esther and Elijah were standing in front of a cream-coloured, semi-detached house with an unkempt front porch. It was the typical sort of house you would find in a working-class London borough, which meant it only looked as inviting as the occupant bothered to make it. From the external appearance of the house, Charlie Robinson did not seem like a man that was worried about aesthetics.

Esther knocked on the door and waited as Elijah hovered behind her shoulder. She remembered that when she had spoken to Charlie on the phone on Tuesday afternoon, his thick cockney accent was even more pronounced than his daughter's. She really had to utilise her full concentration to make sure she understood everything he was saying. Esther heard the sound of the door unlocking.

After meeting Stacy, Esther had expected her father to be quite a large man, but the person who opened the door came as a total shock. Standing in the doorway with a broad smile on his face, Charlie Robinson was the complete of opposite of his daughter. Despite being in his late sixties, he was well-built with wide shoulders and a muscular frame that belied his age. He had silver hair, which he had combed on top, and piercing blue eyes behind his horn-rimmed glasses.

"Well, what do we have 'ere? Is that little Esther now matured into a fine woman?" Charlie said with a charm that was so infectious and warm, he already felt like a long-lost uncle.

"It's nice to see you again, Mr Robinson," Esther said, leaning into the doorway to give him a hug. "You look very well."

"Ah, no need to be so formal. Call me Charlie. You an' your husband can come in. I was just about to put the kettle on."

"Oh no, we're not married," Elijah said promptly, which, for some reason, slightly irritated Esther.

"He's an old friend of mine," Esther quickly added. "Elijah, meet Charlie."

Charlie leaned past Esther and gave Elijah a firm handshake. "Nice to meet ya, mate."

Greetings and introductions out of the way, Elijah and Esther stepped into the hallway and Charlie closed the front door behind them. "Sorry about the strong smell of wood. Been doin' some DIY work upstairs. Fittin' in a new door for the bedroom."

As they followed Charlie to the living room, Esther noticed that Charlie had a lot of boxing memorabilia, and there were framed black-and-white pictures of various boxers on the walls, alongside other images of what looked like shipping docks. Charlie led them into the living room, and Elijah and Esther took a seat on the settee while their host left to prepare the tea in the kitchen. It was a quaint room with a brown wooden television in the corner. Esther could see several framed pictures of Charlie from his younger years inside an oak display cabinet, and he was very handsome, which didn't come as a surprise. There was one picture in particular that caught Esther's attention: Charlie standing next to a short, round woman who resembled Stacy but wasn't her. Then Esther's memory fired an old image of this same woman at her, handing her candy sticks after school when she was still living in Newham in the late seventies. This was Stacy's mum.

Charlie sauntered back into the room, carrying a silver tray with three mugs, a white kettle and a plate of biscuits. He settled them down on the wooden table in the middle of the living room and took a seat in the armchair opposite. Elijah and Esther both thanked Charlie for his hospitality and picked up their mugs.

The tea, resembling the colour of caramel, was sweet but not overly so, with just the right amount of milk. Esther had not realised how much she missed a warm brew, something British people prided themselves on.

"This is really nice tea, Charlie," Esther said with her hands wrapped around the mug. "I've been living in America for so long, and they just don't appreciate a good brew."

"What kinda host would I be if didn't make me guests a great cuppa?" Charlie said. He took a sip of his tea. "Ken used to love me tea too. He loves a pint of ale just as much, your old man."

Esther leaned closer towards Charlie at the mention of her father. "Stacy said you met my father three years ago?"

Charlie's eyes widened in surprise. "Three years? Bloody 'ell that girl has the memory of a goldfish, I swear. I first spoke to Ken again sometime around July in 1996. So almost twelve years ago, actually. He came to see me wife an' me before we divorced. If memory serves me right, your old man was in a right state."

Esther raised her eyebrows. "What do you mean?"

Charlie took another sip of tea and closed his eyes for a moment before speaking again. "The details are a bit fuzzy, but from what I remember, he had fled Nigeria. Some of his closest friends had been executed, an' your old man feared he was gonna be next. 'Wrongly trialled,' he kept sayin'. He came back to England out of fear for his life."

Esther leaned back into the settee, trying to digest what she had just heard. From her father's last letter to her mother, she understood he had fled Nigeria to escape some kind of danger, but she was none the wiser to what this was. Whatever this threat had been to her father, it was clearly serious as it had taken the lives of his friends, whoever they had been.

"But he looked worse for wear," Charlie continued, taking a biscuit from the plate. "Battered an' bruised. I dunno what was happenin' over there in that part of Nigeria you're from, but Ken took a big hit. Never seen a man so rattled."

Esther began to feel regret and shame creep up on her, like an unwanted cold. While her father and mother had been fearing for their lives in Ogoniland, she had been living all the way in Chicago, living her own life without a care. Memories of wild nights in Miami, drowning her soul in a potent cocktail of sex and drugs, only intensified her shame. Esther rubbed her head to wipe away the negative thoughts playing havoc with her mind.

"So why did my father want to speak to *you* when he escaped Nigeria and came back to London?" Esther said, once she felt more composed.

"Well, I dunno if ya remember, as you were so young back then, but me an' Ken used to work together on the docks in east London way back in the seventies. My parents were Irish immigrants, an' since your old man was black, of course, we sorta formed a bond based on our mutual disgust for the British wankers." Charlie let out a belly-fuelled laugh, which prompted uneasy smiles and side glances from both Esther and Elijah. "Anyway, me 'ard-working Irish parents gave me a flat they owned in Brixton to manage. When we lost our jobs on the docks, Ken got some office job in Vauxhall, so I let the flat in Loughborough Estate to him, so he could move in there with you an' your mum. When he came to see me after he had fled Nigeria, he wanted to find out if I was rentin' a room in the flat. He said he didn't need the whole flat no more since your mum was still back in Nigeria an' he was estranged from you." Charlie narrowed his eyes at Esther and paused, as if he was contemplating whether he should utter his next sentence. "He told me you'd abandoned the family to go to America."

Esther felt a lump in her throat and fought back the tears that were trying to force their way out from the edges of her eyes. "So, what happened?" she snapped.

Charlie regarded her for a moment before continuing. "Well, I didn't have the flat no more, I'd given it to me daughter an' her twat of a husband, Simon. Anyways, I didn't hear from or see your old man again until a few months later when I bumped into him by chance at a pub in Cannin' Town. He had taken up a teachin' job at a school in Custom House an' moved in with a woman named Charlotte somethin' or the other, can't remember. But he sounded much happier. I tried to call him some time after but his number weren't workin' no more."

All these new details about her father were spinning through Esther's head, like dirty laundry in a washing machine. She exhaled and put her mug on the table. "Do you remember the name of the school where my father had worked?"

"Yeah, Rosetta Primary School. I wish I could help more, love. But if you're lookin' for your old man, ya best bet would be to go to Cannin' Town an' visit that school. I reckon he stayed there for a while. Teachers always leave behind traces of themselves at schools."

CHAPTER 9

June 2008

The Pentecostal Church of Christ's grand hall was resplendent with purple and gold colours. To celebrate the seventieth birthday of Dinah Oduwole, the entire space had been transformed. Pots and platters, filled with the best Nigerian cuisine had to offer, had been placed on tables at the rear of the hall and guests were not wasting any time filling their plates with mountains of food. There was jollof rice, which was present at any self-respecting Nigerian party, *suya*, *moin moin*, fried plantain and, Elijah's personal favourite, *puff puff*. Mary had cooked a lot of food over the past two days, but still others had brought their own home-cooked Nigerian delicacies stored in woven nylon, tote bags and blue food coolers.

Nigerians and others from the African and Caribbean diaspora in London, who were friends of the Oduwole family, were all in attendance. Every guest wore traditional Nigerian attire in vibrant shades of purple and gold – Elijah's mother's favourite colours. The party was now in full swing as Shina Peters' 'Afro JuJu' boomed loudly from the large rented speakers, and people danced in the middle of the hall, moving their shoulders and waist to the upbeat rhythm.

Elijah stood next to his nephew Joshua and admired his mother. She was in the centre of the room, surrounded by people spraying dollar notes over her head. Even in her golden years, Dinah Oduwole was no slouch. Elijah's mother bounced on the spot in a circular motion, her back slightly arched, glowing in her purple *ankara* gown and her golden head wrap.

Joshua tugged at Elijah's purple trousers. "Uncle, how can grandma still dance so well when she is so old?" he said in his squeaky voice.

Elijah smiled at his nephew and placed an arm around him, pulling the boy closer to his waist. "If you eat yam and *egusi* soup, you will be able to dance like Michael Jackson even when you're one hundred."

Joshua's face fell in disappointment, as if he had just been told that Father Christmas was a fraud. "Really? But I don't like *egusi* soup."

Elijah rolled his head back in laugher. Not many people could make him laugh till his ribs hurt as effortlessly as his nephew could. Elijah recalled the night Joshua was born at King's College Hospital.

Poor Kunle had almost collapsed when the doctors told him that Mary would need an emergency caesarean. All night in the hospital waiting room, Elijah, Jairus and their father had prayed with fervour, as if the existence of the world depended on Mary having a safe birth. Fortunately, God is good: Mary's caesarean delivery was without any complications, and Joseph was born a healthy baby boy.

As the thought of childbirth occupied Elijah's mind, he consciously diverted his eyes to Tiwa. His wife was across the hall with her back to him, clearing some plates from a table. Elijah had not seen his wife for most of the day as she had woken up early to go and help his sister and the other women prepare the hall and the rest of the food for the party. But now, as he watched her, he could appreciate her curvaceous figure wrapped in the violet *ankara* gown with gold petal shapes sewn into the lace. Tiwa briefly turned her head to the side and Elijah caught a glimpse of the left side of her face. She had applied the right amount of foundation to her brown skin and her lipstick, the colour of a rose petal, was a seductive invitation for him to taste her lips.

Telling Joshua to go and find his father, Elijah proceeded to cut through the dancing bodies, like wading through a dense jungle, towards Tiwa. As he reached her, Tiwa turned around with a rubbish bag in her hands. She gave Elijah a faint smile.

"I haven't seen you all day," Elijah said, placing a hand on her waist and giving her a kiss, which she returned, but then quickly pulled back afterwards, as if Elijah's lips were laced with pepper. This action made Elijah feel a pang of rejection but he ignored it and instead gave his wife a compliment. "It's criminal, you're upstaging most of the women here."

Tiwa laughed. It sounded forced, as did most of her interactions with him nowadays. It was like watching an actor following a boring script. "Well, as your wife, it's good to know your eyes still belong to me," she said, turning away from Elijah to place more empty plates into the rubbish bag in her hands. "Have you seen Mary?"

Elijah shook his head.

Tiwa breathed a sign of exhaustion. "If you see her, tell her I am looking for her, please. We've finished all the Guinness, and the big uncles are troubling me about it. Anyway, I have to go. We'll catch up soon."

Elijah knew he shouldn't have let his wife walk away exhausted and irritated. He should have taken the rubbish bag from her hand, pulled her close to him and led her to the dance floor. He should have whispered in her ear: "I know what you're going through, and I am here to talk." But he did none of that. Instead, he simply let her go, watching her trudge away in the opposite direction. *She is in God's hands*, Elijah reminded himself. There was nothing he could do that would give her what she wanted. What they had both wanted.

With a heavy sigh, Elijah turned back around to face the dancing mass in the middle of the hall. He smiled when he witnessed Joshua and a few other children picking up the dollar notes from the floor, but they soon scattered as Kunle dove in, grabbed Joshua by the ear and pulled his son away. Near the rear of the hall, Elijah saw Mary and Jairus talking to Lucien. He had invited Lucien but not really stayed with him. Too many people wanted to speak with Elijah, as usual. Feeling like he needed to be a better host, Elijah walked over.

"Apologies for leaving you alone, Lucien. I hope my brother and sister have not shared any embarrassing details about me," Elijah said, entering their group with a smile.

Lucien beamed at Elijah. He was a twenty-five-year-old man of Senegalese origin with a short-boxed beard and thick brown dreads that reached his shoulders. Jairus gave Elijah a side glance. Unsurprisingly, his younger brother gave off the air of someone who was trying to subdue their irritation.

"There are too many embarrassing moments to tell," Mary said, winking at Elijah from beside Jairus. "Lucien was just telling us all about his church in Paris."

Elijah had met Lucien Carmen on a six-month missionary trip to Paris in 2004. At the time, Lucien was a troubled twenty-one-year-old man, arrested numerous times for delinquent offences and had spent frequent spells in prison. Elijah had the responsibility of educating Lucien and other troubled teenagers at a youth centre in the Paris suburbs about Christianity. Unlike the other missionaries, Elijah seemed to understand Lucien's angry and conflicted young mind without judging him. They soon formed a solid friendship and then one day, Lucien confided to Elijah that he was gay.

From their discussions, Lucien had probably sensed that Elijah was more open-minded than the other Christian missionaries. After Elijah returned to London, he kept in touch with Lucien, checking in on him over the years. Then three weeks ago, Lucien emailed Elijah to tell him that he was moving to London to study. Elijah responded to Lucien's email, asking him if he could lead a sermon for the church's youth service – many of the young black boys and girls, who grew up in south London, needed to hear Lucien's message. Much to Elijah's delight, Lucien agreed and was open to sharing his experiences about crime and life in prison.

"Yes, I was saying how there really needs to be more outreach to the youth," Lucien said, his French accent colouring every word he spoke. "Elijah, when you spoke to me about Christianity when I was a younger man, it saved my life. Troubled young people are open to Christianity if we as Christians come from a place of understanding. Just like you did."

"A Christian who cannot empathise, cannot evangelise," Elijah said with a smile. "We should make that the Church slogan." Elijah turned to Mary. "Tiwa is looking for you. Something about there not being enough Guinness."

Mary rolled her eyes and sighed. "Well, looks like I'll have to leave you, gentleman. It was a pleasure to meet you, Lucien."

"The pleasure is all mine."

After Mary hurried off to find Tiwa, Elijah, Jairus and Lucien spent the next twenty minutes talking about the growth of protestant African churches in France. They then moved on to more trivial subjects such as French food and whether Thierry Henry was the best black French footballer to date.

"Well, I better start heading off," Lucien said, checking his watch and then giving a friendly smile to both Elijah and

Jairus. "It was a pleasure to finally meet you, Jairus." Lucien extended his arm to initiate a handshake. Elijah watched, with narrowed eyes, as Jairus quickly shook Lucien's right hand before withdrawing his own hand sharply.

"I'll see you next Sunday," Elijah said, clasping his hands around Lucien's and beaming at him. "Thank you again for agreeing to speak at the youth service. I really appreciate this."

"Think nothing of it, Pastor. You saved my life so it's the bare minimum I can do, to be honest."

As soon as Lucien was out of hearing distance, Jairus turned to Elijah. "His French accent is so strong, I hope the young people don't struggle to understand him," he said. "I had to really concentrate to understand him at times."

"Why must you be so judgemental?" Elijah said, picking up a bottle of Supermalt from the table behind them. "You are like the Pharisees. Self-righteous to the core."

Jairus chuckled and put small pieces of crunchy, honey-coloured *chin chin* into his mouth from the pile he had in his left hand. "So hypocritical of you to call me self-righteous. You become head of the church after our father's death and what is one of your first acts? You invite a homosexual man to lead the youth worship. Would father have allowed such a thing? You let your compassion guide you too much."

"Maybe you're not compassionate enough," Elijah said, taking a sip of his Supermalt. "Lucien is a Christian, and he's young. He can relate to the youth, and they will relate to him. What does his sexual orientation have to do with anything? Are you so against the idea of accepting a Christian who does not follow what you deem to be sexual norms?"

Jairus scowled at Elijah. "It's not about what I deem to be normal, big brother. It's about what scripture says. It's about what message we're sending to our congregation if they find out a homosexual man is preaching to their children. Our numbers will fall drastically. What will you do then, Elijah?"

"Can we not do this now, Jairus?" Elijah said. He watched his mother take a seat at the banquet table at the front of the hall. "Let's not have one of our usual arguments. Not on our mother's birthday. Please."

Jairus sucked his teeth and finished all the *chin chin* on the palm of his hand. He now wore a sour look on his face, which made him resemble an angry poodle. Amused by this, Elijah grinned at his stubborn younger brother. Just as he was about to pat Jairus on the shoulder and tell him to cheer up, Jairus said something that took Elijah by surprise.

"What are you doing spending so much time with your ex-girlfriend?" Jairus slowly looked into Elijah's eyes and smirked. He seemed pleased that he had caught Elijah off guard.

"Excuse me?"

"I know she came to the church at our father's funeral, I saw you two speaking on the steps of the church. And the next day, after the executive board meeting, I went to Electric Avenue to buy some plantain and saw you speaking to her again. You both walked off together. Then Wednesday this week, I was on the bus and, lo and behold, I see her getting into your car near that fancy white building in Streatham."

Elijah did his best to tighten the lid on a rising steam of anger within him. Not only had his younger brother been spying on him, but now Jairus was questioning what he did during his spare time. Elijah didn't owe his brother any explanation. Still, he did not want to encourage any misguided suspicions in Jairus's mind. Elijah made sure he was level-headed in his response.

"I've been helping her with some personal things that I feel I don't need to disclose with you," Elijah said. "She's just an old friend."

"An old ex-girlfriend."

"Your point?"

"Does Tiwa know?"

The line of questioning was testing Elijah's patience, and it took some self-control for Elijah not to snap at Jairus in anger. He let his mind cool down for a few seconds before he answered, "Yes, she knows."

It was one of those automatic lies that sped out of Elijah's mouth like a track-and-field sprinter, and he could not call it back. But it was not just the act of lying to his brother that took Elijah by surprise. It was the fact he had not told his wife about Esther, and Elijah was suddenly conscious of this. What did he have to hide?

Jairus stared deeply into his brother's face as if he were looking for something that might give Elijah away. "Do not forget your position in the church and the community, Elijah. Remember what Jesus said to his sleeping disciples at Gethsemane."

Before Elijah could ask his brother what he was trying to imply, although he clearly understood the implication of the remark, Jairus walked away.

Elijah watched him, feeling the usual sense of exasperation towards his brother but also a less familiar type of anger – one aimed at himself. He wasn't sure what this anger meant or if he wanted to really understand it, afraid of what it could lead him to. Jesus' words to the sleeping disciples at Gethsemane echoed in his mind.

"Watch and pray so that you will not enter into temptation. For the spirit is willing, but the body is weak."

CHAPTER 10

January 1981

It was a mild and dry Friday afternoon as the bell rang inside Dick Sheppard School and a mass of students came pouring out. Another day of learning, for a small minority of them, playground antics and self-discovery in the form of rebellion had temporarily come to an end. Some students, mostly the younger ones, went straight home either by taking the 2B towards Brixton or in the opposite direction towards Streatham and Crystal Palace, depending on where they lived. For those who lived in Tulse Hill or on the estate, they walked home in groups of two or three. Others loitered in the playground to play football or waited to attend an after-school club. A handful of teenagers headed to Brockwell Park for no other reason than to spend more time with their friends rather than go home – which was another place of rules and routine.

It was for this very reason that Esther never went home straight after school. Although her father had complained many times that she arrived home too late – "Children of God" did not walk the streets at night – he could not punish her. Esther's reason or, more accurately, her lie for coming home late was the alleged extra help she was receiving with her maths homework.

As Esther walked across the playground beside Ayesha, she turned her head and studied her friend's appearance, something she found herself doing often. Esther admired Ayesha's dark skin and her curly afro, but she was not the only one. At school, and across Brixton, Ayesha was recognised for her beauty. Such was her reputation that even boys from Tulse Hill School talked about her as if she was south-London royalty. All the girls in their year coveted a friendship with her. Yet Ayesha had chosen Esther as her female companion and confidante. It was with Esther that she shared her cigarettes behind the science block, and it was with Esther that she talked about the boys she had snogged and wanted to snog. They had not even agreed to be friends; they just had an unspoken and natural connection, like the moon orbiting the Earth.

"Dwayne wants to hang out at Brockwell Park," Ayesha said, turning to face Esther. She was twirling a strand of her curly hair. "He's gonna be with Jermaine, and he wanted me to bring you. Is that alright?"

For the past month, Ayesha had talked non-stop about how she wanted to date Dwayne. He was a slim, fifteen-year-old Jamaican boy, who lived on Railton Road and had just as much popularity capital as Ayesha. None of the boys at school confronted Dwayne because his gangster older brother had stabbed and killed someone in Brixton. Esther had lost count of how many times Dwayne retold this story to all the boys and girls every lunchtime in the playground as if it were proof of his family's criminal prestige. Jermaine was his cousin, and most of the boys in the school gravitated towards the two of them. Any who didn't kept their distance out of either fear or respect.

"Yeah, I'm cool with that," Esther said to Ayesha. "Just the four of us?"

Ayesha turned to Esther and gave her a naughty grin. This told Esther everything about what they would be getting up to at the park. Whether she was looking forward to it, Esther was not entirely sure, but she was going more for her friend's sake than her own.

As Esther and Ayesha walked out of the school gates and into the main street, Esther spotted Elijah standing at a bus stop at the opposite end of the road. He was reading what looked like a small, thick book which, knowing Elijah, was probably a Bible.

"Ayesha, wait for me. I'm gonna quickly speak to Elijah. Two minutes, okay?"

Ayesha looked at Esther with a horrified expression, as if Esther had just told her she was going to impale herself on the school gates. But before Ayesha could voice an objection, Esther had already darted across the road to meet Elijah.

"Hey, Prophet," Esther said with a smile as she put her finger in between the pages Elijah was reading.

Elijah looked up from his Bible and returned the smile. "What's up?" Like most of the black boys in the school, Elijah had a tidy afro, but he didn't wedge his afro-comb in his hair or roll up his trousers. It was these small characteristics that she had grown to like about Elijah. He was not absorbed with the opposite sex or fighting other boys to prove who was the hardest. For Esther, this gave Elijah a certain depth that pulled her towards him like a gravitational force.

"Just came over to say thank you for helping with my maths work in class today. How are you so good with numbers? And please, don't say God."

Elijah chuckled. "Maybe it's my big African head." He lightly tapped his forehead with his knuckles. "Big but useful, eh?"

Esther laughed and was about to invite Elijah to come with her and Ayesha to Brockwell Park, but her better judgement prevented the words from leaving her mouth. While she considered Elijah to be a friend, he could not mix with Ayesha and the other popular boys and girls she hung out with. Elijah was the only person that she could talk to about her love for jazz and soul music and ask questions about religion. But she could never bring him over to the other part of her world where she talked about sex, occasionally smoked cannabis and listened to reggae music with Ayesha. Both Elijah and Ayesha were important to her but for very different reasons. It was more convenient for Esther if they both remained separate parts of her social life.

Elijah nodded in the direction of the school fence, and Esther turned her head to see Ayesha waving at her. She wore an impatient look on her face.

"Looks like Ayesha really wants you to go with her," Elijah said.

Esther sighed and turned back to Elijah. "Yeah, she does. Hey, have a nice weekend, alright? See you on Monday."

"You too. Oh, remember, we have Bible class on Sunday."

Esther rolled her eyes but smiled. It was such a typical comment from Elijah. Not caring what Ayesha would think for once, Esther gave Elijah a hug, the first she had ever given him. She then darted back across the road to meet Ayesha, who was shaking her head with disapproval.

"I don't get it. Why do you hang out with him?" Ayesha said, her tone a mixture of curiosity and repulsion, as she walked alongside Esther through Brockwell Park's grassy field. "Like I really, really don't get it, you know? He's so boring. Mr Bible boy."

"We just go to the same church." Esther shrugged as she plucked a leaf from a nearby bush. "It's the only reason I talk to him." Even as the words left her mouth, Esther was irritated with herself. Why was she not confident enough to tell Ayesha that Elijah was a good friend? Was it out of fear that her best friend would like her less?

Ayesha nodded and played with her hair, seemingly no longer caring about Esther's friendship with Elijah, and the two of them traversed the field in silence, making their way towards an overbearing oak tree with long, thick branches that stretched out like forearms. The branches were covered in thousands of rust-coloured leaves, making for adequate cover if you were smoking a cigarette or kissing someone. Jermaine and Dwayne were standing underneath, and mischievous grins appeared on the two boys' faces as Esther and Ayesha approached them.

"Oi, what took you two so long, man?" Dwayne said, leaping towards Ayesha like an excited kid who was about to unwrap a birthday gift. He pulled her into a tight embrace, his hands already groping the back of her skirt. "You cool, yeah?" Dwayne said, nodding towards Esther.

"Yeah, I'm cool," Esther said with an uneasy smile. Over Dwayne's shoulder, she saw Jermaine leaning against the tree trunk. He stared at Esther, his eyes focusing several inches below her face, and she immediately felt uncomfortable and embarrassed, as if a magician had clicked his fingers and made her clothes vanish. With a slight tilt of his head, Jermaine gestured for Esther to come to him. At first, Esther was not sure if she should, so she turned to get some encouragement from Ayesha. To her annoyance, Dwayne and Ayesha were already entangled in a passionate kiss. Esther sighed. Seeing no other choice, she ambled towards Jermaine with heavy steps.

As Jermaine kissed her neck and squeezed her bum cheeks with his cold hands underneath her skirt, Esther squirmed inside, paralysed by a combination of embarrassment and uneasiness. It was not that Jermaine was unattractive – a light-skinned boy with curly brown hair – but there was something about his demeanour that she found off-putting. This feeling made her muscles tighten whenever he touched her. Thankfully, Jermaine had no desire to kiss her properly; he seemed far more interested in squeezing her bum.

"Listen yeah, me and Jermaine are going to a house party in New Cross tomorrow," Dwayne said. He had come up for air and Ayesha now had her arms wrapped around his waist. "It's a birthday party for a friend of a friend. A few guys and girls from Moonshot Club are gonna be there. You two gonna come with us, yeah?"

Moonshot Club was a popular social club for black youths in New Cross that occasionally hosted reggae nights. Esther had only been there once. One night, two weeks ago, when Esther's mother had been working a night shift and her father had left the house, Esther had snuck out to attend a reggae sound clash with Ayesha and her Jamaican cousin who lived in New Cross.

"That sounds wicked," Ayesha said, looking at Dwayne with dreamy eyes, which irritated Esther but she was not quite sure why. "But you gotta drive us there, yeah?"

"That's cool with me," Dwayne replied.

Ayesha winked at Esther, who returned the gesture with an uncertain smile. She was not entirely sure how she was supposed to attend a party in New Cross on Saturday. Most likely, she would have to sneak out at night and risk the wrath of her father unless he left the house again.

Another fifteen minutes followed of awkward groping, neck kissing and, in the case of Dwayne and Ayesha, intense mouth wrestling before both boys said goodbye to Esther and Ayesha. They had some business to sort out in Brixton. "See you on Saturday," Ayesha called, as the two boys made their way towards the park's exit.

Esther straightened her ruffled skirt and frowned at Ayesha. "You should have asked me first if I wanted to go to this party in New Cross. You know my parents ain't like yours. I can't just do whatever I want."

Ayesha gave Esther a tight hug and did not let go as she spoke. "You're right, sorry. You know I always say things without thinking. I hope you can come. I really want you to."

Esther sighed, and her brief annoyance at Ayesha evaporated. She couldn't stay irritated at her best friend for so long. Esther broke away from Ayesha's embrace and nodded her head.

Then a strange feeling, something Esther had experienced a few times before, passed through her.

Esther's eyes rested on Ayesha's mouth, focusing on her moist, pink lower lip. Her heart rate increased, and she felt like she was standing at the edge of a cliff, ready to jump into a waterfall but not quite sure if she should.

It happened suddenly and silently. Esther's lips locked with Ayesha's. With a longing that Ayesha had never shown her before, she pulled Esther into her and wrapped her arms around Esther's waist. Esther closed her eyes, but she did not need to open them. For the first time in her life, she experienced what it meant to be led entirely by her own desire. Her sexual feelings towards Ayesha, creeping around her mind like a strange guest all this time, had finally become a permanent resident.

Ayesha broke away. Both were panting from the adrenaline rush of their first kiss. It had lasted only a minute, but it had been one of the most intense minutes of Esther's life so far. Although she didn't fully understand it, Esther knew she was not the same girl that she had been at the start of the day. A previously contained part of her had now been given permission to roam free.

"You okay?" Ayesha said. She was smiling at Esther, a warm smile, full of affection and lust.

"Yeah," Esther said, grinning back.

"Let's go watch the boys play football."

Esther nodded.

Walking close together, with their hands interlocked, Esther and Ayesha headed towards the entrance of the park. Esther knew that what had happened between the two of them underneath the oak tree today would now become a secret but vital part of their friendship. Stealing a glance at Ayesha's face, Esther felt her heartbeat quicken just thinking about the next time she would get to taste her lips again.

CHAPTER 11

June 2008

The late afternoon was warm, the sky a cloudless blue and everything seemed brighter as Esther walked alongside Elijah. They were ambling up a narrow suburban street that led towards Rosetta Primary School. In her ripped brown jeans, laced-up, six-inch Timberland boots and her white shoestring cami, Esther looked like she was going to a Mary J. Blige music video. Elijah, on the other hand, looked like he was on his way to a boardroom meeting.

When Elijah had come to pick her up, Esther had noticed how his eyes widened and his jaw dropped when she walked out of the flat. As a forty-year-old woman, Esther was no longer bothered about seeking validation of her beauty from men or women. But she had to admit that she enjoyed Elijah's eyes admiring the grown-ass-woman sexuality that poured from her. It was flattering.

"Can I be nosy?" Elijah said as they walked side by side.

"You're Nigerian; you're nosy by nature," Esther said, turning to grin at Elijah.

Elijah let out a light chuckle. "Why now?"

Esther looked at him, puzzled. "What do you mean?"

"Well, from what I remember, you never really got along with your father. You always used to tell me how he beat you and punished you for trivial things. You haven't spoken to him or your mother for eighteen years, right?"

Esther nodded.

"Just wondering what prompted you to want to look for him now. How did you know he had left Nigeria to come back to London?"

Esther considered Elijah's questions for a moment. Having been estranged from her parents for eighteen years now, it was not a subject she liked to get into. By the time she had turned forty, the memories of her parents had become like fossils – forgotten and buried underneath years and years of other experiences and memories. And then one day, those fossils were unexpectedly excavated.

Esther released a heavy sigh before she spoke. "I'll answer your questions but to give you more context, so you know, I'm currently a teacher at Chicago's School of Music."

"A teacher!" Elijah said in an astonished tone as if she had said she was an astronaut. "Didn't you once tell me that your father had been a teacher in Nigeria before your family came to London?"

"Look at you, with your impressive memory," Esther said. She was touched that Elijah had remembered this detail about her life that she had told him almost twenty years ago. "But anyway, while I was teaching a class, the office administrator came to tell me that someone had called the school from Nigeria asking to speak to me. The person on the line was my mother."

Elijah raised his eyebrows. "Wow."

"I know," Esther said in a faint voice. She still remembered standing in the school reception two months ago, her hands had trembled and her heartbeat was so rapid, she felt it might burst from her chest. "When I heard my mother say my name..." She turned to face Elijah, looking into his dark-brown eyes. "I almost collapsed on the spot. Her voice was so laboured, it was like every breath she took was an effort. Hearing her voice like that after so many years… I cried. It was a lot to take in, you know?"

"Of course. I understand," Elijah said, looking pensive.

"We didn't speak much; the line was so bad. But my mother told me she had tracked me down on the internet with the help of her carer – a young boy called Noah. She said that she and my father had returned to Nigeria soon after I left for Chicago. Then in 1996, my father fled Nigeria and returned to London because he was in danger. She didn't elaborate on why he was in danger. Anyway, she told me that she hadn't received a letter from my father since last December. I told her to send me the letter, and I'd travel to London to find him. Two months later, here I am."

Elijah was silent for a moment as if he were carefully choosing his words before speaking. "God has an unexpected way of working sometimes," he finally said, looking ahead as they reached the school playground, guarded by dark-green gates. "I believe your mother contacting you was God's way of uniting your family."

Esther smiled to herself, knowing Elijah would say something religiously profound. Still, her heart had been comfortably sharing a king-size bed with atheism and cynicism for far too long to really believe it. "That's a nice sentiment, but I'm not much of a big believer in God, Pastor."

"When were you ever?" Elijah said in a teasing voice, lightly elbowing her.

Esther playfully pushed his elbow away. "But I do believe I'm looking for my father for my mother's sake. She deserves closure."

Elijah looked at her, and Esther saw a profound sense of understanding in his eyes. "Maybe you deserve that closure too," he said.

After a quick discussion with the school's caretaker, Esther and Elijah found out that Mrs Herbertson was the headmistress of the primary school. He had given them directions to her office, and Esther now stood in front of Mrs Herbertson's door, with Elijah by her side. She knocked and heard a woman, who was presumably Mrs Herbertson, say, "Please enter," in a very formal and well-spoken accent. Esther immediately had an image in her head of a posh and stiff British woman. She was not proven wrong.

With a gleaming freshwater pearl necklace around her thin neck, chiselled cheekbones and shoulder-length brunette hair, Mrs Herbertson was the epitome of a school headmistress, and she wore her steely authority and by-the-book demeanour like a tailored suit.

At first, the headmistress was quite accommodating when Esther asked if she could confirm whether a man by the name of Kelechi Nubari worked at the school. Mrs Herbertson, in a polite but stony tone of voice, said that she had indeed hired Mr Nubari, who had gone by the name of Ken instead of Kelechi. He had been an English teacher from 5th November 1996, and his employment had officially ended on December 20th 2006. Unfortunately, that was all the information Esther was going to get from Mrs Herbertson. Trying to extract anything else from the stubborn woman was equivalent to bending a steel pole with bare hands.

"I'm very sorry. I simply cannot divulge personal information such as Mr Nubari's address to you," Mrs Herbertson said. She spoke like someone who practised politeness rather than genuinely being a polite person. "Not without written consent from him or the authorities." She rested her elbows on the grey desk, folding her hands together under her chin with a sense of finality.

"But I'm his daughter," Esther said, putting both her hands on Mrs Herbertson's desk, which made the headmistress raise her eyebrows. "I'm desperate to find him."

Without blinking, Mrs Herbertson's thin lips curved into a smile, though Esther knew it was not a friendly one, but a warning that her patience was waning. "Be that as it may, I'm simply prohibited from giving you Mr Nubari's address. Even if you are his daughter, and I'm not disputing that you are, I would need proper proof of evidence or consent from Mr Nubari himself. I'm terribly sorry I cannot be of more help."

Cursing loudly in her mind, Esther grudgingly thanked Mrs Herbertson for her help and turned on her heel to leave the room, Elijah close behind her. As Esther stepped out of the headmistress's office, a young Indian woman, wearing a light-pink hijab, was waiting outside the door. Esther smiled at her politely and then walked past, stopping a few feet away.

"Stupid woman," Esther said, a bit of her original south-London accent piercing through the American.

"Never thought I'd see the day an *oyinbo* would make you leave a room," Elijah said in a joking tone.

"Oh, please, she didn't make me leave. I left because I wanted to, and who says I'm done," Esther huffed. With a renewed determination, Esther was about to march back into the headmistress's office but stopped. The young Indian woman she had passed on her way out of the office now stood directly beside her. She had an inquisitive expression on her face.

"Sorry to be nosy, but I overheard you speaking to Mrs Herbertson about Mr Nubari." The woman spoke with a soft, quiet voice that matched her small and unthreatening frame. "You're his daughter?"

Esther nodded her head in reply, fixing her eyes on the young woman. She was definitely in her very early twenties, with a small button nose, thin eyebrows and almond-shaped eyes. Just from her body language, she seemed welcoming and easy-going. Esther suspected she was a young teacher at the school, still full of warmth and hope, unlike her superior.

"My name is Khadija, I'm a teaching assistant here. I knew Mr Nubari really well. He was my English teacher when I was at school here, almost twelve years ago now. Honestly, he was one of the best teachers I ever had in my life. I can't tell you exactly where he is now, but I can maybe point you in the right direction."

Khadija's classroom felt like the interior of a giant, chaotic toy box. Multi-coloured Lego blocks, stuffed animals and crayons were strewn across the rainbow-coloured mats on the floor. Different shapes, drawn and cut by children, hung from the ceiling like lanterns, held by a string that stretched across the classroom. Esther and Elijah were sitting on two plastic chairs on a circular desk at the far end of the room. Khadija had poured them a cup of tea and was sitting opposite, recounting fond memories of her old teacher, Mr Ken Nubari.

"When I first moved from India to England, I remember feeling so alienated," Khadija said. Both her hands were wrapped around her mug as she spoke, her eyes looking dreamily at the dangling shapes hanging from the ceiling. "This was the first school I came to as an immigrant, and most of the teachers didn't understand what I was going through, but then your father became my English teacher. He was such a kind and understanding man." Khadija looked at Esther with a warm smile on her face. "You're lucky to have him as a father."

Even if she wanted to lie, Esther could not reconcile Khadija's opinion of her father with her own. The memories she had of her father were dark and violent. As Esther considered this, she was pulled back to the night when her father had almost killed her.

It was 1984. Esther had just finished her final year at Dick Sheppard after completing her O-levels. To celebrate, she had gone to see Gregory Issacs perform at Brixton Academy with Ayesha and a few other friends. Although she had smoked enough marijuana during the concert to knock out three Rastafarians, she could not forget that night.

After the concert had finished, Esther and Ayesha had walked through the dark and sinister streets of Brixton. Two girls giggling and singing in a haze of intoxication as deafening police sirens whizzed by and yardies eyed them up like human candy. Probably too high to realise, Ayesha had followed Esther all the way to her block of flats in Loughborough Estate. Before getting a taxi to take her back to Stockwell, where she lived, Ayesha had given Esther a long and passionate kiss. This was a dangerous act to do in public in those days, but Ayesha was always reckless.

Once Ayesha had left in the taxi, Esther made her way up to her parents' flat. It was late at night, so Esther did not expect them to be up. When she twisted the key in the lock and pushed the door open, her father was waiting in the corridor. Esther would always remember how her father had looked at her. She could feel the spite and disgust in his dark eyes. Then he had accused her of being a whore before taking off his leather belt and beating her. As she shielded her face, tears pouring from her eyes, she had pleaded with her father to stop, but he just kept lashing the belt against her skin, peeling off her flesh.

Fortunately, her mother had rushed from the bedroom and pulled her father away. While Esther was curled up on the floor, shaking and bleeding, her mother was on her knees, begging her father not to continue. Thankfully, this worked to calm her father's rage, and he walked away, leaving Esther trembling with pain and a hatred that was as raw as any of the wounds on her body.

Khadija was talking about a man Esther did not recognise as her father at all.

"Have you spoken to my father recently or over the years?" Esther said, bringing herself back to the present.

Khadija shook her head. "No, I haven't spoken to him since I left school." Perhaps sensing that something might be wrong,

Khadija's eyes widened with concern. "Has something happened to him?"

"I don't know, I haven't been in contact with my father for a very long time, that's why I'm looking for him," Esther said. She felt oddly touched that Khadija expressed such concern for her father's wellbeing. "When he was teaching at this school, he had fled from Nigeria. My mother, who's still over there, is very concerned because she hadn't heard from him since December last year."

Khadija seemed taken aback by all this new information, but she remained silent for a few seconds before speaking. "Well, I don't how useful this is to you, and I'm sorry to be the one to tell you this. Your father was having a relationship with a teacher at this school who has since retired," Khadija said, looking directly at Esther. "I remember that we always used to poke fun at Mr Nubari for having a crush on Miss Evans." Khadija smiled to herself. "I actually saw them kiss once, very briefly, near the teachers' lounge. I'm shocked to hear he had a wife."

Esther had begun to feel a touch of pity towards her father. Now, learning that he had started a new relationship with a woman in London, it was rapidly undone. Esther's mother had been left alone in Nigeria, desperately fearing for her husband's wellbeing like a dutiful wife. Meanwhile, her father was in London, sleeping with some British woman. In the last letter he had written to her mother, he had not even mentioned an extramarital relationship, and her mother clearly did not suspect anything.

Esther quelled her anger, ensuring it did not spill into her voice as she spoke. "What was Miss Evans's full name?"

Khadija closed her eyes for a moment, rubbing her forehead, before opening her eyes again with a pleased expression. "Charlotte. That's it! Charlotte Evans. A very quiet lady. As I mentioned, she's retired now, has been for a few years."

Esther had begun to suspect that this was the same woman Charlie Robinson mentioned, and now Khadija had confirmed it.

"I know Miss Evans lived in Canning Town, around an area called Custom House. I remember her always going on about taking her dog for a walk in Cundy Park." Khadija sipped her tea. "I don't know if she still lives there, though. Sorry, I know it's not a lot of information, but I hope it helps."

Esther shook Khadija's hand and thanked her for her help. As Elijah and Esther stood up to leave, Khadija rose to her feet and, with a faint smile, said, "I hope you find your father. He was a good teacher here. He was a good man."

It was nearing 6 p.m. by the time Esther was back in the passenger seat of Elijah's BMW. Next to her, Elijah drove in silence through Rotherhithe Tunnel, heading across the River Thames and back to south London. As he exited the tunnel, Elijah spoke to her.

"So, you've got a name and a rough location, Sherlock. Think you could find out if this Charlotte Evans still lives in Custom House with your father?"

Esther looked out the window, staring at the red double-decker bus that had stopped beside them. She noticed a couple of schoolgirls in their grey uniform step off the bus, giggling to each other. The sight of the young girls awoke a memory. A party in New Cross in January 1981. The night she almost lost her life. Instead, she lost her youthful optimism, replacing it with a burning rage that lasted throughout her teenage years.

"Yes, I think I can. Thank God for the internet, right?" Esther said, still observing the schoolgirls. "But first I'm going to New Cross tomorrow."

Elijah looked at her but said nothing. From his silence, she knew he understood.

The car drove away from the schoolgirls.

"I have to pay my respects," Esther said, more to herself than to Elijah.

CHAPTER 12

January 1981

Elijah had first learned of the terrible blaze from TV.

It was a Sunday evening in the Oduwole household in Denmark Hill. Elijah was sitting at the bottom of the staircase in his orange pyjamas, which had a large picture of Garfield the cat on the front. Mary, his seven-year-old sister, was sitting on the step above him in her pink nightgown, leaning over his back to get a better view of the television.

Peering through the banister, Elijah and Mary could see their parents standing in the middle of the living room. Both were watching ITV Weekend News on the TV set in the corner. They were completely motionless as they stared at the screen.

Elijah poked his ear through the wooden bars so that he could hear the news presenter more clearly.

"Nine people were killed and twenty injured in the blaze which engulfed a house in south London early this morning.

Victims of the fire, all young black men and women, were among guests celebrating a joint birthday party at a house in New Cross Road, Deptford.

One of the birthday girls, Yvonne Ruddock, is seriously ill in hospital.

Evidence suggests the fire started on the ground floor and quickly spread. Revellers were trapped upstairs by the smoke and flames...”

Elijah's father switched off the television. "What a tragedy." He sighed. "We must pray for the young victims at next Sunday's service." Elijah's mother nodded in response and leaned her head on his shoulders.

"Elijah, where is New Cross?" Mary whispered in her brother's ear.

Before Elijah could answer his little sister's question, their parents turned around and spotted them on the stairwell. A frown appeared on their father's dark brown face as he narrowed his eyes. "You both have school tomorrow, and you are spying on us?"

"Daddy, I—"

But Elijah's father waved his hand in annoyance and Elijah knew he dare not say another word. His father sucked his teeth. "You better take your sister upstairs and go to bed, O."

At Dick Sheppard the next morning, talk of the New Cross Fire was spoken in hushed murmurs in the classroom and then in animated conversations in the playground. In just a few hours, Elijah had heard dozens of rumours. During lunch, a West Indian boy called Clarence told Elijah and a group of others how the fire was started. According to Clarence, the fire starters were a group of white boys belonging to the far-right National Front group who had thrown a petrol bomb into the house. Clarence failed to disclose how exactly he knew all this, so Elijah took it with a pinch of salt.

The one rumour that troubled Elijah the most and injected his mind with fear was that Esther was one of the nine people who had been killed in the blaze. On his way to maths class, Elijah had overheard a group of fourteen-year-old girls, on the verge of tears, discussing how Esther, Ayesha, Dwayne and Jermaine had attended the party and all had died, except for Jermaine.

At first, Elijah did not believe it. You could not trust the news floating around the school any more than you could trust fortune cookies. But over the next four days, neither Esther, Ayesha nor Dwayne were seen at school. Jermaine was spotted outside the school gates, but he had gone before Elijah could speak to him.

By the end of the week, the number of people who died in the New Cross fire increased from nine to thirteen. None of the victims had been named yet.

Growing increasingly fretful with each passing day, Elijah included Esther in all his bedtime prayers. The thought of what could have happened to her troubled his mind incessantly. It got to the point where he was reading every newspaper when he walked into an off-licence in Brixton and watched the news every evening for any new developments about the fire.

Even at Sunday service, Esther's fate dominated Elijah's thoughts. Usually, Elijah would be sitting in the front benches, listening like a devoted disciple as his father took the stage to preach to the congregation. But on this Sunday, he was unable to focus. Instead, he spent most of the sermon turning his head this way and that, looking for any sign of Esther or her parents among the churchgoers.

His heart almost skipped a beat when he recognised the familiar balding head, dark-black skin and pencil moustache of Esther's father. But there was no sign of Esther or her mother with him.

When the church service had finished, Elijah squeezed through the crowd of people making their way out of the church. He lost count of how many times he apologised with "Sorry, Auntie" and "Excuse me, Uncle" as he pushed and shoved his way towards Esther's father. Just before Esther's father reached the entrance of the church, Elijah managed to catch up to him and yanked his long, brown *dashiki* robe. Esther's father turned around and stared blankly down at him.

"Uncle, where is Esther?" Elijah asked, still holding onto the robe.

A flash of annoyance crossed Esther's father's face, and he glowered at Elijah. He sucked his teeth, pulling the robe out of Elijah's hand, then, without answering the question, walked out of the church, leaving Elijah in a state of confusion and suffocating worry.

That night, the thought of Esther dying in the fire wreaked havoc with Elijah's mind. Visions of her screaming and burning in the blaze tormented him, and he woke up several times in a cold sweat.

Then on Monday he saw her.

Alighting from bus 2B, Elijah began his usual walk towards the school gates, shivering in the crisp morning air. Without giving it any thought, he looked towards Brockwell Park and a schoolgirl caught his attention. She was wearing a green backpack with her black hair in a ponytail and headphones over her head as she walked through the entrance to Brockwell Park. Although he did not see her face, Elijah intuitively knew it was Esther. Not caring that he would be late for his first class, Elijah dashed across the road and sprinted through the gates to the park.

It did not take long for Elijah to locate Esther. She was sitting by the massive oak tree, her head buried in her knees, surrounded by fallen leaves that had settled on the grass. Taking a deep breath, Elijah walked towards her.

"Hey."

Esther slowly lifted her head to face him. Elijah was stunned to see that her eyes were bloodshot, and lines of tears streaked her light-brown cheeks. He sat down in front of her and crossed his legs.

"Where have you been?"

Sniffing back more tears, Esther wiped her eyes with the sleeve of her school jumper. "I was at the hospital and then with the police. You heard about the fire?" Her voice was brittle, and her sentences came between deep, trembling breaths.

Elijah nodded. "You were there, I know. Is Ayesha alright?"

Esther bobbed her head in response, but she was not looking at Elijah. Instead, she was gazing at the park gates. Elijah turned around, but there was no one standing there. It was like she was looking at a ghost. This thought made Elijah feel uncomfortable.

"I don't know how it happened, Elijah."

Her voice was so low, almost like a whisper caught in the wind, that Elijah had barely heard her. Yet he knew not to respond. Something within him sensed that Esther wanted to talk, and all she needed from him was someone to listen. Nothing more.

"I was just with Ayesha on the top floor of the house. Me, her and Dwayne were dancing. The DJ was amazing, and we were just having a good time. Everyone was. I don't know how it happened." Esther was still looking at the park gates, her expression motionless as tears filled her eyes. Elijah remained silent.

"We heard a bang over the music, but I didn't think nothing of it. Then Yvonne's brother ran upstairs, shouting that there was a fire. I started to smell something burning, and the floor got weird like it had turned into rubber. We panicked. I grabbed Ayesha's hand, and we ran down to the second floor, but there was thick smoke everywhere. I couldn't breathe, and we couldn't see Dwayne anymore." Esther closed her eyes, letting the tears trickle down her cheeks.

"We couldn't go back for him. There was too much smoke. We couldn't breathe, and my face felt filthy…We saw all these people fighting to escape by jumping from a window. We had to jump, or we was gonna die. When I saw the spiked railings below, I was scared, but I thought about my mother, even my father, and just closed my eyes. Ayesha grabbed my hand and we jumped out of the second floor. Someone grabbed me when I fell, but Ayesha landed on the ground, cracked her head open."

Esther turned to look at Elijah and noticing the horrified look on his face, she quickly added: "Ayesha's in hospital. She's okay. Dwayne is…" Esther couldn't finish her sentence. "At least she didn't have to speak to the fucking police."

"What did the police do to you?"

For the first time since Elijah had walked over, Esther's face expressed a recognisable emotion: fierce hatred. Lines etched across her nose as she scrunched it up and sneered. For a moment, her face looked almost contorted. "Fucking cunts. The lot of them. They tried to convince me that I was lying, Elijah. I felt like I'd been bloody nicked. They kept trying to convince me that people had been fighting at the party, and that's what started the fire. To those white men, we was just a couple of rowdy black kids who caused the fire!" Tears started running down Esther's face again.

Elijah found himself shaking with anger at the immense pain his friend was suffering right in front of him. He swallowed a lump in his throat. "Esther—" Elijah did not finish his sentence as Esther spoke again. Her voice was loud and shrill now, her grief naked and raw for Elijah to see.

"If there's a God, Elijah, why the fuck would He let young people die at a party? We was just having a good time, and God sent us to fucking hell." The tears were flowing freely down her cheeks in thick streams. "What kind of God would do that!?"

Overcome with Esther's grief, Elijah embraced Esther and held her tight in his arms, her cheeks warm and wet against his. For what felt like an endless amount of time, Elijah simply held on to Esther and did not dare to let her go, fearing she would be dragged away by the claws of her own anguish.

"Can you feel it in the air?" Esther whispered in Elijah's ear.

"Feel what?"

"How clear the morning is, but there's something uneasy about it. Like when you look at the clouds, and you know a storm is coming."

March 1981

In all her time living in London, Esther had never seen so many black faces all at once. To say it was an army of black people would not have done it justice; it was more like a small island of black people had landed in New Cross. Esther stood just outside Moonshot Club in Fordham Park, a placard in her hand, the phrase *Thirteen Dead and Nothing Said* written in bold, black letters. Beside her stood Elijah, who, like Esther, was still in his school uniform, as they had both walked out of school to attend today's march. In front of them was Ayesha's mother, holding an umbrella in the slight drizzle. Ayesha herself was still at the hospital recovering from her head injury. Thousands and thousands of black people from across all corners of England stood at every corner of the park.

Shortly after the New Cross Fire, the New Cross Massacre Action Group had formed. Esther had volunteered to help in any way she could. The group was a response to the indifference of the police and the pathetic progress of their investigation. To the British establishment, the lives of thirteen black children, burned out like a candle, did not matter. They had just been rowdy black kids – no families, no friends, no lives and now no future. The memory of the police's cold and unsympathetic interrogation of her six weeks ago still made Esther's fists curl until her veins throbbed.

The New Cross Massacre Action Group had organised the march today: the "Black People's Day of Action." It intended to highlight to the nation that black people were done with being ignored and treated like stray urban foxes in this country. This was their country too, whether white British people approved or not. As Esther looked around, she could feel her heartbeat pounding faster. She had read about Martin Luther King and his marches for black liberation, and this sort of felt like the British equivalent. It felt that significant.

"We're making history, you know," Esther said, interlocking her arm with Elijah's. "Fuck the police wankers."

Elijah turned to Esther, raising one eyebrow in disapproval. "Come on, Esther. Be peaceful, yeah."

"Listen to your friend, Esther," said Ayesha's mother, Shanice, in her sharp Jamaican accent. "Deez iz not the Black Panthers, girl. Violence only begets violence."

But their words were unable to traverse the iron wall of anger and grief fortified around Esther's heart.

By 11 a.m., the masses of black people gathered began their march from Fordham Park to Hyde Park in central London. They would walk through New Cross, stride across Blackfriars Bridge into the city and onto Fleet Street. They would march towards the Houses of Parliament before concluding their journey at Hyde Park, the heart of London.

Placard raised in the air, Esther shouted at the very top of her lungs, although she was still having difficulty breathing properly because of the smoke she had inhaled at the New Cross house party.

"Blood ah go run!"

As they walked, banners displaying the faces of the young people who had perished in the New Cross Massacre waved high above the moving assembly and a white truck, carrying a booming sound system, drove slowly with the crowd. Several police officers lingered at the edges with weary looks on their faces. They obviously weren't used to such a sight, afraid of the collective display of unity among Britain's black community.

But as they reached the entrance to Blackfriars Bridge, Esther saw rows of more police officers, their black bobby helmets strapped to their stern white faces, standing guard. It was clear that they were not going to allow this march to go on any further. To them, enough was enough.

Esther could hear the exhilaration and rage ringing in her ears, encouraging her to fight, like coaches goading a boxer before stepping into the ring. Without thinking about it, Esther handed her placard to Elijah.

"Hey, what are you doing?"

But Esther ignored him and, along with a few dozen other black youths, launched herself through the crowd towards the police cordon.

"Get the fuck out of our way!" Esther screamed in the face of one of the policemen. "You bloody pigs. You can't stop us. You fucking hear me!"

Then Esther stumbled back. She felt the cold concrete underneath her as she landed on her backside. One of the police officers had pushed her to the floor with considerable force. This act unleashed the anger of the people on the frontlines of the march. Suddenly, a scuffle between some of the black youths and the police officers erupted as they tried to break through the barrier.

Initially shocked by the police officer's push, Esther was now on her feet and ready to battle. Amid the discord of shoving, grabbing and punching, as the youths fought against the police, Esther's eyes caught an empty green bottle on the floor. Caring little for the consequences of what she was about to do, Esther picked the bottle up. She aimed it at the police officer who had pushed her; it was time to fight violence with violence.

Someone firmly grabbed her wrist.

Esther swung her head around and saw Elijah glaring at her. In all the time they had been friends, she had never seen him so angry, but there was something else within his seething eyes. Deep disappointment.

Clarity tore through Esther's fury like sunbeams piercing through dark clouds after a storm. The green bottle slipped from her hand and landed on the ground with a clink.

With tears in her eyes, Esther hugged Elijah and whispered in his ear. "I'm sorry."

The white truck with the sound system drove past the two of them, its Rasta flag waving in the air. Unable to repel the bullish crowd and faced with the incoming truck, the police broke their cordon, and the black youth rushed onto Blackfriars Bridge.

At last, they were no longer at an impasse, and the march peacefully continued into the heart of London's political and financial infrastructure, carrying the righteous anger of a people with a newfound collective identity.

CHAPTER 13

June 2008

Esther laid the wreath of flowers on the black railings outside house No.439 on New Cross Road in Deptford. She stepped back and examined the brown-brick terraced house. Its bricks were no longer charred from the hellish blaze that had engulfed the building on that fateful Sunday morning. The sounds, smells and sights of the house fire came back to Esther, faint and unclear, as they were old memories now but no less horrific. Esther closed her eyes to halt the onslaught of tormenting visions. Twenty-seven years after the tragedy, she still remembered. Even now, she occasionally suffered from mild breathing problems from inhaling so much smoke.

Feeling that she had paid her respects to the thirteen teenagers that had died in the fire, Esther took one last look at No.439. She then raised the white Sony headphones wrapped around her neck back over her ears and played The Crusaders' 'Street Life', before heading down New Cross Road towards the station.

Like Brixton, the look of New Cross had not altered so drastically from when Esther used to come here as a teenager. But it certainly had a different feel. The high street was still lined with the same barbershops, corner shops, pubs, and the Venue nightclub, which she had attended in the late eighties, but New Cross did not feel like the hostile place it had once been for black people.

In Brixton, during the late seventies, eighties and nineties, the black community was prominent enough that white locals at the time had a weary cautiousness towards black people as if they were uncaged leopards. Deptford was a different jungle. Back when they were teenagers, Ayesha used to tell Esther how her cousins were routinely shot at with pellet guns and had racial slurs hurled at them as they walked the streets of New Cross. Not to mention the racially motivated arson attacks happening across Lewisham that Ayesha would always describe from the harrowing accounts her cousins told her.

As Esther walked past a group of teenagers laughing together, some black and some white, she smiled to herself; at least some change had occurred. All her efforts campaigning and protesting as a young teenager had made a difference for this new generation of young black teenagers. It certainly felt like it.

A few steps on, and Esther strode past Deptford Town Hall, a building with a regal quality about it, before stopping in front of a pub opposite New Cross Gate station called Hobgoblin – a strange name for a pub. Still, the Hobgoblin had a certain warm charm to it, so Esther went inside.

"I'll have a pint of...actually just a glass of rosé, please," Esther said. From what she could see, a lot of international students who went to Goldsmiths University seemed to visit the pub. Maybe that was why the beanie-wearing bartender did not bat an eyelid at Esther's accent like other Londoners did when she spoke.

With her glass of rosé in hand, Esther headed to the lush beer garden at the back of the pub and sat on one of the wooden bench tables. She took off her headphones, removed her laptop from her leather backpack and placed it on the table. From the front pocket of her bag, Esther retrieved the brown envelope that contained her father's letter. Thankfully, the pub had free wireless internet access, so Esther was able to use the web. If she was going to do some detective work and find the location of Charlotte Evans, she would need it.

The revelation of her father's affair with this woman still stung. But before Esther began Googling her father's secret love, there was a name mentioned in his letter that she wanted to research first.

As Esther removed the letter from the envelope and unfolded it, her thoughts wandered towards Elijah. He was at a church function today and could not drive her to New Cross. Not that she minded. It was nice to travel by bus and train and rediscover south London. Apart from Ayesha, and a few others she emailed occasionally, Esther had mostly lost contact with anyone from her formative years growing up in Lambeth. And yet, the universe had dropped Elijah right back into her life. He was helping her just as he had done when they had been friends and then lovers. Over the past two weeks, it was those same reasons why she had slowly fallen in love with Elijah years and years ago that had started to gently tug at her feelings.

It did not take long to connect to the internet. Esther checked the name in the letter again and opened the Google homepage, typing in *Ken Saro-Wiwa* in the search box. In his letter, her father had mentioned Ken Saro-Wiwa as a friend and teacher who had been killed. But he had not revealed the details of the man's death. If she could find out who Ken Saro-Wiwa was and why he had been killed, it might provide an explanation as to why her father had fled Nigeria, fearing for his life.

To Esther's surprise, Google returned dozens of results. *He must have been quite prolific to have so many articles written about him*, she thought. Unable to really determine which of the webpages would be the most useful, Esther took the easy route and clicked on the Wikipedia link. Leaning closer to the laptop screen, she read the first paragraph:

> *Kenule Beeson "Ken" Saro-Wiwa (10 October 1941 – 10 November 1995) was a Nigerian writer, producer, environmental activist, television producer, and winner of Right Livelihood Award and the Goldman Environmental Prize. Saro-Wiwa was a member of the Ogoni people, an ethnic minority in Nigeria, whose homeland, Ogoniland, in the Niger Delta has been targeted for crude oil extraction since the 19fifites.*

Ogoniland has suffered extreme environmental damage from decades of indiscriminate petroleum waste dumping.

Esther stopped reading and pondered this for a moment. She had been born in Ogoniland, in a village called Kegbara-Dere, but in 1973, when she was five years old, her father and mother had left Ogoniland to settle in London. She remembered asking her parents why they had left Ogoniland once, and her father had told her, in a rare moment of vulnerability, that it was no longer a land for the living. Her mother had been just as melancholic, telling her that their home back in Nigeria was sick.

Esther's recollection of her time as a young child in Ogoniland came to her in pieces. But one memory that stood out was the thick, brown mud and oil, as dark as night, that ravaged the fields and rivers like a liquid manifestation of death. Esther massaged her forehead, feeling a headache emerging from all her overthinking, and continued reading the Wikipedia page:

As president of the Movement for the Survival of the Ogoni People (MOSOP), Saro-Wiwa led a non-violent campaign against environmental degradation of the land and waters of Ogoniland by the operations of the multinational petroleum industry, especially the Royal Dutch Shell company. He was also an outspoken critic of the Nigerian government, which he viewed as reluctant to enforce environmental regulations on the foreign petroleum companies operating in the area.

At the peak of his non-violent campaign, he was tried by a special military tribunal for allegedly masterminding the gruesome murder of Ogoni chiefs at a pro-government meeting. Ken and eight others, referred to as the Ogoni Nine, were hanged in 1995 by the military dictatorship of General Sani Abacha. His execution provoked international outrage.

Esther turned away from the laptop, noticing a group of students walk into the beer garden with thick books in their hands. It occurred to her that she knew almost nothing about Ogoniland. Esther had long buried any desire to know more about her Nigerian heritage, for it linked her back to her father. Instead, she had chosen to embrace her identity as a liberal black British woman, and later, once she had gained her American citizenship, she saw herself as an African American woman.

And yet Esther found herself fascinated by the recent history of her battered homeland. Had her father fought alongside Ken Saro-Wiwa as well? Had he fled to London to escape the same fate that had befallen Ken Saro-Wiwa and the other Ogoni Nine? Despite loathing her father, the thought of him as a rebel fighting alongside his fellow countrymen to protect his land filled Esther with a grudging pride. Maybe she was more like her father than she realised.

Esther spent another hour reading about Ken Saro-Wiwa and the Ogoni people's suffering with an intense interest that tempted her to keep reading well into the evening. But she forced herself to move on to the matter of searching for the whereabouts of Charlotte Evans.

To Esther's delight, it took less than ten minutes to find a promising lead. The first link from the online results for *Charlotte Evans Rosetta Custom House* was a website called 192.com, which contained residential and business records across the UK. There was only one Charlotte Evans who lived in Custom House. To access the specific details of her address, Esther had to pay a fee, which was more than she expected, but she did not have much choice.

After paying the fee and signing up, Esther was able to view Charlotte Evans's profile, and there it was:

13 Throckmorten Road, E6 5XA

It was slightly terrifying that she could locate a stranger's address with such ease.

Still, Esther was finally close to finding her father. Suddenly, it felt all too real: the thought that she was going to confront a man she had not seen in eighteen years. It filled her with juxtaposing feelings of excitement and utter dread.

As she closed her laptop and began packing her items into her bag, Esther's mind wandered back to Elijah without permission. She could not wait to call him this evening about the significant progress she had made today. Then, like a needle piercing into her skin, Esther painfully recalled that Elijah lived with his wife. It would not be a wise decision to call him tonight without warning. Foolishly, she became somewhat irritated at that fact.

Esther heaved her backpack onto her back and made her way out of the pub. As she walked across Deptford High Street towards New Cross Gate station, Esther's thoughts were still circling around Elijah like bees swarming around honey. If Ayesha were with her now, Esther knew that her friend would be sternly warning her to avoid reigniting feelings for an ex-boyfriend, especially when he was a married man. Had she had an inkling before that she was still mildly attracted to Elijah, Esther would have stayed away from him, but it was too late for that. All she could now was discipline her feelings, as if they were reckless children, so they would not lead her to something she would later regret.

CHAPTER 14

January 1982

For the past week at Dick Sheppard, there had been a feverish excitement that infected every student, classroom and corridor. Everyone was eagerly anticipating the visit from Prince Charles and Princess Diana. None of the students, and especially not the school's staff, could believe that members of the Royal Family would be stepping foot in Tulse Hill, least of all to pay a visit to a comprehensive school in Brixton.

Elijah first heard the news of the royal visit from Mr Donald, his long-nosed maths teacher, during one of his morning lessons. Sitting next to Esther, Elijah joined the rest of the class in a collective gasp of surprise at the announcement, followed by animated discussion about what this royal visit meant. One student suggested that, since Princess Diana and Prince Charles were expecting their first child in the summer, the royal couple were potentially considering Dick Sheppard School for their unborn child to attend when he was older. It was so ridiculous, the idea that a member of the Royal Family would attend a school in Brixton, that the entire class had collapsed with laughter for a good five minutes.

The actual purpose of the royal couple's visit was a lot less exciting. Mr Donald told them that Princess Diana and Prince Charles were visiting the school's fundraising fair, which aimed to raise enough money to send sixteen students from the school to Zimbabwe. The royal couple wanted to show their support for the cause by visiting the fair.

While the rest of the class was gripped by royal fever, Esther seemed unsurprisingly immune to it.

"It's pretty cool that we actually get to see the royals," he said. Esther did not immediately answer. She was using the rubber at the bottom of her pencil to erase the answer to an algebra equation. "We only ever see them on TV."

Esther stopped pressing the rubber against her sheet of paper, looked at Elijah and shrugged her shoulders. "It's not like them coming here is going to change anything. Police will still treat us like shit, and whites still want us out of this country. So who cares really? Might as well be Davie Bowie visiting us."

Although Elijah was slightly annoyed at Esther's indifference to the fact that members of the royal family were visiting their school, he had also expected her response. Esther was no longer the same girl she had been when they had first become friends. Ever since the New Cross fire, Esther had developed a passionate anti-establishment belief, which had brought to life the raging political radical inside of her. Before her awakening, Elijah's conversations with Esther used to be about jazz and soul artists and religion. Now she would wax lyrical about how she detested right-wing groups like the National Front and neo-Nazis and found any opportunity to insult Margaret Thatcher, whom she often called "the carrot-nosed witch."

Last year's Brixton riots, which happened a month after the Black People's Day of Action, had only thrown more coal into Esther's burning furnace. Esther's mother, who had been travelling to her nightshift at King's College Hospital in Denmark Hill, was caught up in the middle of the rioting, and amid the chaos, she had been knocked to the ground by a police officer and sprained her arm.

Fortunately, Elijah and his family were at home when it started. The rioting escalated to such a degree that he remembered the police knocking on the door of his house, ordering his father to ensure that the family remained indoors for their own safety.

Once the rioting, which lasted for three days, had stopped, Elijah returned to school. He and Esther met up that morning and walked through Coldharbour Lane. Brixton had never been a pretty place, but Elijah was shocked to see that it now looked like it had been bombed. There were smashed windows, the twisted wreckage of demolished cars, debris from torched buildings scattered across the pavements and roads. Yet Esther had seemed excited about it. While they trotted past the Ritzy Cinema, she told Elijah that this was only the beginning and that "the whole of Britain will now see that us blacks will fight back against those racist pigs." The naked hatred in her words had troubled Elijah.

Unlike Esther, Ayesha, who had fully recovered from the head injury she had sustained at the New Cross house fire, did not seem to share this hatred of the police and the government. In fact, soon after the maths lesson, Elijah overheard Ayesha speaking to a group of popular black girls, which included Esther, in the cafeteria. With a barely concealed sense of self-importance, she was telling them that the headteacher had selected her as one of the few students who would have the privilege of speaking with Princess Diana and Prince Charles privately about last year's riot in Brixton. When Elijah thought about it, it only made sense that Ayesha, the princess of south London, would meet Diana, Princess of Wales. As Elijah walked past, he saw that Esther's face had remained stony after her friend's announcement.

On the day of the royal family's arrival, it felt like the entire school had become a Hollywood movie set. Students, teachers, and staff were all in frenzied spirits. Elijah could tell that everyone felt this would be the only time Dick Sheppard School would have any national relevance and so the school needed to be seen in its best light. No rolled-up trousers. No inappropriately short skirts. No smoking behind the swimming pool building. Everybody had to be on their best behaviour, and everyone was happy to oblige. This was the royal family, after all.

Metal crowd control barricades had been set up around the front entrance of the school to control the inevitable swarm of residents in Tulse Hill, and everyone else in south London, who wanted to catch a glimpse of the royal couple. Like almost every student that day, Elijah arrived at school earlier than usual. By the time he did, there was a massive gathering of people behind the barriers. Even film and camera crews had turned up, along with a few dozen police officers who stood at either side of the fences.

Unable to locate any of his friends, Elijah stood behind a row of other younger students and their parents. Despite several attempts to squeeze into the throng of people, he could not get a good view of the main street where the car carrying Charles and Diana would pull in. There were too many eager people in front of him.

Elijah sighed, giving up any hope of seeing the royal couple. Then he felt someone tap his shoulder and he turned around to see Esther standing behind him. Her signature silver Walkman headphones with their orange ear pads hung around her neck.

"You're not gonna see them from here, you know," Esther said.

"Yeah, I know. It's like I came early to school for nothing, man…" Elijah sighed then raised an eyebrow. "I'm surprised you're here early."

Esther shrugged her shoulders. "I knew there was gonna be a lot of traffic this morning because of the whole royal family visit. So I just came to school earlier. You know what, I actually found a good spot where we can see them arrive."

Elijah felt like throwing his arms around her. "Wicked. Hey, I thought you didn't care about the royal family visiting?"

"I'm not excited, but I know you are, and if I'm gonna see the royal family come to our school, it might as well be with you."

Elijah smiled at Esther and gently held her hand. "Come, let's go."

The spot Esther had located was on the middle floor of one of the school's grey building blocks. The corridor, barren and silent, had a long landscape window that stretched the whole width of the hallway, providing a panoramic view of Tulse Hill estate and the crowded streets.

Standing close together, Elijah and Esther fixed their eyes on the street below. It was a swelling mass of students, teachers, camera crew and police officers, dotted with the colours of the Union Jack flags waving in the breeze.

"Hey look, that must be them in that limo!" Esther said, pointing towards the far end of the street. Elijah followed the direction of Esther's finger and, sure enough, a black limo was driving through the road. It parked just outside the school gates, where the jubilant crowd were now clapping and whistling from behind the metal fences.

With the elegance and grace expected from a member of the British monarchy, Princess Diana stepped out of the limo. Even when Elijah had seen pictures of her in newspapers or magazines, an aura of charm and beauty radiated from her. Like rays from the sun in summer, she seemed to brighten her surroundings, warming the heart of even the staunchest critic of the royal family.

Elijah watched Princess Diana wave at the crowd; she looked like she had been plucked out from the pages a fairy tale. Squinting his eyes, he could just about make out the finer details of Princess Diana's ensemble as she came closer to the school's entrance. She wore a vibrant blue coat decorated with floral designs at the collar. Sparkling earrings hung from her ears, somehow accentuating her crystal-blue eyes – the finishing touch to her brilliance. Prince Charles followed her into the school, waving at the crowd and looking rather bland compared to his stunning wife in his black suit and plain tie.

"Even I have to admit that she's beautiful," Esther said.

Elijah turned to look at Esther. She was staring at the royal couple with a look of deep interest.

"Could you imagine being a British woman and looking like her," Esther said. "All blonde hair and blue eyes. No one would treat you like shit. No one would glare at you on the street as if you had leprosy. You wouldn't have to look at your black skin every morning in the mirror and be angry at God for cursing your life by making you a black girl."

Elijah frowned at Esther, puzzled by her words. "What are you talking about?"

"Black girls aren't beautiful like her, Elijah. Our skin is too brown or too dark. Our hair is too nappy or rough, not golden and smooth. There's nothing we black girls can do about it. I can't exactly peel off my skin like an onion and find my white skin underneath. I can't change the texture of my hair."

"Esther," Elijah said, in a soft voice, his eyes exploring her face. An invisible spotlight seemed to shine on her as if she were the star in a stage play. Not for the first time, Elijah found his heart beating faster and he felt lightheaded as he took in Esther's light brown skin, her slightly round cheeks and her lips, pink and curved. He wanted nothing more than to feel those lips against his own.

"Why would you want to peel off your skin when you're already beautiful? God hasn't cursed you; He has blessed you. To me, you're more beautiful than the princess at our school today. You're a black and beautiful princess."

Esther turned to him with an unreadable look in her eyes and Elijah became very conscious of how close together they were; their lips separated by a single movement. At that moment, he could not resist the urge that gripped him and pushed him forward.

Her lips were just as soft, and warm as he had imagined they would be. Elijah kissed Esther and kept kissing her as if he had been starved of her lips for too long. And she returned his passion, pulling him even closer to her, so her small breasts pushed against his chest.

It was the first time Elijah had kissed a girl and the first time he understood what it meant to be in love.

CHAPTER 15

June 2008

Esther pushed the black metal gate, feeling its paint peel off underneath her fingers, and held it open with an outstretched arm so that Elijah could follow her onto the stony front porch of Charlotte Evans's home in Custom House, East London. Esther had spent her first years in Britain not too far from here. The search for her father was unearthing memories and experiences she had long buried.

As it was Friday, Elijah had come straight from work and Esther noticed again how effortlessly dashing he looked in a suit. He had decided to wear contact lenses instead of his glasses, which made him look younger but no less masculine. Esther had ditched her usual colourful and bright clothing for something less loud. Today, she wore a loose, black blouse with grey trousers. The red bandanna she often wrapped around her head was gone, and she had tied her curly afro into a puff.

It had been eighteen years since Esther had seen or spoken to her father. And yet, even as a forty-year-old woman, she felt she needed to tone down her usual fashion sensibilities in front of him. Throughout her teenage years, Esther had often deliberately gone against her father and, by extension, her Nigerian culture by dressing and acting more like a white British girl. But today, faced with the real prospect of a reunion, a part of Esther did not want him to look at her and be disappointed as he always had been. She wondered whether every woman desired approval and acceptance from their father, if it was part of their DNA.

"The moment of truth," Elijah said, resting his hands calmly on her shoulders. Esther felt his hands on her body, and it relaxed her nerves. Although she hadn't told Elijah, she found his presence comforting.

"Thanks for coming again, Elijah," Esther said, stopping in front of the house's red door. She turned around to face him. "I hope your wife doesn't mind that you've been spending so much time with me."

Elijah chuckled, but Esther caught a hint of nervousness behind it. "Oh, she's fine. I'm just helping an old friend. Anyway, how are you feeling?"

Esther wanted to remind Elijah that she was more than just an old friend but decided not to. It would not be appropriate right now. Instead, she gave a weary sigh. "I'm potentially about to meet my father, and he's going to find out I'm not married at forty and have no children. He'll probably disown me again on the spot." Esther laughed to herself.

Elijah shook his head. "I've prayed for you. It's going to be okay."

Esther turned back to the door and gave Elijah a warm smile over her shoulder, he responded with a cheerful wink. Feeling less nervous, but only slightly, Esther took another deep breath. The moment of truth. She pulled the flap of the letterbox twice. It made a loud clanking sound.

After a few tense moments of waiting for Esther and, she felt, Elijah too, since he had probably become just as invested in this quest to find her father, the door opened. A young boy in a navy-blue school uniform, looking no older than ten years old, stood in the doorway. He had thick blond hair, bright blue eyes and was chewing gum very loudly. His eyes darted from Esther's face then to Elijah's and back to Esther's.

Before Esther could ask the boy if Charlotte Evans was at home, a mature female voice came from behind him.

"Colin, you know you shouldn't open the door without asking who it is first."

A woman strode down the corridor to the doorway. She stopped behind the boy, who was presumably the "Colin" she had been referring to. With the same bright blue eyes as Colin, the woman examined Esther and Elijah for a moment in a way that was curious rather than suspicious.

"How may I help you?" the woman said with a soft Northern lilt.

"Good afternoon. I'm looking for Charlotte Evans. I believe she lives here?"

The woman smiled and her eyes lit up with genuine warmth. She stretched her right hand out and shook Esther's hand. "Charlotte Evans, how may I be of help?"

Esther took a deep breath to calm herself, feeling oddly anxious that she was standing in front of her father's lover. "It's a pleasure to meet you, Ms Evans. My name is Esther, and I'm looking for my father, Kelechi Nubari. Or you might know him as Ken Nubari. I believe he was living with you here?"

At the mention of Esther's father's name, Ms Evans staggered back as though she had been knocked off balance.

For the first time, Esther looked at the woman properly and realised that she was younger than Esther had expected. She was by no means a young lady, with bright white hair styled in a classic bob, faint wrinkles around her upper lip and dark circles forming under her eyes, but she looked no older than her early fifties, which would make her at least ten years younger than Esther's father.

Ms Evans shook her head and composed herself. "Not in my wildest dreams did I ever imagine you would be on my doorstep one day." She seemed stunned, and Esther wanted to hold her up, legitimately afraid the woman might faint.

"Colin, please go upstairs," Ms Evans said, patting the blond-haired boy on the head.

Colin bolted back into the house, pleased to have escaped their strange conversation, and Ms Evans looked at Esther with a melancholic smile. "You better come inside as well. I have a lot to say about your father."

Esther found that the interior of someone's house was often an outward manifestation of their mind and soul and, consistent with her well-mannered disposition, Ms Evans's home immediately announced that she was an educated woman with a taste in high-brow culture. Several bookshelves lined the corridors, and as Esther glanced at the spines, she realised Ms Evans seemed to have encyclopaedias on every subject she could think of, from learning Latin to Chinese cuisine. Black-and-white paintings of famous women, one of whom Esther recognised as a young Aretha Franklin, covered the walls of the ground floor, making it feel like a museum of prolific female talent.

Ms Evans led Esther and Elijah to a spacious kitchen with laminated flooring and wooden shelves stacked with plant pots. As Esther and Elijah sat on two transparent plastic chairs around the dining table, Ms Evans offered them tea or coffee, to which Esther and Elijah both requested tea at the same time. Ms Evans boiled the kettle and was soon handing them mugs filled with tea that had a hint of lemon to it.

"That young boy you met outside, Colin, is my nephew," Ms Evans said, taking a seat opposite Esther and Elijah. "A wonderful lad but very mischievous even if he doesn't quite look it."

Esther smiled at her, and Ms Evans returned the smile before putting her mug to her lips, her eyes still on Esther. A silence settled over them as all three sipped their tea, with only the soft sounds of slurping to break the quiet.

"So, you're looking for your father, did you say?" Ms Evans had placed her mug on the glass table and was now looking at Esther with a curious expression.

Esther nodded her head and then told Ms Evans the whole story of her journey to find her father. Judging by his absence and Ms Evans's startled reaction to his name, Esther strongly suspected that their relationship had ended some time ago.

Ms Evans closed her eyes and her thin lips formed into a small smile. She shook her head, and Esther thought she might cry. "Yes, your father and I were in a relationship. I had just moved to London from Yorkshire in the summer of 1996 to start a new life as a teacher in the big city. Your father, who told me his name was Ken, had come from Nigeria to start a new life here too. Here we were, two different people, from two different cultures, but with the same dream."

"And you became a teacher at Rosetta Primary School, where you met my father?"

"Yes, I met Ken at Rosetta Primary School. I interviewed him for an English teacher position. We shared a love of Shakespeare, Charles Dickens and Jane Austen. I would never have guessed a man from Nigeria could be so knowledgeable about British literature, but then I remembered how influential the Commonwealth once was."

As Ms Evans spoke, Esther studied her. Apart from the fact they were both women, she was the antithesis of Esther's mother. Like most Nigerian women from Ogoni, Esther's mother was not highly educated because there was no need for her to be. In Ogoni culture, the man worked, and the woman nurtured the household and children. But Ms Evans was certainly not the type of woman who would settle for a life of nurturing. She seemed independent, smart and successful. By comparison, Esther's mother was docile and submissive.

Ms Evans took a gulp of her tea and stared at the kitchen window as if her memories lived within the glass pane. "We gradually formed a bond over four years, your father and me. The school's governing body knew about our relationship. They didn't mind as long as we didn't make a fuss about it. We were like a husband and wife in all but name."

"But Esther's father isn't living with you anymore?" Elijah said.

Esther had been so fascinated by this woman who had an unfathomable relationship with her father, that she had forgotten to ask the million-dollar question.

Ms Evans closed her eyes and shook her head as if she were trying to rid herself of something painful lodged in her skull. "Ken and I became lovers very quickly. We moved in together in 1997, and he stayed with me till the end of 2006. Some of the best years of my life. I loved him dearly, and so I asked him to marry me. This was around the winter of 2006."

Esther widened her eyes in shock. The idea of her father walking down the aisle with Ms Evans seemed farfetched. *People really do fall in love with the most unexpected people.*

"But your father could not marry me," Ms Evans continued. Now her voice seemed like it was going to crack any minute. "Ken finally told me that he had a wife in Nigeria and had been sending letters to her without me knowing. He also told me about a daughter he hadn't spoken to in almost two decades." Ms Evans opened her eyes and seemed to be on the verge of crying, but no tears fell, as if she had cried them all out. She looked directly at Esther and her tone took on a sharper edge.

"I can be honest with you and say I was heartbroken by your father's revelation. He had kept his wife secret from me for nine bloody years. I felt like a fool for never suspecting a thing." Maybe Esther was reading too much into it, but she felt like Ms Evans was projecting the pain her father had caused onto her. Maybe, in Ms Evans's mind, if Esther and her mother had not existed, she would have had a blissfully married life with her Nigerian lover who was fond of British literature.

"What happened after my father told you about his marriage to my *mother*?" Esther emphasised the last word of her sentence. Part of her wanted to remind Ms Evans that she would never replace her mother, even though Esther knew that she never had that intention.

Ms Evans smiled, and for the first time since they had arrived it was not sad or kind. It was bitter. "I kicked him out, of course.

We had a massive row, and I told him to pack his bags and never call me or scc me again."

"When was this?"

"I can't recall exactly, sometime around early December, I suppose. Shortly after parting ways, he quit his teaching position at the primary school." Ms Evans caught Esther about to open her mouth and answered her question before it materialised. "Since then, I haven't spoken to or seen your father, and I don't know his whereabouts. He never tried to get in touch with me after the end of our relationship."

Esther felt crestfallen. Ms Evans was the last person who would have known where her father was, and since she did not know, the trail had gone cold again. For all Esther knew, her father was not even in London anymore.

As if reading Esther's disappointment, Ms Evans reached across the table to place her hand over Esther's. "I'm sorry I couldn't be of more help. But I do have something I'm sure you'll find interesting, if not useful."

Before Esther could ask her to elaborate further, Ms Evans had sprung from her chair and darted from the kitchen. Esther turned to Elijah, who looked at her with a puzzled expression and shrugged his shoulders.

A few minutes later, Ms Evans returned, holding a black book in her hand. She sat down on her chair and offered the book to Esther.

"What's this?" Esther said, giving the book a curious look as she took it from Ms Evans's outstretched hand.

"It's a journal your father kept while he was still living with me," Ms Evans said, her voice sounding strangely far away. "I never read it. I felt no need to after your father told me about his other life. I didn't want to know about any other secrets he had kept from me, and I had been hurt by him enough. For a long time, I've been questioning why I kept it around. Perhaps I was supposed to give it to you. It may help you find him."

Esther flipped through the pages, noting that her father had written a few entries. A resurgent hope swelled in her as she thought about the potential clues within the journal that might indicate where her father would have gone after moving out of Ms Evans's home. As Esther's eyes skimmed over her father's neat, cursive handwriting, she suddenly felt like she was in possession of an ancient text which held deep insights into a human soul, never to be shared with anyone but her.

After finishing their tea, Elijah and Esther thanked Ms Evans for her help. She told Esther to think nothing of it and led the two of them to the front door. Just as Esther was about to step out into the front porch, Ms Evans touched her arm.

"Thank you for coming today," she said with an earnest tone. Esther could not quite understand why, but Ms Evans seemed happier than before. "Your father's journal was the last piece of him that I had, and I think it's the final closure I needed to move on from my memories of what he did to me."

"I understand," Esther said, smiling.

"A piece of advice. When you do find your father, don't hold on to the bad memories you have of him. Forgive him. Holding on to a grudge can be like having shackles on your feet, and you will only be able to move through life with joy when you choose to take them off. Believe me. Today, you've helped me take off those chains."

CHAPTER 16

June 2008

"Can I just have a pint of Guinness, please? Cheers," Elijah said to the ginger-haired bartender, who had a beard so bushy and plentiful that he looked like a modern-day Viking.

"And I'll have a glass of Graham Beck Brut Rosé," Esther said, reading from the menu. "Make it a large. Thanks."

Once they had taken their drinks from the bartender, Elijah and Esther walked over to a wooden table close to the pub's front windows. They had a clear view of the intersection between Coldharbour Lane and Atlantic Road. Elijah took a sip of his cold stout, letting the roasty, slightly metallic taste he had grown to love as an adult wash down his throat and refresh him.

"I can't believe they renamed this place Dogstar. Seriously?" Esther said, toying with the stem of her wine glass. "I preferred The Atlantic. Remember that? God, Brixton has changed a lot since I left. It's lost so much of its ghetto charm."

"It's definitely lost a lot of its ghetto charm, but I'm not sure that's a bad thing," Elijah said, glancing at Esther's full, pink lips, vaguely remembering how he had enjoyed kissing her all those many years ago. Elijah shook his head and diverted his gaze out the window to focus on something else. He noticed a young, well-dressed white couple crossing the street into Pope's Road.

Just like The Atlantic, Brixton had gone through its own rebranding. Three major riots – one of which Elijah and Esther had once found themselves unwittingly in the middle of – rampant crime and widespread poverty had brought much notoriety to Brixton. And yet, Brixton's urban grittiness had attracted the young, the educated and the comfortably well-off in droves in the early nineties.

By the time 2008 came around, rent prices had risen faster than the cost of a pint. Many of Elijah's old friends from school had already moved out of Brixton, unable to cope financially as it became a bohemian playground for the middle-class and reasonably wealthy. If not for his own well-paid job and his wife's modest salary, Elijah would probably have had to drag himself out of Brixton as well. There was a reason why many of the area's original residents, who still attended his church, called him the "Last Prophet of Brixton." Still, Brixton remained very much multicultural, and its Afro-Caribbean flavour had not been washed out thoroughly; it was still the best place to buy ackee and saltfish pie in London, but it had lost some of its edginess from the seventies and eighties, for better or worse.

"Do you think I'll ever be able to find my father?" Esther was looking at him now. She had untied her black afro so that it sprung out from all sides in curls and twists. Elijah loved her hair like this; it was uncompromising and bold, much like Esther herself – until it came to the subject of her father.

"You will. Have faith. You have your father's diary now, which will hopefully give you something. I would say you could ask the police to file a missing persons report too, but I remember you aren't exactly their biggest fan. Unless that's changed?"

"Nope, that definitely hasn't changed," Esther said. She took a big swig of wine, finishing more than half the contents in her glass, before continuing to speak. "They don't show us black people any more love in America than they do over here. It would probably take those knuckleheads a decade to look for my father; his name would be right at the bottom of the pile. Police or cops. Whatever you want to call them, I would trust the jaws of a lion before I trust them."

Elijah chuckled at Esther's remark. He was reminded of the political and rebellious spirit that had burned so fiercely in her youth.

The Dogstar was starting to get busier as it neared 8 p.m., and workers, students and committed alcoholics began filling the place. These newly arrived residents, tired from the heavy toll London took on their bodies and minds, had taken seats at several wooden tables around the pub. The chandeliers dangling from the green ceiling turned on, announcing the arrival of Friday night.

"You know, there's something you still haven't told me," Elijah said. While he had polished off his Guinness – and would not be drinking any more as he was driving home – Esther had almost finished her large glass of wine, and Elijah suspected she would order another. They would be at the pub for a while.

"Really? What haven't I told you?"

"Why didn't you release your album? I'm dying to know. You had four great songs and were well on your way to dethroning Beyoncé, tell me, come on."

Esther laughed, but it was a bitter sound. She drained her glass before answering, "Our dreams don't belong to us, Elijah. We just think they do."

Elijah raised his eyebrows at her in puzzlement. Had the wine already gone to her head?

Reading Elijah's expression, Esther laughed again. "As a pastor, I thought you would appreciate my philosophical musings."

"Very funny."

Then a deep sadness extended across Esther's face like a shadow at noon. "When I first arrived in Chicago, I was this wide-eyed, enthusiastic, ambitious twenty-two-year-old girl. I had left everything in London, and I was determined to start my new life as a musician in America. A girl from Brixton chasing the American dream."

Esther let out a deep sigh which felt heavy with the weight of regret and swayed slightly. The wine was clearly having an effect.

"I worked and hustled hard, Elijah. I was sleeping on other people's couches. Working waitress jobs at different restaurants in Chicago. Then one day, after three years of living just above the poverty line, I managed to get a spot singing at The Green Mill: a swanky bar in uptown Chicago. Think Moulin Rouge. Anyway, that's where I got my big break, as Americans love to say."

The Dogstar was a hive of activity now. Pints, cocktails and beers littered the tables in various stages of consumption, and people were laughing and talking with the type of energy that comes from knowing you have no work tomorrow. Amid all this cacophony of life, Elijah was engrossed in Esther's story.

"At The Green Mill, the head of a major record label, I mean, we're talking big-time, Elijah, heard me sing one night and he was 'impressed,' in his own words. Backstage, he gave me the address of the hotel he was staying in and asked me to deliver him a mixtape. So I did. Three weeks later, I was on a plane to Miami to sign a record contract under his label."

"You didn't sign it?" Elijah said.

"I did sign it. Worst mistake of my life." Esther turned to the bar. It was filled with people either yapping to each other or waiting to be served. "Do you mind getting me a glass of wine, please? The same brand I was drinking last. And don't give me that look. You know I can handle my drink, Pastor."

Elijah chuckled, shaking his head. "I'm only getting you another glass because I'm driving you back. I don't condone alcoholism," Elijah said with a playful tone as he stood up. It only took him five minutes to make his way to the bar and return to Esther with her glass of wine. She took a long swig of wine and continued her story.

"So I signed the contract. Finally, I had achieved my dream. But like I said, our dreams don't belong to us. Being so young, I was naive. After the overnight success of 'Choices', I, ironically, started making all the wrong choices. I was partying almost every night in Miami, taking all kinds of drugs, and having sex with anyone and everyone. One day, I looked in the mirror and didn't recognise myself anymore, you know? This is what those child movie actors go through. I'd become a sad cliché."

Esther laughed, and this time it was stained with sorrow. Elijah could tell she was laughing as a way of pitying herself. At that moment, he thought how different things might have been for Esther if he had got on that plane to Chicago with her eighteen years ago. Maybe he would have been able to protect her from those who had exploited her. Maybe he could have steered her away from the destructive tendencies she was sometimes prone to. Of course, they would never know. But Elijah did not speak these thoughts aloud, he simply listened. Esther was offering her soul up on a silver platter, and he knew she did not need him commenting on its taste.

"George Michael once compared being signed to a music label as a form of professional slavery, and he wasn't wrong," Esther said. She downed the last remnants of wine in her glass and requested one final glass. Reluctantly, Elijah agreed to get her another glass but not without a promise from Esther that it would be the last one for the evening. When Elijah returned from the bar with Esther's glass of wine, she took it from his hands and finished it in one loud gulp before speaking again. "I hadn't even read my record contract when I signed it, so I was shocked by how much control they had over everything. Marketing, my image, my sound. I wanted one of the songs on the album to be about a woman falling in love with another woman, and the record execs were completely against it. They told me that I wasn't to speak about that part of myself. Bisexual female artists don't sell records, apparently. I wasn't happy anymore. I don't think I'd been happy once since signing the contract."

"So what did you do?" Elijah said.

Esther waved her hand in a dismissive gesture, almost knocking over her glass. "I bloody quit, that's what I did. I remember telling them to sod off with their contract, not that a bunch of American record label execs understood what that meant. It was so funny. Thankfully, they didn't fight me in court or anything; I was clearly suffering from depression and exhaustion by this point, and I guess they didn't want any bad press. So they released me from my contract."

Elijah shook his head. "I'm so sorry you had to go through all that."

Elijah was glad she did not request another one. "In hindsight, it was an experience that I'm glad I went through," Esther said, propping her elbows on the table and resting her chin in her hands. "Baptism by fire, Pastor. And it wasn't all bad. I'd already made a decent amount of money in royalties from my singles, enough to buy my own apartment in uptown Chicago. I worked a few odd jobs after my whole music contract fiasco before finding a job as a music teacher at Chicago's School of Music. It wasn't my dream, but I've been teaching there for years now, and I'm happy. I guess sometimes we have our dreams and plans, and life just laughs at it. Life has its own plans for us."

Elijah thought about what Esther had said earlier. "*Our dreams don't belong to us.*" Elijah had sacrificed so much, including his previous relationship with Esther, to achieve the dream of becoming senior pastor at his late father's church. Now that he was leading it, and facing resistance from his own family to make it more inclusive, was he happy? Even his marriage to a dutiful Christian wife, which appeared perfect on paper – was it really fulfilling?

Before he could dwell on these thoughts further, Esther pulled him out from sinking, like quicksand, into the recesses of his mind by asking him a question. "So now that I've shown you my soul, are you going to show me yours?"

"Sure. Go ahead."

"You're married," Esther started, glancing at Elijah's wedding ring, "you have a well-paid job, and you're finally the pastor you always wanted to be. You have it all...except kids. A successful Yoruba man like you, living the good life in London, I'm surprised you don't have any yet."

Elijah sighed, wishing he could order another pint of Guinness. "I wanted kids, but my wife, Tiwa, she can't conceive." Elijah realised his voice sounded detached and cold even as he said it.

Perhaps he had told this cruel fact to other people and himself so many times it had lost any emotional meaning to him.

"Did you know she couldn't have kids when you met her?"

Elijah shook his head. "No, I didn't know, and neither did she. We tried many times, and at first, I thought maybe something was wrong with me. But then the doctors examined her and discovered that she can't get pregnant. A problem with her ovaries."

Elijah was surprised when Esther stretched out her right arm and placed her hand over his. She squeezed it lightly. "I'm so sorry to hear that, Elijah. I hope your wife is coping okay. How do you feel about it?"

"She's coping as best she can," Elijah said, smiling at Esther, not asking her to remove her soft, warm hand from his own. "Me? I don't question God's choices, but I do wonder, and I shouldn't think this, but what if this is punishment for a choice I made a long time ago? When I decided not to have the baby God had given me." Elijah looked deeply into Esther's eyes.

Esther gave him a smile, one that carried the weight of an incurable sadness, and she shook her head. "We were too young then, Elijah," she said, stroking his palm. "And we both made that choice. Don't think like that."

"Yeah, you're right," Elijah said, half-smiling. "I just wonder sometimes…if we did the right thing?"

Esther shook her head and shrugged her shoulders. "We did what we thought was best at the time, I guess."

There was a moment of silence between them and the chattering of the Dogstar's clientele suddenly sounded louder to Elijah. Esther spoke again. "So how did you meet your wife then?" Her words were slurring slightly. She removed her hand from Elijah's.

"I met her in Paris when I was doing missionary work there," Elijah said, thankful that Esther had changed the subject. It felt odd that he was speaking to her about how he met his wife. He would never have imagined that one day he would be having this sort of discussion with Esther at what used to be The Atlantic. "She was working at a local church while studying."

"In Paris, how romantic. Love at first sight, then?"

Elijah let out a laugh. "Yeah, something like that. How about you? Any special man or woman in Chicago?"

"I'm glad you considered both sexes," Esther said, grinning at Elijah. "But no, I'm married to my teaching. And don't you dare feel sorry for me, Pastor."

Elijah was about to say something he hoped would have made her laugh when Ben E. King's distinctive voice filled his ears. 'Stand by Me' was playing at full blast.

"We have to dance to this, Elijah," Esther said, already making a move to stand up. "You remember this is one of my favourite soul records, right?"

Elijah shook his head. "I remember, but no, no, no, I can't dance. Look, you're clearly tipsy anyway. Can you even move your feet properly for a dance?"

Esther sucked her teeth and grabbed both of Elijah's hands. "Stop being a boring pastor and get up and dance. God gave you legs, did he not?"

Knowing that he would end up dancing, whether he agreed or not, Elijah sighed and stood up from his seat, allowing Esther to led him to the dancefloor by the hand. Surrounded by drinkers and revellers, Elijah and Esther moved their bodies to Ben E. King's melody. Elijah found his rhythm with hers, and they smiled at each other, enjoying the closeness, feeling like they had both earned this moment. Then, to Elijah's surprise, Esther rested her head on his shoulder, her eyes closed as they swayed together, Elijah's legs between hers. Her perfume, zesty and floral, tickled his nose and her body resting against his felt right, like it had when they had been young lovers. Elijah slipped his hands into her own and, finding solace in each other's embrace, they danced together for the duration of the song.

It was nearing 9 p.m. by the time Elijah arrived at Pullman Court with Esther sleeping in the passenger seat. Her head swayed from side to side and her eyelids fluttered as if she were in a trance. Elijah grinned at her.

"Hey, wake up. We're at Pullman Court."

With a moan, Esther slowly opened her eyes. "I think I drank way too much wine, Elijah."

"I know you're a grown and independent woman, but you'll be okay getting up to the flat by yourself, right?"

"I'm forty, not twenty. The days of stumbling up the stairs drunk are far behind me," Esther said in a slightly garbled voice as Elijah watched her search her pockets for her flat keys. When she located them, she dangled the keychain in front of Elijah with a big, toothy smile on her face, like a treasure hunter who had just found the keys to an ancient tomb.

"Okay, just text me tomorrow, so I know God safely guided you back to your flat."

"I will."

There was a moment of silence as they looked at each other. Elijah's eyes once again rested on Esther's pink lips. Their hearts raced, knowing that either one of them could act on the feelings that were binding them together, like a rope tightened to their waists, pulling them closer and closer. Yet, just as quickly as the moment came, it passed. Esther broke their eye contact, and with that, the rope was cut.

"Well, goodnight, Elijah."

"Goodnight, Esther."

As Esther exited his BMW and closed the passenger door, Elijah felt a surge of disappointment and regret, but he knew these were foolish feelings. Esther was his friend now; she had not been his lover for eighteen years. Tonight, all they had shared was a harmless drink and dance. He was a married man and a pastor. There was no point in wasting mental energy dwelling on what could have been with her.

With that thought, Elijah started the engine and drove back to his house in Streatham, praying that his wife was asleep.

CHAPTER 17

March 1982

There was a spring to Elijah's gait as he dawdled through Electric Avenue on a brisk and busy Monday morning. It was the type of spring that a made his steps feel lighter as if he were walking on thin air instead of concrete ground. Elijah whistled and nodded his head to the reggae music coming from one of the market stalls. A policeman passed and gave him a wary side glance, but not even that could taint his mood today. He was a boy in love, and she loved him back.

It had been a month and a half since Elijah and Esther had started going out. After sharing their first kiss, Elijah had felt elated and confused at the same time, like he had just stepped off the teacup ride at a theme park. He knew, deep within himself, what the kiss meant, but he did not know how to articulate it to Esther.

On the Sunday after their first kiss, Elijah had been at church. Throughout the service, he was unable to keep his eyes off

Esther as she sang with the choir. For once, Elijah was not even paying attention to his father's sermon. He was utterly focused on Esther, who would occasionally smile back at him when she caught him looking at her. The rush it gave him was addictive.

After their Bible class that Sunday, Esther had met Elijah behind the church. Even now, walking through Electric Avenue, Elijah smiled as he recalled their conversation:

"I liked kissing you," Esther said. Even though she was wearing a long, plain black dress, Elijah was mesmerised by her. He saw her in a new light, like a beautiful black-and-white picture that had been painted in full colour.

"I liked kissing you too," Elijah replied. He stepped closer to her, wanting nothing more than to kiss her for that whole afternoon.

"So, you wanna go out with me then?" Esther sounded uncertain, as if she were afraid Elijah would not reciprocate her feelings. Of course, he did.

"Yeah, I do." No sooner had Elijah replied than his lips were already with hers. On reflection, he was surprised he had not cared that someone from church might have spotted them kissing. The thought of it made the kiss even more thrilling.

After they had agreed to go out with each other, their relationship continued in the same way: talking about soul and jazz music, Elijah trying to explain Bible verses to her and Esther sometimes ranting about black injustice in Britain. The only difference was that, after school, when they went to Brockwell Park, they would spend a lot of time kissing and gently touching each other's faces and arms. The opportunity to taste Esther's lips and feel her caramel-brown skin was now an experience he looked forward to at the end of each school day.

It was Esther's fourteenth birthday today, and Elijah knew he needed to get her an impressive card, even if it meant using most, if not all, of the pocket money his father had given him.

Elijah took a left out of Electric Avenue and dodged out of the way of a few short black women with headscarves, pushing wheelie bags. He strolled past the butchers, stinking of raw meat, where his mother often bought chopped lamb or chicken if she was cooking stew, and a group of Jamaican yardies in their slacks and suspenders, wearing sunglasses. One of them, who Elijah recognised as someone who attended his father's church, gave him a nod of acknowledgement. Just before coming to the end of Brixton Road, Elijah stopped in front of a card shop with a variety of wrapping paper designs, cards and cheap gifts displayed in its windows. He walked inside.

"Good day, mate. What can I do for ya?" The Indian boy behind the counter smiled as Elijah approached.

"Good morning, mate. Errrr…I'm looking for a birthday card for a girl," Elijah said, feeling embarrassed. He suddenly became aware that he had never bought a gift for another girl, apart from his little sister.

"Ahh, got a sweet bird have ya?" the boy said, adding a wink as he finished his sentence. "Don't worry bruva, I got sumffin' for ya."

Elijah waited expectantly as the boy left the till and walked towards a stack of cards on one of the blue display stands. He leaned forward and examined the cards while stroking his rugged chin as if he were deciding what to eat from a menu. "That's the one." He picked up a card and walked back to the till.

"Wot ya fink, mate?"

Elijah took the card from the boy's outstretched hands and scrutinised it. It had a red background with white hearts dotted around the edge and red musical notes drawn in the centre. A short poem was written inside in bold letters:

To my wonderful girlfriend
I hope you listen to your favourite song today
And everything you do will go your way
And when you've opened all your presents today
There's just one thing I wanted to say
I can't wait to give you a kiss on your special birthday

Elijah looked at the boy and smiled. "It's perfect."

Surrounded by bright amber leaves, Esther leaned against the oak tree in Brockwell Park with her headphones on, listening to her Walkman. Her eyes drifted shut as she nodded her head to Al Green's 'Let's Stay Together', allowing herself to fall into the song's melody as if she were landing on a velvety blanket that wrapped around her and brought peace to her mind and soul.

It had come as a surprise to her that Elijah had kissed her the day Princess Diana visited Dick Sheppard, but when his lips touched hers, it felt so natural and satisfying, like raindrops on your face after spending the whole day in blistering heat. From the few experiences she had kissing boys, Esther had never liked it – in fact, it made her squirm, even if the boys were good-looking.

She did not think she was like Ayesha – who had confessed to her one afternoon that she liked both boys and girls but fancied girls a lot more. Instead, Esther had thought that she was a lesbian, a term she had only just learned. By reading magazines like *Cosmopolitan*, *Woman's Realm* and *Vogue* that her mother left lying around, Ayesha had become far more knowledgeable about sex than Esther was and passed her knowledge on to her friend in the manner of an experienced sex therapist. The only book in Esther's flat was the Bible and a bunch of old plays written by Shakespeare that her father loved to read.

But Esther's self-assessment that she was a lesbian could no longer be accurate now that she was going out with Elijah, and she took pleasure in this realisation. The idea that she was attracted to both boys and girls excited Esther, it was like she had opened a new door into her identity, revealing previously hidden parts of her character. But what would Elijah think if she told him that she found girls attractive too?

Esther was so engrossed in her thoughts that she jumped when she opened her eyes to see Ayesha standing in front of her.

She stopped the tape playing in her Walkman and pulled down her headphones.

"Hey, sorry, I didn't hear you come over."

Ayesha stared at Esther for a moment and then tilted her head to the side as if something on Esther's face wasn't quite right. "You're waiting for him, aren't you?"

Esther felt a sharp pinch of panic, which she failed to hide. "What? Who? No…I'm just…chilling…y'know…before school starts and…"

Ayesha sighed heavily and started twisting the curls in her short afro. "I know you're going out with Elijah." Her tone of voice was understanding, which Esther had not expected.

"We haven't done anything with each other in, like, two months, and I've seen how you look at him when we're in class. You forget I'm really, really good at reading body language."

Esther felt backed into a corner with no opening through which she could escape. There was no point lying. "Yeah, I'm going out with him." Esther searched her friend's face for a sign of disapproval, but Ayesha smiled warmly at her.

"You've always kinda liked him, you know," Ayesha said. She walked towards Esther and leaned against the tree trunk before turning to face her. "You sorta make a good couple. Me? I couldn't go out with a boy that religious. Just no. Obviously."

Esther chuckled, feeling a great sense of relief that she would not have to choose between Ayesha and Elijah.

"It's your birthday, right?" Ayesha said, her eyes no longer looking at Esther's face but gazing at her lips.

Esther gulped. "Yeah, it's today."

Ayesha's voice was soft now, almost a whisper. "Can I at least give you one last kiss, you know, for your birthday?"

Elijah alighted from the bus and raced towards Brockwell Park with Esther's birthday card in his hand. He almost knocked over another student as he slid between the boy and his friend and shouted an apology back to him, increasing his pace towards the park. He had spent longer than he intended buying a card for Esther and school started in fifteen minutes.

No one knew that Elijah was going out with Esther, and he preferred to keep it that way. While other boys at school would have boasted about going out with Ayesha's best friend, Elijah did not need or want that kind of attention. He was known as a "church boy," which meant that if the other kids discovered that Elijah and Esther were going out, he would be on the receiving end of many a joke. *"The church boy has abandoned Jesus for a girl. Oh, the shame."* He could already hear the jibes his friends would make. Not only that, but a few kids at school went to Elijah's church, and he did not want the attention there either. Keeping his relationship with Esther secret made it more special, something that belonged only to the two of them.

As they had both agreed, Elijah made his way towards the big oak tree in Brockwell Park. He raced across the grassy fields until the tree came into view, and Elijah saw two people, wearing the grey Dick Sheppard school uniform, leaning against it. Moving closer, he realised it was Ayesha and Esther, standing side by side but turned to face each other. It looked like Ayesha was whispering something to Esther.

Then Elijah saw their lips touch. It was not just a small peck on the lips, the type of innocent kiss a girl might give her friend. It was a passionate kiss – the kind reserved for lovers, not shared with just anyone like some gummy bear from a packet of Haribo. It was a kiss that Elijah had thought Esther shared with him and him only.

For a few seconds, Elijah watched them kissing before turning his head away. The sight of two girls' lips locking together, an act that was meant for a boy and a girl, was revolting. To Elijah, it was like watching a human kiss a horse – disgusting in its unnaturalness.

Fist clenched in anger, Elijah stomped away from the oak tree. He flung Esther's birthday card in the bin as he left the park, his eyes stinging with tears.

It was unusual for Elijah not to have shown up at their agreed time and place. As Esther left the park with Ayesha by her side, she wondered what had happened. Elijah was one of the most reliable and organised boys she knew. It was that sort of maturity, which she found lacking in many other boys at school, that played a part in why she liked him so much.

Religious studies was Esther's first lesson. After saying goodbye to Ayesha in the corridor, Esther made her way to her class. As usual, the classroom was in a state of mayhem. Squeezing past two black boys arguing about football, Esther sat two desks away from Elijah as the other desks close to him were already occupied. She noticed that he was glaring down at his book. When she tried to grab his attention by waving at him, Elijah ignored her although she knew that he had seen her wave.

The religious studies lesson became painfully uncomfortable. Every time Esther leaned over her wooden desk to look at Elijah, he was either scowling at his book, concentrating on the teacher or looking out the window. Not once did he look at her, and she began to suspect that Elijah was deliberately ignoring her. Esther could feel her heartbeat quicken in panic as her mind scrambled for an explanation as to why Elijah would be so angry.

Once class finished and Mr Freeman dismissed them, Elijah stood from his desk, slung his bag over his shoulder and dashed towards the door, without a glance in her direction. Knowing she needed to get to the bottom of the problem Elijah seemed to have with her sooner rather than later, Esther picked up her schoolbag and rushed after him.

Elijah was at the end of the corridor, about to make his way to the science block when Esther grabbed his shoulder. He turned to face her and, with a force that he had never shown her before, shrugged her hand away.

"Don't touch me."

Esther was taken aback; Elijah's voice sounded so venomous. It felt unnatural coming from him, and she recoiled as the words hit her. *What have I done?*

"Elijah, what's wrong? What did I do?"

"You know what you did," Elijah snarled, his face contorted with pain.

"No, I don't know, that's why I am asking."

"I saw you kissing Ayesha in the park."

A tidal wave of realisation washed over Esther and her mind became clear. Now she understood, all too well, Elijah's fury towards her. She froze on the spot, her jaw clamped together like it was wired shut.

"You're disgusting, you know. You're sick."

Still, Esther said nothing. She stood in front of Elijah in a silent and suffocating chamber of embarrassment.

"You're dirty, and you're sinful, and you're going to burn in hell."

Fierce anger suddenly filled Esther. With gritted teeth, she raised her hand and slapped Elijah hard across his right cheek, causing his head to wobble from side to side.

Three schoolkids had witnessed the slap and now stood watching Elijah, mouths agape and eyes bulging at the drama unfolding before them. Elijah was clutching his cheek with his right hand. He wore the facial expression of someone who could not quite understand what had just happened to him.

Esther's flash of anger vanished, leaving her feeling stunned and lost. The rope that had brought them closer and tied them together had been severed.

She stared at Elijah. It looked like tears wanted to fall from his eyes but were too stubborn to emerge. For a second, it appeared as if Elijah was going to say something to her. Instead, he turned around and pushed the door open behind him, vanishing into the playground.

For a few minutes, although it felt like longer, Esther stood at the end of the hall alone, allowing the tears to trickle down her cheeks before falling, like droplets before a rainstorm, onto the floor.

CHAPTER 18

June 2008

"Thank you again, Lucien, for agreeing to come today," Elijah said, shaking Lucien's hand and smiling at him.

They were standing at the front of the church hall. The leading church service had finished, but a few members of the congregation had waited behind to talk to their friends or gossip, something that Elijah tried to discourage. Around them, several children were chasing each other around the brown benches, and Joshua had climbed up behind the wooden podium, mimicking a pastor by shouting random verses from Ephesians with a Bible in his hands.

"Get down from there, Joshua," Elijah said with a loud voice as he narrowed his eyes at his misbehaving nephew.

Joshua stopped pretending to preach and frowned at Elijah. "But Uncle, if I want to be a pastor like you, I have to practice."

Elijah grinned, smothering his compulsion to laugh, as he knew that doing so would only encourage his nephew. "You can practice another time. Now you better get down from there before your father finds you."

Joshua's eyes widened in horror at the possibility of his father scolding him, and he quickly jumped down from the platform and dashed towards the other kids, no doubt in search of another opportunity to cause mischief away from the watchful eyes of adults.

"Kids are as addicted to trouble as they are to candy," Lucien said, watching Elijah's nephew join the other hyperactive children. "But like it says in Psalms 127: 'Children are a heritage from the Lord.'"

"It would not surprise me if my brother-in-law read that Psalm every day to remind himself why he got into the business of raising kids in the first place," Elijah said.

Both men shared a moment of laughter.

"Before we start the youth service, may I ask where your toilet is?" Lucien said.

Elijah gave Lucien instructions to where the toilets were located and watched as Lucien walked, with a brisk pace, in that direction. As soon as Elijah turned around, he saw Jairus marching towards him. As was often the case with his younger brother, a look of disapproval was plastered onto Jairus's long face.

"Judging by the fact that I've just seen your gay friend in the church, am I right to assume that you're still going ahead with it?"

Elijah sucked his teeth and shot a disapproving look at Jairus. "Why are you so rude? What's wrong with you?"

Jairus squared up to Elijah as if they were both about to engage in a fight. "Me?" he said with barely concealed disgust in his voice. "There's nothing wrong with me, brother. It's what is wrong with you that bothers me. You're letting someone who freely and knowingly lives in sin preach to our children."

"He's a Christian and a good man."

"He is no different from an adulterer and should have no right to preach to our children. You are not only shaming God and this church, Elijah. You shame our father."

"Enough!" Elijah said, louder and with more rage than he intended. "I am the senior pastor of this church, and I've prayed to God about this. I know this is right. If you don't like it, then leave, Jairus."

Jairus's lips parted as though he was about to say something in response but then he seemed to decide against it. Instead, he shook his head at Elijah, and his mouth twisted into a snarky smile. Giving a final disapproving look at Elijah, Jairus sucked his teeth and flounced out the hall, towards the entrance of the church.

As Jairus stormed off, Elijah felt like calling him back to explain to him, in a calmer and less harsh tone, why Lucien deserved to preach to the youth service, but he decided not to. What would be the point? Like the older Nigerian Christians Elijah had grown up around, Jairus was a conservative Christian, and in his case, the word Christian was written in capital letters and underscored. Unlike Elijah, Jairus did not drink, had never smoked and, to the best of Elijah's knowledge, had not even engaged in sex. Both had grown up differently: Jairus in Nigeria and Elijah in England, and much of the misunderstanding between them was due to this fact. Jairus had once told Elijah that his upbringing in London caused Elijah treat sin as if it were a witty and charming criminal, whom he played cards with even if he did not follow the criminal to rob a house.

With a sigh, Elijah turned away from his brother. Lucien was now walking towards him, with a friendly smile, and together the two of them made their way to the meeting room in the church where the youth service was to be held.

Brixton and other areas in Lambeth borough were going through a gang epidemic. There were youth gangs in every council estate where poverty, anger and violence grew into the lives of young people like mouldy fungus grows on food that is exposed to harmful air. For Elijah, this was nothing new. Brixton and its surrounding areas had always been a place with patches of violence and destitution. Yet the Pentecostal Church of Christ provided a safe haven; a place where young people, spiralling into gang life, could find some steady ground and a helping hand.

Given Lucien's background as a former teenage criminal and the fact that he was still young enough to relate to the teenagers who attended Sunday's youth service, Elijah was confident that they would appreciate Lucien's talk.

A mix of third-generation, British-born African and Caribbean teenagers sat in the spacious white room where the youth service was taking place. Many of them had been chatting among themselves or consumed by their smartphones. As soon as Elijah walked into the room with Lucien in tow, everyone ceased their activity. With his long brown dreadlocks, small beanie hat and jeans, Lucien did not look like or dress like anyone at the church, and this caught the teenagers' attention, stroking their curiosity, as Elijah knew it would.

Lucien stood at the front of the room to introduce himself, and Elijah ambled towards the corner of the room where Tiwa and Mary sat, taking a seat beside his wife. Tiwa turned to face him, her shoulder-length braids swaying gently as she moved.

"I hope this goes well, Elijah," she said. "You still haven't told their parents that a homosexual person will be preaching to their children?"

"No, I have not."

Tiwa threw Elijah a look of disapproval and shook her head. In return, Elijah playfully poked her elbow.

"His sexual orientation is not important, Tiwa," Elijah whispered, as Lucien began talking to his audience. "He's a Christian, and he has a message that will resonate with the youth of this church. That's all that matters."

Tiwa eyed him for a moment and then sighed softly. Thankfully, she knew there was no point questioning Elijah's decision on this. Unlike his brother, his wife did not try and undermine his authority at every chance.

Much to Elijah's delight, although he had expected nothing less, Lucien's talk was brilliant. He spoke to the teenagers, some of whom had been arrested, honestly and candidly. Using relevant verses from the Bible and his own personal anecdotes, Lucien held the youths' attention with a firm grip for almost two hours – no easy feat.

The service concluded at three o'clock, and the teenagers made their way out, thanking Lucien as they walked past him.

"Wow, he was terrific," Mary said, leaning over Tiwa to speak to Elijah. "I didn't expect him to be such a natural speaker. He certainly knows his scriptures."

Elijah smiled at his sister. "Never judge a book by its cover, Mary. It's always what's inside that counts."

That night, while lying in bed next to Tiwa, who was already in a deep sleep, Elijah decided he would allow Lucien to minister to the youth regularly at the church, effectively becoming a second youth pastor. Lucien had not only displayed a strong understanding of scripture but was charismatic, with a relaxed approach to public speaking.

As Elijah placed his Bible on top of the small wooden bedside table and prepared himself to fall asleep, he considered the fact that he would face some resistance at the church; his brother's disapproval would no doubt deafen his ears. But Elijah had a vision, a dream to make his father's church more modern and inclusive. After praying to God on this issue, he felt even more determined to see it through.

The next evening after another uneventful day at the office in Canary Wharf, Elijah drove to Peckham to pick his wife up from the school she taught at before driving to the church for the board meeting. He had not told Tiwa about his decision to make Lucien a youth pastor at the church. He knew perhaps he should have, but he wasn't entirely sure what his wife would think and was too tired for a debate.

"You seem to be in an unusually good mood after work," Tiwa said as they both walked through the church's halls towards the room where the board meeting took place. "Promotion?"

Elijah chuckled and turned to his wife as they reached the wooden door of the meeting room. "My work already thinks they overpay me. No, I'm just in a good mood about a decision I've made."

With a firm grip on the handle, Elijah twisted the doorknob and opened the door. He did not expect the sight that greeted him. A few dozen adults, who he recognised as regular churchgoers and whose children attended the youth service, stood in the room with looks of displeasure aimed squarely at Elijah. His eyes darted to the corner where Elijah's mother sat, draped in a long, green *ankara* blouse, with her wrinkled hands wrapped around her chestnut walking stick. Mary stood next to their mother with Kunle by her side; neither of them would meet Elijah's gaze.

"Ah, Elijah, you're here at last," Jairus said from the front of the crowd. He had a look of immense satisfaction glowing on his dark face.

Elijah looked around at the faces in the room, genuinely puzzled. "Good evening, everyone. I hope you are all blessed. What is this all about?"

Chidi, a big-bellied and equally big-headed Igbo man in his late forties with two sons who attended the church, stepped forward and pointed his sausage-shaped fingers at Elijah. "Are you mad, Elijah?" he said in harsh Yoruba.

Taken aback by the forcefulness of Chidi's 's tone, Elijah responded in Yoruba, "Okay, calm down."

Atinuke, a forty-five-year-old woman whose daughter also attended the youth service, stepped forward to address Elijah. "We've been told that you let a homosexual man speak to our children at yesterday's youth service."

Elijah turned his head sharply towards Jairus, who countered Elijah's scowl with a Cheshire-cat smile.

"How can you allow that type of person to preach to our kids, Pastor?" Atinuke said, staring directly at him. "Does this church approve of homosexuality now? Is that what this church is becoming under your leadership, Pastor?"

All at once, mouths began to move in quick succession as the crowd talked over each other. How could the pastor give a gay man a platform at the church and allow him to preach the Bible to their children? From the tone of some of their voices,

Elijah would have thought he had invited a child killer to the youth service.

Elijah cleared his throat as loudly as he could, and the chattering gradually quietened. "Look, I completely understand your concerns," he said, making sure he did not look at his brother's face in case he could not fight the temptation to slap him. "But the man who spoke to your children, Lucien Carmen, is a friend of mine. A good man and a devout Christian—"

Chidi cut Elijah off with a loud voice. "Nonsense! People like that are false believers. I do not want such people speaking to my children. I don't send my sons to church to listen to people who are gay. They're exposed to enough of that rubbish at school."

Again, the room filled with the sound of angry chatter as everyone's opinions flew through the air at once. This time it was Jairus who cleared his throat, and everyone turned to face him in silence. Although he was no longer smiling, Jairus still had the look of someone who had overthrown a king.

"I think I speak for most of us in this room when I say that we do not want homosexuals speaking to our children. They can come to our church, and we will, of course, help them overcome their sinful nature, but we will not give them a stage to preach the Bible."

Elijah surveyed the room, his earlier good spirits trodden on like a discarded newspaper as every person nodded their head in agreement. He looked at Tiwa, who seemed to be avoiding his gaze on purpose. Then Elijah turned towards his mother, but she shook her head slowly, her dark eyes unmoving. The matriarch of the Oduwole family had spoken.

With a defeated sigh, Elijah spoke. "Apologies if I have unintentionally caused upset among any of you. Of course, this is a church that listens to its congregation. I give you my word, with God as my witness, that this incident will not happen again."

The crowd murmured in agreement. Satisfied with Elijah's response, they began to disperse, and many nodded their head at Elijah as they walked past him and into the main hall of the church.

Jairus was the last to leave. Walking towards Elijah with the air of a man who had just consumed the most satisfying meal of his life, his younger brother smirked at him. "You need to pray harder, Elijah. You may lose your way, but this church cannot afford to."

Elijah did not respond, knowing that the words that would come out of his mouth would be inappropriate for a place as holy as the church.

CHAPTER 19

June 2008

Esther poured herself a glass of Chateau Grand-Puy-Lacoste, a wine that looked as expensive as it sounded, from Ayesha's impressive wine collection. She took a small sip, savouring the tease of the rich taste on her tongue, and then walked over to the mahogany four-poster bed located in the corner of the open-plan flat.

Her father's journal lay on the white bedsheets. After her drinking session at the Dogstar last week, Esther had felt groggy for two days – hangovers were increasingly becoming harder to shake off at her age – so she had not been in the best state to start reading the journal immediately. Taking one more sip of wine, Esther placed her glass on the bedside table and picked up the journal, throwing herself onto the springy mattress.

She ran her fingers across the partially battered leather cover. Here, in her grasp, was a piece of her father's spirit. His thoughts, feelings and desires were all written and contained within the brown pages of this book.

Even if she did not love her father with the type of compassion or devotion that a daughter is supposed to show the first man in her life, over time Esther had developed an all-consuming desire to understand him. Perhaps it was because she was getting older, but she had this need to make sense of her father, the man who had bruised her skin as well as her soul.

Feeling the rhythm of her heartbeat quicken with anticipation, Esther leaned against the pillow and opened the first page of her father's journal.

Monday 8th January 1996

When I first arrived in England in 1973 with Zina and our five-year-old daughter, I remember stepping out the immigration office and feeling an ice-cold wind hit me. Not just the weather, but the white faces, too. They had ice-cold eyes. Ice-cold skin. And an ice-cold talk. An ice-cold country for an ice-cold people.

I had convinced Zina that we should leave our oil-stricken lands after Nigeria had forsaken our people, for the Ogoni are the forgotten Nigerians or, should I say, the ignored Nigerians. We may have had independence for thirty-six years, but Nigerians only pretend to be unified. In reality, we are just a bunch of disparate tribes who were forcibly brought together, and we Ogonis are the outcasts of Nigeria, worse off than the Igbos, not prolific like the Yorubas or the Hausas.

But I vowed to return to my homeland and reclaim it. After living in the cold country of England for twenty long years, with nothing to show for it, I decided to return to Ogoniland to fight alongside my brothers. To fight alongside my friend, Ken Saro-Wiwa.

Now irony, having its fun with me, has put me back in the cold country once again. I had to leave my wife to protect her. My daughter – I lost her a long time ago. My brothers, their blood soiling the Ogoni fields, killed by the hands of our so-called Nigerian brethren, are hanging from ropes. And I am alone.

But as I lay in this desolate squat in east London and despair taunts me to take a knife to my throat, I am reminded of James 1:12:

"Blessed is the man who remains steadfast under trial, for when he has stood the test, he will receive the crown of life, which God has promised to those who love him."

Fascinated, Esther flipped to the next page in the journal, and a sheet of paper fell out. She realised that the journal was missing a few pages, which had probably fallen out as the book's binding weakened over time, and upon closer inspection some of the ink had faded. Esther could not make sense of the writing on several of the pages, so she kept turning through the journal's entries until she found one that she could make sense of.

Tuesday 6th August 1996

There is an English saying I like. When life gives you lemons, make lemonade. And though I have often tried to mix the bitter lemons this country has given me into the proverbial lemonade, success has continued to elude me.

But it seems I have finally grasped it. When I first arrived in England in 1973, I was unable to find a position as a teacher. So I settled for jobs working on the ice-cold docks (coldness loves to follow me in this country like a second shadow) followed by eleven years as a clerk in Vauxhall, filing records for solicitors in a cold concrete basement. This is a generous description; I liken it to an English dungeon. And now that I have returned to the land of colonisers, I find myself working as a security guard.

Working as a security guard by night, I have been studying for my English teaching qualification by day with the little money I save. Doorman by night. Student by day. It is the usual dichotomy of ambitious Africans who travel abroad.

But, glory to God, my sacrifice and hard work has given me something sweet, like palm wine squeezed from a sap. I now have a qualification to be an English schoolteacher in this country. My God is awesome.

God, to His glory, places people in our lives to help us. I recall as a young boy, sometime around 1956, I visited Port Harcourt with my seven older brothers. Befriending danger, as one does when they are young, I walked too close to a ledge by the river, and I fell into the water, unable to swim. My brothers had not seen me fall, and as I thrashed my limbs, feeling the water pulling me down as if it were hungry for young human flesh, a fisherman came to my rescue and pulled me from the river.

God, to His glory, had placed the fisherman on the river that day to save me, unbeknownst to him. Today, God has put someone else in my life to save me, unbeknownst to her.

Miss Charlotte Evans interviewed me for the English teaching position for children age seven and above. She is head of the English department at the school. Her name is so plainly English, too simple for such sophisticated beauty: shoulder-length, silky soft hair, blinding with its lemon-blonde strands, and her eyes, a crystal blue like the purest sapphire. When I first saw her, I realised, for the first time, why some African men find their eyes following an English woman.

Today, I received a letter confirming I have been giving the teaching position. And I know it was because of her, Miss Charlotte Evans, with her hair bright like a lemon. Life gave me lemons, and she has turned them into a glass of refreshing lemonade.

Esther turned the pages of the journal until she noticed Charlie's Robinson's name on an entry marked 27th December. She started reading:

Friday 27th December 1996

This evening I met my Irish friend, Charlie "Deft hand" Robinson. As I write, I am drunk, so God, I beg for your forgiveness.

I want to say it was a chance encounter, but I met Charlie at The Barge, a pub on the junction of Victoria Dock Road and Freemasons Road in Canning Town, which we used to frequent when we finished our shift on the docks, way back when we were younger, slightly less-jaded souls. I would like to think God wanted me to meet him again. Why? I may never know. The Lord works in mysterious ways. I find it amusing that this often-used phrase is not mentioned anywhere in the Bible, but it does not make it less accurate.

Over several pints of ale we shared our stories, just as we used to share our contempt for Englishmen in the same pub. It always made me laugh that Charlie and myself had such similar lives. We were both Christians, though he was Catholic, and I was Protestant. We both despised England for dividing our respective homelands, and we were both vilified by the English.

So, of course, Charlie is now estranged from his wife and no longer speaking to his daughter, like myself. Here were two men of vastly different cultures, Nigerian and Irish, connected by the universal truth of Jesus, our Lord and Saviour, abandoned wives and ungrateful daughters.

I recounted to him a story that I am sure I had already told him, and he had no doubt already forgotten, about the trouble in Ogoniland. He called me a coward for running away. A blunt man, Charlie is. And he was right.

God knows the hearts of men. What do I have to hide from him?

In my heart, I know, and He knows, that I returned to my homeland in 1990 to join my brothers and my friend, Ken Saro-Wiwa, and his political movement, MOSOP.

For more than four years, I was one of MOSOP's steadfast activists. While Ken Saro-Wiwa was travelling across Europe and bringing international attention to our just cause, I was on the frontlines. I helped families escape during the conflict with the Andoni and Okirika people, both of which claimed the lives of five of my older brothers. I fought against the Shell workers, disrupting their harmful oil drilling. With passion, I spoke against Sani Abacha, our worthless President.

But when they hung Ken Saro-Wiwa along with our other friends, I knew it was only a matter of time before I would join them. The military was searching for me. I was the sword of MOSOP, and once the Nigerian government had dealt with MOSOP's leaders in a rigged trial, its triumphant and murderous eyes turned to the warriors. So I fled. I did not want to be a martyr, and I fled back to the cold country.

I hope when we meet again in the afterlife that my dear friend, Ken Saro-Wiwa, will forgive me for abandoning our cause. When the storm bore down on the Ogoni people, I allowed myself to be swept by the tide.

Although Esther had begun to comprehend, from reading her father's last letter to her mother and speaking to Charlie Robinson, why her father fled Nigeria, she now had the complete picture.

It dawned on Esther that for many black people, whether in Africa, Britain or America, the struggle would always hover above them like thick, grey clouds, ready at any moment to rain destruction and misery upon them. History had made sure of it. Her father had fought against his own prejudiced government for the rights of the Ogoni people, and she had fought against a prejudiced government in Britain for the rights of Black Britons. Two different generations, fighting for black justice on both sides of the Atlantic. The black struggle was universal.

Esther turned to the final entry in the journal, dated 8th March 2002. She widened her eyes in surprise. There appeared to be several references to her. By the time her father had written this, it had been twelve years since they had spoken to each other. As her heart rate increased with the rising sensation of excitement, Esther read her father's final entry:

Friday 8th March 2002

She had sounded different, of course, but vaguely familiar. I felt like I was hearing my daughter's voice through another woman's mouth.

Charlotte had turned on the radio after we had a disagreement. One thing I have noticed about her is that she does not like to admit when she is wrong. If she is angry, it is because I have made her angry. If I am frustrated with her, she will find a way so that it is my fault I am mad at her. It is a condition unique to western women.

Anyway, I do not listen to secular music, so I did not know what BBC 1xtra was. But the presenter had said that they would be playing music from UK female artists to celebrate International Women's Day. I did not expect to recognise any of these female artists; I am an old man with old ears.

But the third singer I recognised as my daughter. They had introduced her as "Esther" but there was no mention of her last name. I cannot even recall the name of her song, but I can remember her voice. A parent does not forget their child's voice, our ears are designed to pick up its soundwave like an antenna – a kind of parental mechanism created by God so that we can instantly hear when our children are screaming or crying out for help.

Esther, my only child. I named her after Queen Esther, from the Book of Esther, one of my favourite chapters in the Old Testament. Queen Esther was a courageous Jewish queen in Persia, who thwarted the genocide of the Jews.

It is more than a decade since my daughter decided not to follow her father and mother back to her homeland but travel to America at only twenty-two. More than a decade ago, I told her never to come back. But I knew, long before, that she had more of a connection to the concrete slabs of Brixton than to the coastal sand plains of Ogoniland.

For a long time, I only looked at my daughter through a lens of anger and deep-rooted disappointment. By the time Esther was thirteen, she was a child of England. She spoke and behaved like a white British girl, she listened to their music and wore their culture. The only sense of spirituality I could see in my daughter was her angelic voice.

When I was a teacher at the school I built in Kegbara-Dere, I prayed that God would give me a precious daughter like the girls at my school who were proud to be from Ogoni, the pride of the River States in Nigeria.

But my daughter knew nothing of her heritage and did not care to learn it. Many times, I rowed with her and beat her. Once, I even threatened to return her to Nigeria. She had almost died in a fire at a house party she went to without my permission. I had thought that such a near-death experience would bring her closer to God and to me, but it did the opposite.

I recall that she had begun to see the boy who later became her boyfriend. I do not remember his name now. He was the son of a pastor whose church I visited while we were living in Brixton. I remember the boy's mother, for I had once become close to her. I thought at the time that God had put this boy in her life to make her more spiritual. But as always, I did not see any change in her.

But the day I knew I had lost her forever still haunts me. I am no longer sure precisely when the incident had happened, maybe the mid-eighties. Those days, we lived in a horrible block of flats in Brixton, and that night, I was having trouble sleeping and stepped out of the apartment. From the balcony, the surrounding blocks of flat almost invisible in the blackness of the night, I saw my daughter kissing another woman. As a father, it was too much to bear; to witness how this country had ruined my daughter completely. It had already pained me to see her reject God, but to witness her behaving so unnaturally shattered my heart and gave rise to a hatred I did not know I possessed.

Even as I write in this journal, I remember how severely I beat her when she returned home. I was incensed with rage, pain and shame. I wanted to kill her. I can only thank God that her mother intervened, or maybe I would have taken my daughter's life that night. At the time, I thought it was better to have no daughter than a daughter who was rotten.

Charlotte did not see the tears in my eyes as I listened to my daughter's voice on the radio. In that moment, I realised how much I still love my daughter. For so long, I have been so angry that I came to Britain. Angry that I wasted many years of my life coming here the first time and now I am back here again. Over the years, I resented my daughter for being moulded by British culture rather than her own. But hearing her voice on that radio today, I finally realised she was a wonderful blessing that God had given me. I was just too bitter to appreciate it. Too resentful to love my daughter as she was.

I never cherished my daughter. I was the one who abandoned her. And it pains my old soul that I will never have a chance to tell her I love her and to apologise for how I treated her. Sorrow and regret make easy friends, indeed.

For what seemed like hours, although it was only a few minutes, Esther stared in silence at her father's final journal entry. Even before she realised she was crying, her tears formed wet marks on the journal's brown paper. In all the twenty-two years she had lived with her father, this was the first time he had said he loved her. Even if it was communicated through written words on old paper, it did not lessen its impact. Not only did her father love her, but he knew that she was bisexual. Now she understood why he had beaten her almost to death that night in 1984, but more importantly, it seemed her father had accepted who she was later in his life. The revelation of all these truths, these once hidden facets of her father's soul, overwhelmed her, and Esther took a deep breath, allowing this sudden realisation to breathe new understanding into her reality.

As Esther wiped away the tears in her eyes, she heard her iPhone vibrate on the armrest of the sofa where she had left it. She gently placed her father's journal on the duvet and walked towards the phone, feeling remarkably lighter, as if she had suddenly lost weight. Elijah's name was flashing on the screen.

"Hey, didn't expect to hear from you this late in the afternoon."

Elijah chuckled from the other end of the phone. "I thought I would surprise you with some good news."

Esther sniffed as she smiled. "A pastor who brings good news. How unexpected."

"Alright, I set myself up for that one. Wait, are you okay? You sound like you've been crying."

"You're right, I have. You're too good at reading my moods, you know that? I just finished reading my father's journal, and I have so much to tell you."

"Wow, well that's a coincidence."

Esther sat down on the armrest and wiped her eyes again with the sleeve of her blouse. "What do you mean?"

"The reason I'm calling is that I think I may know where your father is. I've found a possible address. Can I come over?"

CHAPTER 20

June 2008

Sometimes, silence can be loud enough to tell you everything about the state of a marriage. This is what Elijah thought as he sat at his desk in the church's green office. In the left corner, a few steps away from the door, Tiwa was typing on a computer, her intermittent tapping breaking the sharp silence between husband and wife.

Surrounding the married couple were old photos of the founding members of the church. On the left wall, beneath a golden crucifix of Jesus, hung a black-and-white framed picture of Elijah's late father standing in front of the church after he completed his first ever Sunday service, his face frozen in a smile of immense accomplishment. Beside the portrait of his father was another framed image of Elijah's mother, and next to that, a picture of his father's late younger brother, Samuel Oduwole.

Being a senior pastor of the church his family built, a finance director, and a man who liked to keep his personal life separate from work, Elijah had three email addresses corresponding to the separate parts of his life. Currently, he was scrolling through his senior pastor inbox, looking at dozens of emails from members of the church. Usually, most messages he received were from church members seeking his advice on a variety of personal matters ranging from money issues to sexless marriages. Others were long-winded questions about Biblical passages and spiritual salvation. But this evening, a lot of the emails were about Elijah's friend, Lucien.

Inviting a gay preacher to speak was always going to lead to some backlash from the stubbornly conservative congregation and the clergy. That was why Elijah had wanted to keep Lucien's sexuality a secret from the church attendees. Although Elijah now felt his decision may have been an erroneous judgement; in his heart, he knew God wanted him to have Lucien speak at the youth service.

Yet, Elijah could not have told those inner-city London teenagers beforehand that Lucien was homosexual. It would have been like placing a large cardboard sign with *gay* written on it around Lucien's neck. The teenagers would no longer be listening to Lucien's words but focusing on the cardboard sign, their own learned prejudices blocking their ears like two fingers.

Jairus had betrayed him. Of course he had. Elijah felt like a fool for believing that his brother would not disclose Lucien's sexuality. For once, Elijah had thought Jairus would put the harmony of the church above his enormous appetite for undermining Elijah's leadership. He had put too much faith in his younger brother.

Now that everyone knew, the complaints from parents were expected. The lack of support from his mother, his sister and brother-in-law was expected. What Elijah had not prepared for was the complete absence of support from his wife.

Tiwa might as well have been a statue. As the mob of angry parents had surrounded him, accusing him of failing in his role as senior pastor, Tiwa had not opened her mouth once to defend him. She had not even looked him in the eye. To add salt to his wounded ego, Tiwa had still not acknowledged what happened this afternoon. Instead, she nonchalantly tapped away on her keyboard as if her husband being humiliated within his own church had never happened.

Tiwa turned around on her swivel chair to face Elijah. "I've managed to update the church member records," she said, and something about her Nigerian-accented voice irked Elijah. "Not everyone has filled out the forms properly. Honestly, it's like half the congregation cannot use a computer."

Elijah looked at Tiwa, curled his lips and returned to the laptop screen. Her voice had released the lid pinning down his aggravation, like a cork popping from a wine bottle. "How hard can it be to support your husband?" he said, scrolling through the emails but not reading any of them. Even he could hear the bitterness colouring his every word.

"Excuse me?" Tiwa said. She sounded more confrontational than Elijah had anticipated. "What do you mean by that?"

Elijah narrowed his eyes and locked them on his wife. "Where were you today? You were noticeably quiet when your husband was being criticised in his own church. I would have appreciated your support."

Tiwa shook her head as if what Elijah had said was absurd. "And how would you have wanted me to support you?"

"Are you serious right now?" Elijah said, outraged by her blatant disregard for him. "You could have opened your mouth, Tiwa. Defended my stance, but instead you stood by and watched me be made a fool of."

Tiwa let out a short, biting laugh. "And what good would that have done? Since becoming the senior pastor, you don't listen to anyone at this church anymore. It's a community, and you cannot just ignore it to push forward your own agenda."

"My agenda?" Elijah said in a tone of disbelief. "I'm trying to make this church more inclusive. A church that is centred around love and understanding, not exclusion and judgement. Is that what you believe in? That a man or woman has no right to preach the Bible because of who they choose to love?"

"It doesn't matter what I think. It matters what your congregation thinks. And you hold them all in contempt as if you're better than them. Somehow more enlightened. You should listen more to the people who have been coming to your father's church for decades."

Elijah shook his head and sucked his teeth. He was hurt that his wife did not have any faith in his leadership. She had even referred to it as "your father's church" as if he would never be able to fill his father's pastoral robes. "The fact is you didn't show up for me. That's what I expect from my wife.

At this, Tiwa shot Elijah a look of contempt that surprised him. "Like you've been showing up for me?"

"What is that supposed to mean?"

Tiwa laughed, almost maniacally and shook her head, smirking as if she was keeping a secret. At this gesture, Elijah began to feel his irritation swell into seething anger.

"Answer me, Tiwa. What do you mean by that?" Elijah said, struggling to maintain the volume of his voice.

Tiwa stood up from her seat, picking up her brown leather jacket, and sneered at Elijah. "When were you planning on telling me about all the time you've been spending with your ex-girlfriend?"

As soon as the question left Tiwa's mouth and glided into Elijah's ears, his mind became momentarily blank, as if her words had caused his brain to short circuit. He had not suspected that Tiwa knew about the time he was spending with Esther. But Elijah quickly regained composure; he was not going to let his wife use it against him.

"Of course Jairus told you, that brother of mine has such a big mouth. I was planning on telling you that I've been helping her find her missing father, but I've been so busy, it slipped my mind. And anyway, would you have listened or cared? Do you even notice me anymore?"

"Missing father?" Tiwa said, raising an eyebrow. She let out another maniacal laugh which made Elijah seethe. "You think I haven't noticed you coming home from work later than usual these past weeks? You think I haven't smelled the strange perfume on you? Have you been sleeping with her? Her name is Esther, right?"

Elijah stood from his desk with the force of someone jolted with a bolt of electricity. Rage and frustration now had firm control of his mind and, by extension, his mouth. "I'm not sleeping with her! I'm helping her search for her father. Besides, I'm surprised it even matters to you." Elijah could no longer hear the words coming out of his mouth even as he spoke them. His ears were deafened by white-hot anger. "You haven't touched me in almost a month. And when we last had sex, it was almost as if you didn't want to. You just lay there. For the past year, we've only been having sex to create a baby that you cannot even conceive. Nothing else."

Tiwa stared at him as if he had slapped her. Elijah looked back at her wide eyes and slightly parted lips, and he suddenly realised what he had said. The gravity of the words pulled him back to his sensibilities, and a wave of regret and shame overcame him. "Tiwa. *Ife mi.* I'm so sorry. I shouldn't have said that."

Tiwa gulped and bit her lip, avoiding Elijah's imploring eyes. "Don't worry about driving me to Grace's this evening," she said in a voice that struggled to carry her words. "I'll order a taxi to Camberwell."

"Tiwa, wait..." But Tiwa had already turned on her heel and marched to the door.

Elijah called for her once more, but Tiwa outright ignored him as she opened the door of the pastor's office and walked out, leaving Elijah in a fog of regret. Only the framed pictures of his mother and his deceased father and uncle kept him company now, and their unmoving smiles seemed to mock him.

A few minutes after his wife left the office, Elijah decided he had to go after her. Allowing this schism to remain between them would only cause it to widen, like the ground splitting during a powerful earthquake, until they were too far apart to jump over the crack.

With a heavy sigh, Elijah made for his blazer hanging on the coat rack when he noticed that Tiwa had not logged out of the computer. In fact, the database software the church used for storing information about members of the congregation, past and present, was still open. Out of a sense of duty, Elijah walked over to the computer to close the program.

Leaning forward with his right hand on the mouse, Elijah moved the cursor to shut down the database. But something caught his eye. In one of the columns, a name had been inputted in capital letters that Elijah instantly recognised:

K NUBARI

"No way," Elijah whispered to himself as he reread the name, to make sure. He felt his heartbeat quicken with excitement. Elijah took a seat on the swivel chair, his eyes never leaving the screen.

Once he had sat down, Elijah clicked on the name to find out what other information about this man they had stored in the database. The screen froze for a minute, the slow program processing Elijah's command. Just how old was this software? After two minutes of loading time, the screen finally transitioned to the next page. All the columns requiring personal information, apart from occupation, had been filled out:

NAME: K NUBARI
AGE: 70
SEX: MALE
OCCUPATION: N/A
ADDRESS: 32 FORMOSA STREET
W9 2QA
LAST UPDATED: SUNDAY 20TH JANUARY 2008

Was he leaping headfirst into the conclusion that this was Esther's father? Elijah rubbed his forehead, scavenging through half-formed memories to find one that suggested he had seen Kelechi Nubari at the church in the last year. But to no avail. Just as he had told Esther almost a few weeks ago, he had not seen her father since 1990. Or so he believed.

So many people came to the church every Sunday that at times Elijah rarely focused on anyone. It was entirely feasible that Kelechi Nubari had indeed visited the church in 2008 and Elijah had simply taken no notice. More convincingly, the age of the man tallied with how old Esther's father would be at this time.

He clicked on the address. After another few minutes, as the software silently struggled to carry out Elijah's command, it finally transitioned into another screen. This new page revealed that someone else also lived at the same address and had attended the church with *K NUBARI*, the person who may or may not be Esther's father.

NAME: E Dankworth
AGE: 58
SEX: MALE
OCCUPATION: UNIVERSITY PROFESSOR
ADDRESS: 32 FAMOSA STREET
W9 2QA
LAST UPDATED: SUNDAY 20TH JANUARY 2008

It could have been a coincidence, but this new lead was too promising to be dismissed entirely. Suddenly Elijah felt excited, his earlier irritable mood evaporated by the comforting thought that he now had an excuse to see Esther. He reached into his blazer and took out his mobile phone to give her a call.

Elijah drove his BMW through the long stretch of road that was Brixton Hill as he headed towards Pullman Court. Esther had sounded thrilled when Elijah told her that he had found an address where her father might be staying. He had been light with the details on the call in the hope that they could talk about it in person. When she agreed for him to come over, Elijah was ecstatic. It was a feeling a teenage boy might get after his school crush told him he could go around while her parents were not in. It had been a while since someone in his life had made him feel wanted.

Elijah's Blackberry vibrated on the passenger seat where he had left it. Someone had sent him a text. When Elijah stopped at a red traffic light, he picked up his phone to read it. His mood dampened when he saw it was from Tiwa, who had sent him a brief instruction:

Pick up some garri from the market on your way back.

Irritation crept in again, shoving his optimism aside as if it were occupying space in his spirit that it did not deserve. With some reluctance, Elijah did a U-turn and made his way towards Brixton market.

It was nearing 6 p.m., and Brixton market was winding down. As the traders packed up their stalls after a long day of selling in this busy district of south London, Elijah walked through Electric Avenue with a briskness to his steps.

By the time Elijah had bought the *garri*, he was starting to feel hungry. Feeling its weight in the blue carrier bag he was holding, Elijah paced through Brixton village. He passed numerous shops selling everything from *ankara* lace to vintage clothing. As

Elijah walked past a record shop, he caught something familiar from the corner of his eye. He backstepped and looked at the vinyl record displayed in the shop window that had grabbed his attention. There was a picture of a woman he recognised on the record cover.

Needing to confirm if his suspicions were correct, Elijah walked into the record shop.

Anyone who was a fan of vinyl could quickly lose hours of their lives in this treasure trove of music from years past. Vinyl covers, ranging from the funk music of the seventies to the reggae of the eighties, were lined neatly in rows on the display shelves.

With fondness, he recalled the days of his youth when he would sit with Esther in Brockwell Park and share her headphones, nodding their heads to whatever cassette was playing from her Walkman. Jimmy James and the Vagabonds, The Real Thing, Junior Giscombe, George Michael and Lisa Stansfield were just a few of the records on display that he recognised. Still, Elijah had not come into the record shop to soak himself in the soundtracks of his youth.

Elijah walked towards a display stand facing the window and picked up the vinyl record that had piqued his curiosity. He looked at the picture of the young black girl on the cover and chuckled to himself.

"How much for this?" Elijah asked as he placed the record on the wooden counter.

The young man behind it, skinny with spotty white skin and untidy dreadlocks, gave Elijah a pleasant smile. "This record is a little gem, you know," he said, picking up the vinyl and inspecting it as if were a delicate and rare item at an auction. "Not many people know about her. She had some fame in the nineties. All the cooler that she's one of Brixton's exports. You're a fan?"

Elijah smiled. "Yes, you can say that. In fact, I'm on my way to meet her right now."

CHAPTER 21

June 2008

Esther opened the door of the flat, and Elijah stepped in, carrying a blue plastic bag in his right hand. As Elijah surveyed the living room, Esther felt a sudden closeness to him. Here he was, bringing her some news about her father's whereabouts, going out of his way to help her like he always had. She hoped he would stay for a while; his presence relieved her of the sense of loneliness and boredom that came with being alone in the flat.

"This is a really impressive place," Elijah said, his eyes focusing on the retro television. "Feels like I'm in an episode of *The Jetsons*. How did Ayesha afford this again?"

Esther closed the door and walked over to stand beside Elijah. "She won a massive divorce settlement from her rich ex-husband. He owned a PR company or something."

Elijah shook his head, smiling. "Sounds exactly like something Ayesha would pull off."

Esther chuckled and gestured at Elijah's blazer. "You don't have to be all formal and stiff. Loosen up."

As Elijah removed his jacket and placed it on one of the chairs, Esther moved towards the kitchen. "I'm whipping up a chicken stir-fry if you want some?" She turned around and gave Elijah a wry smile. "And no, there isn't any jollof rice, Pastor."

Elijah laughed as he slumped into the couch like a man beaten down by the day's stress. "There's more to this Nigerian man than jollof rice, you know that. Stir fry sounds great. Thanks."

Esther brought over two plates piled high with steaming chicken stir-fry and placed them on the purple glass table in the living room. She then got two glasses and a jug of water from the kitchen before taking a seat next to Elijah. For a few minutes, they both ate in silence.

"So, you found a possible address?" Esther said after gulping down some water.

Elijah sucked a single noodle dangling between his lips, which made Esther smile. "Yes. My wi—I was going through the church's database, which is a record of all the recent attendees. I came across the name K Nubari and an address, 32 Formosa Street. It's in Maida Vale."

Esther's eyes widened in shock. "Well, the name definitely matches my father's. But what else makes you think it could be him? I thought you hadn't seen my father since 1990?"

"I don't recall seeing him since then, but that doesn't mean he didn't attend the church this year. You remember how many people come to my church? It can be more than two hundred people sometimes. I might not have noticed him in the sea of faces." Elijah took another forkful of noodles, put it in his mouth and chewed. Once he had swallowed, he spoke again. "Besides, his age matches your father's. I can't believe we didn't think to check the church records. We're clearly not Sherlock Holmes and Dr Watson."

Esther let out a quiet laugh and put her knuckles on her chin, resting her elbow on her knee as she leaned forward. "It can't be a coincidence. And you said there was another person who attended the church that lived at the same address?

Elijah nodded. "Yes, a man by the name of Mr E Dankworth, which is the most British name I've ever heard. He put his occupation down as a university professor. It shouldn't be too hard to find out which one he works at."

Esther nodded her head in agreement, feeling a sense of renewed hope in finding her father. She thought she had met a dead end and had already started thinking about what to tell her mother when she returned to Chicago three weeks from now. But this new information was promising. It at least confirmed that her father might still be alive and in London.

"This so helpful, thank you," Esther said, patting Elijah's thigh and smiling. "I hope the chicken stir fry you're chowing down like a man who hasn't eaten his whole life shows my appreciation."

"It's good, I'll give you that," Elijah said, putting his fork back on the plate. He took a sip of water before continuing. "So what did you find out in our father's journal. You said you had so much to tell me?"

Esther let out a sigh. "Where to begin. Well, I discovered that my father knew I was bisexual as early as 1984."

"Wow, that's great. One less thing you'll have to explain to your father when you find him. It'll make your reconciliation a lot easier without that elephant in the room."

"True," Esther said, nodding her head. "He also mentioned why he fled Nigeria…The government was searching for him because he'd been a militant fighting against the oil companies destroying Ogoniland. Then a group of his friends were hanged for opposing the Nigerian government, and my father feared he would suffer the same fate, so he escaped Nigeria in 1996 to save his life."

Elijah's eyes widened and then he smiled at Esther. "The more you tell me about your father, the more he reminds me of you. You used to fight for the rights of black people and black women in Britain back in the day. The apple doesn't fall too far from the tree. Although you're a little bit more charming than your father. Just a little bit."

"Look at you, in a funny mood today," Esther said, pushing Elijah playfully on the shoulder. "He also mentioned in one of his journal entries that he was close friends with your mother at one point. I didn't know that. Did you? Do you think she's been in contact with him since?"

"I never knew they had a close relationship," Elijah said, taking a sip from his glass of water. "But I doubt my mother has been in contact with him. She mostly keeps to herself these days. I mean, I could ask her, but old-school Nigerian parents rarely tell their children everything about themselves. They keep their secrets close to their chest."

"Yeah, that's true," Esther said as she wrapped a lone noodle around her fork. "Just from reading my father's diary, I realise I barely even knew him at all, and I lived with the man for twenty-two years! Still, it's interesting though, since your mother never liked me at all. Remember? Maybe your mother and my father grew close from sharing a mutual disgust for me."

They both laughed at Esther's remark before continuing to eat. After swallowing his last mouthful, Elijah reclined into the couch, as if he were ready to slide from it. He rubbed his eyelids from underneath his glasses. Even after all these years, Esther could still read his mood like a sheet of music.

She poked him on the shoulder. "You look stressed. What troubles the good pastor?"

Elijah smiled at her and sighed so deeply that Esther could feel his exhaustion leave his body like a spirit. "You really want to know?"

"I'm sure you spend a lot of your time listening to the insecurities and stresses of your congregation. But who listens to the pastor? Come on, how about you vent, and I will offer you my non-religious advice?"

A flash of the younger and more playful Elijah, the one she had fallen in love with all those years ago, briefly lit his face.

He sat up straight from his slumped position as if Esther had breathed new energy into him.

"Alright, although I want you to know I'm dubious about any advice not steeped with Biblical analogies," Elijah said, giving Esther a mischievous smile.

"I'll do my best to add in some Biblical references."

Elijah chuckled. "Well, since becoming senior pastor, it's not exactly gone as I thought it would."

"You're not enjoying it? Isn't this what you wanted?" While it no longer pained her, Esther had still not forgotten that Elijah had severed their relationship to pursue his "calling." Deep within her, where pettiness resided, she took a little pleasure knowing that Elijah was not enjoying his position as a senior pastor. But it was a feeling she knew was wrong to have and so did not revel in it.

"I'm trying to modernise the church," Elijah explained, and Esther could tell he was trying to outwardly justify his convictions. "I want it to be more inclusive of people and to reflect our changing society, but I'm facing resistance from my family and the church's members. Elijah scowled. "My brother constantly undermines my leadership."

"Oh, Jairus, right?" Esther said, remembering that she had met Elijah's younger brother once at dinner with their family. At the time, she had not been very fond of him, and she was sure the feeling had been mutual.

"Yes, him," Elijah said, with a hint of quiet but unfiltered anger in his tone. "I invited a close friend of mine to the church, who happens to be gay, to preach at the youth service. And my family and the wider congregation were appalled. Outright refused to allow him to preach at the church again."

"I'm not surprised," Esther said, leaning against the armrest and looking at Elijah. She let her eyes briefly rest on his lips and the stubble around his chin. "If you remember, that was one of the reasons I stopped going to your church back in my twenties. I could never be my authentic self. For many African Christians, same-sex love is an aberration. It's nothing but lust in their eyes. They think true, deep, emotional love can only exist between a man and woman."

"I once thought like that as well," Elijah said.

Esther nodded her head. "Yeah, I know."

"And that's why Christians must be careful not to allow themselves to become so dogmatic about the Bible that they lose sight of the greatest lesson the Bible teaches us."

Esther smiled at Elijah. "Love, right? You told me that once. Do you remember?"

Returning her smile, Elijah nodded. "Yes, I do. Above all, love each other deeply, because love covers over a multitude of sins."

"1 Peter," Esther said, inwardly shocked that her brain had managed to somehow retrieve that knowledge from the dusty and neglected corners of her memory.

"Wow, I'm impressed. So you were actually paying attention at Bible study class all those years ago."

"And our many discussions about the Bible. Remember those too?"

"Yes, I do.

They smiled at each other, and Esther felt like she had shifted closer to Elijah although she had not moved closer to him on the couch.

"I know you've always loved preaching, Elijah. But you need to ask yourself, do you enjoy being a leader of a church as well? Look, I'm the last person with any authority on religious doctrine or whatever, but can't you serve God without having to lead His people as well?"

Elijah looked away from her and stared at the window, seemingly contemplating Esther's proposition. She did not want him to be in such a deep, introspective mood for the rest of the evening, so she decided to change the subject.

"What's in the bag?" Esther said, gesturing towards the blue plastic bag Elijah had brought with him that was now resting against the sofa.

Elijah looked confused for a moment as he stared at it. Remembering where he was, now that Esther had pulled him from his thoughts, Elijah grinned, returning to a more cheerful mood.

"You're not going to believe what I found at a record shop in Brixton market."

Still grinning, Elijah reached into the plastic bag and pulled out, from what Esther could tell, a vinyl record, with a jarring orange colour scheme, and handed it to Esther. She took it from his hands and turned it over so she could see the front cover.

"Get out of here, no way."

Esther could only smile outwardly and cringe inside as she looked at the vinyl record of her first and most successful single 'Choices'.

Everything about the vinyl record, from its design to its bright orange colours, boldly announced that it was a relic of the nineties. Right on the front cover was a picture of twenty-six-year-old Esther with a massive curly afro, much bigger than it was now, hands on her hips as she leaned forward. The nineties Esther was wearing a pink belly top, white jeans and pink Timberland boots and huge hoop earrings dangled from her ears in the shape of the peace symbol.

To a bystander, Esther looked like a fiercely independent and strong woman, a woman in control of her destiny. Yet, Esther remembered that she was anything but at the time. This image of her was a manufactured caricature of who the record labels expected her to be. She was merely playing the prewritten part, like a puppet dancing to the movements of its puppeteer's strings.

"Some of the best and worst times of my life," Esther said, moving her fingers slowly across the image of her younger self. "I still get the odd royalty cheque from this. Nothing huge, but it lets me buy myself an expensive dress now and again. I haven't listened to this in years."

"We should listen to it."

Esther laughed at Elijah, shaking her head in resistance. "Oh, come on, you really want to listen to this?"

"Of course. Come on, it's your masterpiece; your *pièce de résistance*. Aretha Franklin has 'Respect', and you have this."

"Okay, enough with the exaggerated praise," Esther said with a playful tone, although she was flattered by Elijah's enthusiasm. She stood up from the couch, the record still in her hands. "I'll play it if we can find a turntable somewhere in this flat."

Elijah and Esther began opening various drawers and rummaging through boxes until Esther finally managed to locate the turntable.

"Do you know how to...erm...put it on?" Elijah said, standing behind Esther as she placed it on the table.

"I'll figure it out. After all, I am a music teacher *and* a former R&B superstar."

It was not complicated at all. Being a modern turntable, all Esther had to do was plug it into a power socket, and it came with its own in-built speakers. After adjusting the tonearm, Esther switched on the turntable. She then slid the vinyl out of the packaging and slipped it carefully into place. With a delicate movement, the tonearm turned and touched the smooth, black surface of the spinning record.

As expected with music played on vinyl, the quality of the sound was crisp and sharp. Better than anything digital. For a moment, Esther was transported back to the recording studio in Miami where she had first recorded the song. A twenty-six-year-old girl living out a dream she would later realise never belonged to her.

But that was then. Regretting the past was an insult to the present. And in the present moment, Elijah was with her, moving his hips to the rhythm of her music.

"Come dance with me," Elijah said, waving both his hands in a circular motion, gesturing for her to come closer. "God gave you feet, did he not?"

Esther bit her lip to stop herself laughing aloud and sashayed closer towards Elijah, swaying her hips to the tempo. It felt a little disconcerting to listen to her own singing voice, like reading a diary from when you were thirteen years old. Still, she was enjoying being so close to Elijah again. He put his arms around her waist, and Esther allowed him to pull her closer to his chest.

It had been a while since Esther had enjoyed the touch of a man. But Elijah was not just any man, he was the one who appreciated and accepted her completely. She felt his soft lips brush against her neck and the sensation sent a familiar, arousing tingle through her body. His cologne tickled her nose and only made the thought of undressing him more tantalising. She did not think about what was happening, although she clearly understood since she was allowing it to happen.

Her lips met his just as the song came to an end, and they stood in the middle of the dimly lit living room with their arms around each other. Esther closed her eyes as her mouth reacquainted itself with the texture of Elijah's lips. Her body seemed to ignite with an intense heat every time he pulled her deeper into his chest as if he wanted to absorb her body into his own. Soft moans floated from Esther's mouth as Elijah gently bit her neck, pulling at the skin with his teeth. She wanted nothing more than to feel Elijah inside of her, stretching her. Almost desperately, she wanted to experience the feeling of fullness, of physical completeness that a man gives a woman when he is making love to her.

Without saying a word, Esther held Elijah's right hand and led him to the spare room. As if in a trance, Elijah followed. Inside the room, their lips found each other again, but Esther pulled back and stared into Elijah's eyes. They were alight with the depths of his own desire.

Once more, they kissed each other deeply, as if their lips could not stay apart. Then Elijah began to undress her.

CHAPTER 22

August 1985

Elijah stood in front of Brixton Recreation Centre – an imposing brown-brick building, shaped like a rectangle – waiting for Mary to finish her gymnastics class. Still wearing his Brixton TopCats uniform from practice, Elijah was holding his basketball up to his face, staring in awe at Michael Jordan's signature.

Over the past week, the only thing Elijah and his friends had discussed during basketball training was which one of them would be worthiest of playing against Michael Jordan when he came to visit the Brixton Recreation Centre. This was Michael Jordan's first visit to London. At twenty-two, the sports star was five years older than Elijah, but he was already blazing a trail of glory in the NBA after just one season with the Chicago Bulls. For many black boys in Brixton, including Elijah, Michael Jordan served as inspiration for how far they could go, even if they were living in a place where their skin colour marked them out as dangerous, untrustworthy, and undeserving of the opportunities to better themselves.

Growing a little impatient that his sister was taking so long, Elijah started bouncing his Michael Jordan-signed basketball between his legs. He took extra care not to scratch the fresh Nike Air Jordans his father had bought him as a reward for achieving eight outstanding O-levels.

In fact, Elijah had managed to achieve the highest number of A grades at Dick Sheppard in his final O-level exams, excelling, particularly, in maths. It was the highest achievement for a black boy at a comprehensive school in the whole borough. His father and mother had been so overwhelmed with pride that they threw him a party at the church, gathering every Nigerian in Lambeth. So significant was his educational achievement, during a time of high unemployment among black male youths, that Elijah had been interviewed by *The Voice*, Britain's only newspaper written for and by black people. It had been one of the best summers of his life: he was the golden child of Brixton.

But with great accomplishments came great expectations – especially in a Nigerian family. Upon completing his O-levels, Elijah had left Dick Sheppard and was now taking his A levels in maths, economics and statistics at South London College. Everyone in his family and at the church – sometimes it felt like the whole African community in south London – were looking forward to another display of black academic excellence.

But if his O-levels had been like *Star Wars: A New Hope* – safe and optimistic – then his A-levels were like *The Empire*

Strikes Back – challenging and complicated. To take his mind off the pressure that sometimes threatened to overwhelm him, Elijah had joined the Brixton TopCats basketball team.

Elijah stopped bouncing the basketball between his feet and looked at the concrete staircase that led to the upper floors of the centre. Mary, wearing a green and blue campri ski jacket over her leotard and black tights, was skipping down the stairs towards him. Only eleven years old, she was already becoming one of Brixton's promising young gymnasts. Greatness seemed to run in the Oduwole clan.

"Did you get to see him?" Mary asked, staring at Elijah expectantly.

"Sure did," Elijah said, beaming as he showed his sister the Michael Jordan signature on his basketball. Mary's eyes widened with wonder as if Elijah had shown her a basketball made of diamonds.

"That's so cool."

"I know," Elijah said, tucking the basketball against his waist. "Anyway, let's get going, sis."

It was a warm and busy Saturday afternoon in Brixton as Elijah and Mary walked through Brixton Station Road. They passed a row of traders under pop-up canopies who encouraged them to peruse the tables littered with counterfeit watches and jewellery. Taking a turn into Brixton Hill Road, Elijah and Mary made their way underneath Brixton's railway bridge as the sound of a train passing above them rumbled in their ears.

When they reached the main square in Brixton, Elijah decided that it would better to take a bus than continue the rest of the journey home on foot in case they missed lunch – pounded yam and corn beef stew.

Just as Elijah was about to verbalise this to his sister, he noticed a group of black women standing in front of Lambeth Town Hall. Some of the black women were middle-aged, and some were older, but the majority looked like teenagers. There was a wooden table beside them with various leaflets displayed on top. Some of the women were handing them out to weary passers-by while others were chanting:

"Our rights. Our liberation. Black women of this country. Where is our salvation!?"

Standing at the front and shouting loudest was Esther Nubari. Elijah froze on the spot as his eyes met hers.

Elijah had not spoken to Esther for almost three years. After Esther had slapped him in the corridor, a memory determined to cause him anguish for the rest of his time at Dick Sheppard, Elijah and Esther had purposefully avoided each other. They returned to their respective social groups at school; Elijah buried himself in his studies and the Bible, only sharing company with the more academically ambitious students at Dick Sheppard, of which he could count on one hand. Naturally, Esther embedded herself deeper into the higher echelons of the popular girls, which she co-led with Ayesha. By the time they had finished their O-level exams, Elijah and Esther existed on two separate sides of the same land, like the Berlin Wall Elijah had learned about that separated East and West Berlin. He did not know if Esther had gone on to do her A levels at the sixth form or in another college, or whether she had even achieved any O Levels or taken the less impressive CSE exams.

Looking at Esther's dark eyes and seeing the same relentless passion and energy that had always drawn him to her, Elijah suddenly felt a longing to speak to her.

But there was something else. Now that Esther was seventeen, she had become even more attractive. Her black-and-white chequered skirt accentuated her hips and hourglass figure, and Elijah noticed that her breasts had grown rounder and more prominent underneath her white tank top. While before she always tied her hair in a ponytail, Esther now wore it loose so that she had a puffy, curly afro, which better suited her bold personality.

Still, Elijah had not forgotten Esther kissing Ayesha three years ago. The betrayal had stung, and the act itself made him look at Esther as if she were a freak, like an alien from a sci-fi film. Yet the passing of time and the growth of his own maturity had made Elijah feel significantly less angry about the incident, even though he was still confused by it.

Much to his surprise and delight, Esther gave him a friendly smile. Elijah took that as a green light to go and speak to her.

He turned away from Esther and the other group of women to look at Mary. "Go home without me, yeah? Just tell Mum I saw a friend from school. You're okay getting home by yourself, right?"

Mary snorted and put her hands on her hips. "Excuse me, I am not a baby. Jeez. I'll tell Mum but don't be too late. You know Mum and Dad get all funny when we stay out too late."

Once Elijah had seen Mary get on the bus and was satisfied he had done his duty as a big brother, he crossed the road towards Esther. As he got closer, he noticed the titles of the two leaflets laid out on the table. One was called the *Feminist Review*, and the other was *Speak Out: Black Women's Group Brixton*.

When Elijah finally stopped in front of Esther, he had forgotten what he wanted to say to her and became very conscious that he was standing in front of a dozen impassioned female activists. Esther grinned at him, probably reading his awkwardness, and gestured for him to follow her to the corner of Lambeth Town Hall where they could speak privately.

"Hey, it's been a long time, Elijah," Esther said with a cheerful tone. Elijah became more relaxed now that she had spoken first. It seemed there were no hard feelings after the terrible things he had said to her the last time they spoke.

"Yeah, I know, right." Elijah's mind was working overtime, trying to think of what he could say to her, but Esther's hips and breasts were distracting him too much and muddling his mind. Fortunately, Esther realised he was at a loss for words so carried the conversation.

"We're demonstrating against the lack of real job opportunities black women face in this community," Esther said. "Those pink-faced Conservative politicians call us loud and angry black woman and I take it as a compliment. We gotta be loud and angry to be heard."

Elijah nodded his head, smiling at her and finding himself inwardly impressed by her rebellious nature. She had not lost her fiery political spirit. He suddenly realised that he had not seen her at church for a long time, but before he could ask her why, a woman wearing a brown headscarf popped her head around the corner of the town hall.

"Come on, sister, we need you over here," the woman said, looking directly at Esther and ignoring Elijah completely.

"Yeah, give me a minute, Madeline." Esther turned her attention back to Elijah and smiled. "You kinda got me at a bad time. Hey, you wanna meet up later?"

Elijah said yes before he had even thought about it properly.

"Cool. I work at The Atlantic in the evenings at 8 p.m. It's a pub just off Coldharbour Lane. You know it?"

"Yeah, I do." The Atlantic was probably the most well-known black pub in Brixton and with that came a particular reputation – one of the notorious kind. Elijah had heard stories of drug-dealing yardies and frequent police raids. He recalled, from watching the news reports at the time, that much of the rioting in Brixton four years ago had happened around Coldharbour Lane. Elijah was surprised that Esther was now working at an establishment with such a dubious image.

Regardless, Elijah agreed to meet her at The Atlantic at 8.30 p.m. He had no clue how he would pull off such a feat with his strict Nigerian parents, who were terrified of Brixton's streets at night. Esther gave him a final smile and sauntered away to join the rest of the black female activists. As Elijah watched her go, her hips swaying with newfound sexuality and feminine energy, he wondered to himself if he had ever really stopped loving her.

The playful and reggae-soaked melody of Mighty Diamonds' 'Pass the Koutchie' bounced across the main room of The Atlantic. The air was heavy with the familiar smell of marijuana, and this, along with the rhythmic and fast conversations of Jamaican patois spoken by The Atlantic's most popular clientele, West Indian men, fused together to create a lively atmosphere. Yet there was an undercurrent of danger and dread. Emboldened by the liquor burning in them, some of the men were already sizing each other up.

Esther was at the bar, cleaning a glass as she surveyed the room. As expected, The Atlantic was busy tonight, and like most nights, the pub was filled with a medley of West Indian men and a few of the region's women. Many of the men, some with dreadlocks, tidy afros or wearing Rasta beanies, would often dance in the middle of the floor and Esther liked to watch them, impressed by their leg work.

But it was the women who caught and held Esther's attention. She loved the energy of West Indian women, particularly Jamaicans. She found them to be the most passionate in bed. Even now, Esther's eyes fell on a pretty woman, who looked

Jamaican, standing by the window with a group of men. She had almond-shaped eyes and a brunette ponytail which complimented her glowing complexion. The mysterious woman met Esther's stare from across the room, her eyes like a beacon, signalling her sexual desire. But Esther only gave the woman a weak smile in return and nothing more. She had an appointment tonight. She checked her Casio digital watch. Five minutes to nine. Where was Elijah?

The sudden sound of the door opening jolted Esther's attention away. She glanced at the door and a smile formed across her face. Elijah walked into the pub. He looked very weary and cautious, like a rabbit that had strayed into a den of foxes. She waved her arm in the air. Elijah noticed her, and his expression relaxed considerably.

"Hey, I'm happy you came. For a sec, I was thinking you wasn't gonna show up," Esther said as Elijah stood in front of her at the bar. He smiled nervously at a Jamaican man, with thick, long dreadlocks that reached the bottom of his spine, who gave him an unfriendly side glance. He then turned his attention to Esther and gave her a wink.

"It's cool. I kinda had to tell my parents I was helping a friend with homework. Luckily, they didn't ask questions."

Esther smirked, impressed by Elijah's boldness, although not totally surprised. He always had an understated mischievousness about him. "You want anything? And don't worry. It's on me."

"Cheers, but I'm cool. Still kinda full from supper."

"I'm gonna be on a break in five minutes. Grab a seat by the window over there, yeah?" Esther pointed towards an empty bench with a green cushion. "I'll come over and meet you."

Five minutes later, Esther was sitting in front of Elijah, staring into him with prying eyes. For almost three years she had not spoken to Elijah and pretended, as tricky as it had been, that he had never been a part of her life by completely ignoring him like he was just part of the school's walls. But when Esther had seen him at Brixton earlier today, something made her smile at him. The first thing she had noticed about Elijah was that he was taller, and his face was less like a round, umber-coloured potato – now it was thinner, more chiselled and masculine. He still had his small afro, but there was a new patch of stubble growing underneath his chin, announcing his transition into a young man. Whereas before she had found Elijah cute, now that he was at the edge of male puberty, she found him attractive, in a way that was no longer innocent.

"So are you in college now?" Elijah asked.

"Nah. I mean, I was smart enough to take O-levels and I got enough decent grades to do my A levels, but I didn't go to sixth form. I just left Dick Sheppard and went straight into any kind of work I could find, which ain't easy. Barely any jobs around. I was doing some vocals for a reggae band up in Harlesden then I got a job here, and I've been here for like almost a year. How about you?" Although Esther had asked the question, she partly knew the answer. She had read about his exceptional O-level results in *The Voice* newspaper.

"Yeah, I'm studying at South London College. Taking A-levels in maths, computing and politics. It's really hard, man."

"Yeah, I bet. I kinda want to study politics, but I'm not sure if it's for me."

Esther's dealings with the police after the New Cross Fire four years ago had made her aware of the political disadvantages black people faced in Britain, and it opened her curiosity. When she had left Dick Sheppard, in between looking for a job, singing and smoking marijuana, she would go to Brixton library and read about political ideologies, such as Karl Marx's theories of socialism. However, the more she read, the more she realised that there were not any significant political writings by black authors, and she became frustrated once again.

Like a boat sailing down a rapid river, Esther's intellectual journey into political theory led her to essays on black feminism, a far more relatable flavour of feminism for her than the mainstream one espoused by educated, liberal white women. She had read *The Heart of the Race* by Beverley Bryan, a book about black British women's post-war experiences. The writings in that book threw more coal into her political furnace, so she joined Brixton's Black Women's Group – an activist organisation formed by women who had been members of the now defunct British Black Panther movement.

"You was always into politics. You should do it," Elijah said with an encouraging smile.

"I don't know. Like yeah, I find politics interesting, but music is more my passion, you know. I want to spend the rest of my life making soul music."

Elijah nodded at her. For a moment they sat in silence, listening to the insistent chatter of The Atlantic's merry drinkers and the reggae music coming from the sound system. For a change, Elijah was the first to break the silence between them.

"Why don't you come to church anymore? I still see your parents every Sunday."

Esther looked away from Elijah, feeling his eyes burrowing into her, like a mole digging into the ground. She had stopped going to church for the same reason she had slapped Elijah. Judgement and shame. It had been a hard choice because a part of her was still moved by the wisdom of Biblical scripture, and she loved singing Christian hymns with the church choir. But Esther was unable to reconcile her sexuality, her feminist beliefs and her bohemian lifestyle with the doctrine of the Bible. She had chosen instead to be spiritual rather than religious.

As if he had read her thoughts, Elijah spoke. "Is it because you like girls? Because you're a...lesbian?" Elijah whispered the word as if the police might burst into the pub and arrest him for uttering it. But instead of being annoyed at Elijah, Esther was understanding. He was a Christian, one who came from a family of steadfast and renowned Nigerian Christians. The fact he was even having this conversation with her was a significant step forward for him.

"I'm not a lesbian. Well, not really. I'm bisexual."

"You're what?" Elijah's eyes widened in such a comical fashion that Esther bit her lip to stop herself from laughing.

"Bisexual. It means I fancy boys and girls."

At first, Elijah just blinked at her silently, as if his mind were trying to process this new concept. "Wow, I never knew someone could like both boys and girls in that way," he said eventually, looking a little bemused. "Do you like, I don't know, like one more than the other?"

Esther shrugged her shoulders. "Not really. I've been with more girls, but I've liked guys obviously. It's hard to explain. It often comes down to the person. You know, who they are on the inside."

"Oh, that's cool," Elijah said, still wearing a bewildered expression on his face. He leaned back against the bench, and his mouth slowly formed into a warm smile. "I don't understand it, but this is how God has made you. I think it's quite amazing that God has given you the ability to experience real love with both a man and a woman. After all, love is the most important thing in the Bible. Jesus died because God loved us, you know."

"Yeah, I guess so. I mean, you're the Bible expert," Esther said, grinning.

Elijah's demeanour shifted and he cast his eyes down. "I'm sorry about the things I said to you back then. I just didn't...I didn't..."

"It's okay," Esther said calmly. She placed the left palm of her hand over Elijah's fist resting on the table. "To be honest, yeah, you had every right to be pissed off. Like, I shouldn't have kissed Ayesha. Not when I was going out with you. I'm sorry, too."

Elijah looked up at her and squeezed her fingers gently, and Esther realised how much she had missed his touch. "You wanna hang out again?" he asked. "You know, like old times?"

A broad smile, the type that forms on your face when you receive a Christmas present, stretched across Esther's face.

"Yeah, that would be cool. I'd like to be friends again."

CHAPTER 23

July 2008

Something within him felt different as Elijah stood at the altar of the church on the first Sunday of July.

His Bible was placed on the purple cloth draped over the podium and opened to Proverbs 6:32. In front of him were the expectant faces of the Sunday congregation. African women and their British-born daughters of all shapes and sizes wore bright, multi-coloured *ankara* blouses and elaborate head wraps. African men and their British-born sons, dressed less flamboyantly than the women, wore a shirt or a shirt with a tie, though some of the younger men had worn their *dashikis*. All the congregation were waiting for the thrilling sermon from the "Last Prophet of Brixton."

And yet all Elijah could do was stare at Proverbs 6:32, his body completely rigid and his mind as blank as a white sheet of paper. Last night, he had made his annotations and notes for today's sermon on Proverbs 6:32 without any problem. But as he stared at the verse now, he felt the words piercing him like a sharp dagger.

Proverbs 6:32: But whoso committeth adultery with a woman lacketh understanding: he that doeth it destroyeth his own soul.

Though he tried to resist, Elijah was pulled back into the memory of that Monday evening, a week ago now, when he had shared a bed with a woman who was not his wife. In front of him, the whole church hall had somehow morphed into the dimly lit spare room in Ayesha's flat and Elijah witnessed their encounter like he was watching a staged play. His lips sliding down Esther's neck. Undressing her, removing every item of clothing on her body, gripped by lust as a new piece of her caramel-brown skin was revealed to him. Pressed on top of her, her breasts pushing against his chest as he entered her. Her moans of pleasure with every thrust of his hips, every time his hands squeezed her thighs, pulling her whole body into him as they both climaxed.

The vivid memory of this act was simultaneously revolting and exhilarating. Elijah placed his fingers underneath the rim of his glasses and rubbed his eyes.

"Elijah, are you alright?"

Elijah looked up and saw Mary beside him with her hand on his shoulder. "You've been standing here for a minute without saying a word."

In front of them, a melanin-skinned mass of confused faces watched with trepidation. Their mother was sitting on the front bench next to Tiwa. Both wore worried expressions.

"I'm sorry, I'm not feeling too well," Elijah said, realising that his palms were sweaty. "Mary, do you mind taking over? I'm going to go to the lavatory."

Mary inspected him for a moment before nodding her head. "Of course."

As he made his away across the altar, Elijah could feel the many eyes of the congregation upon him. But he paid them no attention. He walked down the steps of the raised platform at the front of the church and caught Jairus sitting by the electric keyboard, flanked by the drummer and the guitarist who formed part of the church's band. Elijah did not miss Jairus narrowing his eyes at him as he exited the stage and hurried to the restroom.

In the cool of the stone-walled lavatory, Elijah removed his glasses and placed them on the sink. He ran the tap and began splashing water on his face, childishly thinking for a moment that the cold droplets would cleanse him of his shame. After carefully placing his glasses back on his face, Elijah looked at his reflection in the mirror. He felt like he was staring into his inner soul.

On that Monday night, when he had returned home from Esther's, the physical intimacy had left him feeling high and light-headed with pure satisfaction. He realised that he had not experienced such a sensation in a long time, and it emphasised how perfunctory the act had become with Tiwa. Elijah had taken a quiet shower and then carefully slipped into bed next to his snoring wife. But the pleasure of making love to Esther evaporated and he was gripped by a state of shock. Elijah now had to face the truth that the sexual desire had been vacuumed from his marriage. And it was not just the physical act of sex that had felt cathartic but the emotional connection that he and Esther had rebuilt. He knew it made his betrayal to Tiwa more severe.

Elijah was not a fool and he was not blind to the fact that he had spent too much time with Esther. It was the reason he had not told Tiwa about it directly. But he had not expected the emotional and physical connection to Esther to have materialised so naturally. Then again, maybe it was to be expected. She was his first love, in every sense.

Staring at his reflection in the mirror, Elijah sighed deeply, bowed his head and closed his eyes in prayer. He begged God to forgive him and to provide the moral strength and resolve he needed to cut ties with Esther.

But in his heart, Elijah knew it was a half-meant prayer. His body still craved Esther's, and he was unsure if he could fight this temptation of the flesh that consumed him. But if he did not, the consequences would be devastating.

By the time Elijah returned to the main church hall, the congregation were now on their feet. Many of them had their eyes closed or were waving their hands as they sang a well-known Yoruba worship song.

Mary was still standing in front of the podium, leading the worship as she sang into the microphone. As Elijah approached her, Mary turned to face him.

"Are you alright now?"

Elijah took the microphone from her hand and smiled. "I'm fine now. Just needed some water. Thank you."

Mary responded with an odd expression, somewhere between a smile and a suspicious stare, and then walked off the stage. Elijah gripped the microphone and shouted into it.

"Praise the Lord!"

The congregation, seeing only the showroom confidence and energy Elijah was projecting, and not the conflict raging internally, answered with a thunderous "Hallelujah!"

Elijah lay on his bed, adjusting his glasses as he read his Bible. The bedroom was mostly shrouded in darkness except for speckles of moonlight filtering through the windowpane and the dim glow of the lamp by his side.

Occasionally, Elijah would pick up his phone and check if there was a message from Esther. He had not been in contact with her since that Monday night. Partly out of shame and partly because the feelings he had for her were unclear to him. It felt like more than just physical lust, but did he still love her, after all these years? How did Esther feel about it? These were questions Elijah was not sure he should be seeking answers to.

Engrossed in his own thoughts, Elijah had not realised that Tiwa had vacated their king-size bed until he heard her retching in the en-suite bathroom. He removed his reading glasses and placed them on the chest of drawers beside the bed, but as he got up to check on his wife, she emerged from the bathroom. Tiwa was wearing her silky, pink nightgown and clutching her belly with her right hand.

"Are you okay?" Elijah asked, studying her face as she leaned against the doorframe. She looked incredibly tired. "You've been throwing up again."

"I'm fine," Tiwa said in a weak voice but the resentment in her tone was sharp and unmistakable. "Go back to reading your Bible."

Elijah started to move towards Tiwa, but she sidestepped away from him and stopped by the closed bedroom door, clutching the handle.

"Leave me alone, you liar. Until you can tell me the truth about what is going on with that woman, we don't need to talk."

"I told you, nothing is going on," Elijah said, regurgitating the phrase with as much force as his wife had been vomiting minutes ago. "She's just an old friend who I'm helping out."

Tiwa closed her eyes, shook her head and began to cackle bitterly.

"What is this? What are we doing right now?" Elijah said, his bare right foot touching the Persian rug between them as he took a single step towards his wife.

"Stay away from me, Elijah," Tiwa said as she opened her eyes. They radiated such raw sadness and pain that Elijah could not bear to look at them for a moment. "I'm sleeping in the spare room, don't follow me."

"Tiwa, stop this, please."

But Elijah's pleading did nothing to dissuade Tiwa from opening the door and walking out of the bedroom. On her way out, she slammed the door behind her.

There was no point going after her, so Elijah made his way back to bed and just lay on the mattress, staring at the white ceiling. For the first time in a long time, he was unsure of what God wanted him to do or why God was testing him so brutally.

Was this the end of his marriage? As a religious man, Elijah knew he should not even let such an idea manifest but manifest it had. The question lingered in his mind, waiting for God to give him an answer, but none came, there was only the silence of his bedroom.

As troubled as his spirit was, Elijah eventually allowed sleep to come and whisk him away to the realm of dreams. Even there, he had stubborn visions of Esther's naked body, the colour of caramel and just as sweet.

CHAPTER 24

July 2008

"Back up again, babe. You had sex on my bed? And I hope you're not finishing all of my alcohol!" Ayesha's voice echoed from the laptop.

Esther was staring at the laptop on the kitchen island in front of her with a champagne glass in her hand, filled half-way with Dom Pérignon.

From the slightly fuzzy image on the screen, Esther could see Ayesha in a skimpy bikini, showing off her toned, dark-skinned body. She was holding what looked like a pina colada in her right hand as she relaxed on a tropical beach, with white sand and lush palm trees, somewhere in Montego Bay.

"First thing, I had sex in your flat but not on your bed. We had sex in the spare room." Mentioning the word sex made Esther feel dirty for the first time in her life, for she had not just had sex with any man – it had been with a *married* man. "And secondly, if I finished all your liquor, I would be speaking to you from a hospital bed while the doctors pumped my stomach."

Ayesha burst out laughing, spilling some of her pina colada on the sand. "I wish you were here with me. We would get into so much crazzzzziness, babe." She pulled her Ray-Bans down and gave Esther one of her signature cheeky smiles. "But it looks like you don't need *moi* to have fun. Sleeping with your married ex-boyfriend. I would tip one of many Prada hats to you if I were wearing one right now."

Esther shook her head at Ayesha and managed a half-hearted laugh, although she was not in a playful mood. The memory of Monday night was still fresh in her mind and on her skin as if Elijah's touch had left an imprint on her.

As much as Esther tried to block the thought from her head, the fact was: Elijah had a wife. There was another woman who wore a matching wedding ring to the one on his finger. And yet, when she had allowed him to kiss her, to hold her and undress her, she had felt that same love he had given her eighteen years ago.

It was not a feeling a woman forgets. Elijah's touches had not been quick and overexcited, like those of a man whose only desire for her was sexual. They had been tender and patient, as if her body were a delicate oil painting and he was rediscovering its texture. They made love mostly in silence, broken sporadically by faint moans of pleasure as they relished each other's flesh, which felt familiar yet different: a little fuller and softer than when they were younger lovers. After they had both climaxed,

Elijah clung to her for five minutes, as though she might suddenly dissolve if he did not. They still didn't speak a word to each other as they put on their clothes. Esther suspected that they were both still in a daze from what they had done, like waking up from a vivid dream and trying to acclimatise to your surroundings. Once all his clothes were on, Elijah had merely said, "Have a nice evening. Call me when you're ready, okay?" before he left the flat.

It had not felt like sex for the sake of release – the kind where two people crave another person's touch and nothing else. It was something more. Yet Esther was unclear on what that *"more"* was or what it even meant.

Ayesha slurped her pina colada through the twisty straw before speaking. "Was he the first guy you slept with in a while? How did it feel getting some of that…?" She made a lewd gesture with her hand.

Unsurprisingly, Ayesha was more interested in the sexual details, rather than the moral dilemma whirling Esther around like a spinning top. "I've slept with other men this year, if you must know," Esther said with a tut to match the disapproving look she shot Ayesha. "And to answer your question, it was great sex, but I feel…"

"Dirty and ashamed?"

Esther sighed. "Yeah, there's those feelings, obviously, but also…I'm not sure what it meant. When I usually sleep with someone, it's purely physical. But with Elijah, there's always been something else underneath it. And that something is still there after such a long time. It's so clichéd, but he's the only man I've ever slept with where the sex is physical and emotional. Where I can completely lose myself."

Ayesha sat up on her deck chair and removed her sunglasses. Feigning the exaggerated movements of a therapist, she crossed one leg over the other and fixed her eyes on Esther. "Look, I know he broke up with you, like, a lifetime ago, but maybe you never stopped loving him? Maybe he never stopped loving you? Come on, babe, it took just under a month for you two to end up having sex, and it felt so right."

Esther shook her head, at a loss for what to say. At this point, she didn't even know what to feel.

"Listen, babe, you know me. I've slept with married men and women without giving two fucks about them beyond whether they can give me an orgasm – pure pleasure. Once I get what I want, I never think about them again. But the fact you're still thinking about Elijah after the act...it's clear you still love him."

Esther put her hands over her face and let out a muffled noise of frustration. At forty years old, she felt like an emotional teenage girl fretting about whether some boy she'd had a one-night stand with would call her back.

When she had seen Elijah outside his church, which felt longer than four weeks ago, it was nice, if not somewhat awkward, to see him again, though no more meaningful than a conversation with a long-forgotten ex-boyfriend. But as they spent more time together, some of the love Esther had for Elijah all those years ago had unknowingly crept back in through the door to her heart. But did she still love him? And if she did, what would she do? Esther had returned to Brixton to find her father, not to rediscover love with an ex-boyfriend who had broken her heart eighteen years earlier.

Completely lost in her thoughts, Esther was startled when she heard Ayesha's voice, jolting her out of her contemplation.

"I'll ask again, seeing as you were in your own world for a minute. Have you phoned him since Monday night?"

Esther rubbed her forehead and took a large sip of champagne before responding. "No, I haven't called him yet, and he hasn't called me. Knowing him, he's probably battling all kinds of shame and guilt right now. He's a pastor, remember."

"Yeah, I can imagine he's been spending the whole week in the confessional box."

"He's not Catholic, Ayesha. He's Protestant."

Ayesha waved her hand dismissively. "Whatever, babe. All I know is, you need to call him at some point and talk to him. Anyway, enough about sex, religion and married men. How goes the daddy search?"

Glad for the change of topic, Esther smiled at Ayesha. "To be honest, I'd almost given up, but it just so happens that my father might have attended Elijah's church earlier this year."

"Wow. And Elijah told you this, right?"

Esther nodded her head and took another sip of her champagne. "And he gave me details of an address my father might be sharing with some university professor. I'll be doing some snooping on the internet tonight, hopefully I can find out what university this professor is working at and pay him a visit. I'd rather not go straight to his home address unannounced."

"Well, sounds like you're getting close." A very dark-skinned, topless man came into view and Ayesha bit her lip as he bent down to take her empty glass away. "Anyway, babe, I gotta bounce. I'm going snorkelling this afternoon, and I haven't swum in fucking ages. Keep me updated, okay?"

"Try not to sleep with any of the lifeguards," Esther said, sticking her tongue out at Ayesha. And with that, Ayesha ended the Skype call.

Carrying the laptop in one hand and her champagne glass in the other, Esther made her way to the four-poster bed in the living room. Once she was settled on the bouncy mattress, she opened the Google homepage, typed *E Dankworth* into the search box and pressed ENTER on her keyboard.

The internet was a truly life-changing invention, and Esther wished Google had existed when she was a young girl. Within seconds, Google trawled through its billions of interconnected online documents and returned a list of links related to her query. Esther looked closer at the screen, examining the search results. The first link appeared promising:

Professor Edward Dankworth | Staff | SOAS University of London

Esther clicked on it and found herself on Professor Edward Dankworth's staff page. The first thing she noticed was the thumbnail image of a middle-aged white man who looked no older than forty with long, greying brown hair tied into a bun and a grey Van Dyke beard. She turned her attention to the small description written underneath the photo.

Professor Edward Dankworth
Senior lecturer in African Minorities
Email address: edankworth@soas.ac.uk
Telephone: 020 7946 0111
Address: SOAS University of London, Thornhaugh Street, Russell Square, London WC1H 0XG
Building: Russell Square: College Buildings

Biography

Professor Edward Dankworth studied at the University of Cape Town before earning an MSc and PhD in African Studies from the University of Oxford. He previously taught at the University of Oxford and the University of South Africa.

Professor Dankworth is the author of several peer-reviewed journal articles and books including Apartheid Untold: Stories of Racial Segregation *(Dante Publishing, 1999),* The White African: A Study of Race and Identity in South Africa *(World Forever Publishing, 2001) and* Dividing an African Pie: A Critical Analysis of European Colonisation and Trade in Africa *(World Forever Publishing, 2004).*

His latest book, Killing the Niger Delta: How Foreign Oil Devastated the Niger Delta's Minority Ethnic Groups *(World Forever Publishing, forthcoming December 2008) is an in-depth study that examines foreign oil exploitation of the Niger*

Delta's natural resources at the expense of the region's minority ethnic groups.

Engaging her detective instinct, Esther considered what she had read for a moment. If this Professor Dankworth was indeed the same man who had attended the church with her father earlier this year and seemed to be living with him, then she could already see the connection. It could not be a coincidence that he was writing a book about the Niger Delta, a region where her parents' homeland, Ogoniland, was situated. But what could Professor Dankworth have wanted with her father? Had he contributed to this new book?

Esther dug further into Professor Dankworth, who turned out to be a very prolific writer. He had written numerous academic journals, papers and articles around the issue of oppressed or long-suffering ethnic minorities in Africa. Despite having skin as white and lined as the average Caucasian male, Edward Dankworth seemed to care a great deal about people whose skin was far darker than his own. Over the years, Esther had met a few white people – upper-middle-class and highly educated types like the professor – who seemed obsessed with the suffering of Africans. Sometimes, she felt this stemmed from the guilt they felt over their forefathers' brutal acts of slavery. But other times, when Esther had heard these white academics speak, it seemed like the plight of Africans merely made for an interesting study in which to indulge their intellect. Until she met

Professor Edward Dankworth in person, Esther could not tell which category he belonged to.

Now feeling a little lightheaded from the champagne, Esther closed her laptop. First thing tomorrow, she would visit the university and hopefully be able to locate and speak to Professor Dankworth. She had two weeks left in London and could not rely on him responding to an email. The time she had to find her father was running out.

Would she ask Elijah to come with her? Esther looked at her iPhone, laying on top of the bedside table. Part of her wanted to text him but then, it being a Sunday night, he was probably with his wife. She shook her head, trying to rid the thoughts of Elijah's wife from her mind as if they were droplets of water stuck in her ears after having a shower. She would visit the university by herself. Afterwards, once she had made peace with her feelings, she would give Elijah a call.

CHAPTER 25

July 2008

Inside the SOAS University of London, the receptionist gave Esther the directions to the Brunei Gallery auditorium where Professor Dankworth would be giving a lecture on "The Conquest of Africa: An Introduction to New Imperialism."

After thanking the receptionist for her help, Esther was soon making her way through the bustling corridors of the university's campus in Bloomsbury. Animated young people, a mixture of different ethnicities, talked loudly with others or played on their phones, walking past Esther without so much as a glance. Posters advertising a mind-numbing amount of club nights and guest talks were plastered over every wall. One poster, which made Esther chuckle inside, preached the virtues of practising safe sex.

By the time Esther reached the Brunei Gallery auditorium, she had five minutes until Professor Dankworth's lecture started. She pushed opened the heavy wooden door and stepped inside.

Standing a few feet from Esther on a raised platform at the front of the auditorium was Professor Dankworth. He paused midway through fiddling with a projector and looked at Esther with a raised eyebrow. Just like the picture on his staff profile, Professor Dankworth had long brown hair, twisted into a bun, which was far shabbier today than in the photograph, and a greying Van Dyke beard. With a surname like "Dankworth," Esther was not surprised that he dressed like someone who could successfully audition to be Doctor Who: brown loafers and jeans, a blue turtleneck jumper and a red scarf. But if Professor Edward Dankworth looked like a typical middle-class English man, he certainly did not sound like one.

"Hello. Pardon my curtness, but are you a student in my lecture?" Professor Dankworth said in a flat South-African accent as he took a few steps towards Esther. "I ask because I don't recognise you."

He certainly had British politeness and the tendency to apologise for any perceived slight – something Americans lacked. "Hi, Professor. My name is Esther Nubari," Esther said, walking up the steps to the platform. When she reached the top, she extended her hand and shook Professor Dankworth's. He was still looking at her with the genial but perplexed expression of someone receiving a handshake from a person they don't quite recognise but feel as though they should. "I think you know my father, Kelechi Nubari."

Professor Dankworth's brown eyes widened with both shock and comprehension, a familiar look Esther was getting used to seeing when she told people she was Kelechi Nubari's daughter. It made her feel strangely like the daughter of a celebrity. Now that she knew about her father's past as a rebel, fighting for the sake of his people, Esther thought that maybe he was deserving of some of this fame.

"My goodness, what a surprise," Professor Dankworth said, gaping at Esther as he examined her face. "I can see the resemblance. My gosh. It's a pleasure to meet you."

"Yes, it's nice to meet you too." Esther paused. "So, about my father?" At the second mention of her father, a solemnity washed over Professor Dankworth's face, and he sighed heavily. "Of course, you are here to speak about your father, but now is not a good time, Ms Nubari. All I can tell you right now is that he was living with me, but we need to sit down and talk properly."

Was? What did that mean? Before Esther could enquire further, a crowd of chattering students entered the auditorium all at once.

"Ms Nubari, if you could please give me your contact details, I will call you later this evening to arrange a time where we can speak properly. Please excuse my curtness. You were a surprise I was not expecting, although no less welcomed."

"That's fine. But can I ask…"

But Professor Dankworth did not let her finish. "Expect a call this evening, and we can arrange a time for us to speak. I would be delighted for you to come to my home, should you like to?"

"Yeah sure," Esther said. The students were beginning to take their seats. As Professor Dankworth saved Esther's number on his BlackBerry, she knew that this was her last chance to ask him the question that had been on her mind for weeks.

"Professor, I have to know before I go, is my father still alive and still in London?"

Another strange, melancholic expression fell over Professor's Dankworth's facial features. "Yes, yes, of course, he is alive, and he is still in London. I speak to him regularly, in fact. But please, let us talk more about this at an agreed time."

Esther breathed a sigh of relief and clasped her chest, feeling as though her heart just skipped a beat. *My father is alive!* She thanked Professor Dankworth, shook his hand again and then walked down the platform steps. As she headed towards the auditorium's exit, she could feel Professor Dankworth's eyes following her.

Walking through the corridor as she headed back to the reception, Esther kept thinking about the grave look on Professor Dankworth's face when he had confirmed to her that her father was alive and still residing in London. Why had he seemed so sad when talking about her father if he was still in contact with him? Esther felt like she needed to speak to someone about this new development. The first person to spring to mind was Elijah. But was she prepared to call him, and what would happen if she did?

It was 7 p.m. and Elijah found himself at the Dogstar, sitting opposite his brother-in-law, Kunle. They had spent the best part of an hour discussing the subject of marriage. Both had been at the executive board meeting earlier today and once it had concluded, Elijah had invited Kunle for a drink. The crisis threatening to untangle the binds of his marriage was growing with each passing day, and Elijah wanted another married man's perspective on how to resolve it.

Forty minutes before meeting Kunle at the Dogstar, Elijah had dropped Tiwa off at her support group. Since learning about Esther, Tiwa had now shut him out emotionally, communicating only with passive-aggressive actions. She had not uttered a single word to him in the car and had not looked at him as she stepped out and closed the door with enough force to break it.

Part of Elijah wished to cross this chasm between them, reach out to her and salvage their marriage, but how could he after what he had done? All he could think about was Esther and whether there was still a chance for them again. It sounded illogical and yet Elijah could not stop these unchecked thoughts from carrying away into a fantasy that part of him wanted to become real.

That morning, before Elijah drove to work, he had prayed over this dilemma, but still God had given him no solution. The fact that he was able to reignite his relationship with Esther so quickly was making him question the validity of his marriage. Tiwa was as devoted a wife as they came, and although she could not give them a child, it had not lessened her as a woman in his eyes. His father had loved her; his mother loved her, and so did the rest of his family. Tiwa was the type of woman any man of the faith would marry without hesitation. But somewhere in their journey, passion had fallen by the wayside. And Elijah was not sure how to find it again or if he even wanted to.

But this missing passion had been easily recreated with Esther, so easily that it had driven him to go against his own better judgement as a man of God. If he still loved Esther, then what did this mean for his marriage? Divorce? No, he could not possibly go through with that, could he? The ramifications of such an act would cause a seismic shift, like the moving of the tectonic plates, across the Oduwole family, undermining his position at the church. If not divorce, then what? Elijah tried to form an answer from the fragments of his thoughts, but he could not piece one together.

"*Oga*, marriage is not easy," Kunle said, placing his pint of Guinness on the wooden table. Froth from the stout stained his moustache, and Elijah made a gesture for him to wipe it off as he looked too ridiculous to take seriously. Before Kunle spoke again, he got rid of the foam with his sleeve. "We have this big wedding day. Everybody dresses up, and all our families and friends see us marrying a beautiful woman, and we are smug with pride. Look at me! See how God has blessed me, O! Five years later, you find yourself pleading to God to make your wife disappear just for a week so you can watch Arsenal play football and drink your Guinness in peace."

"You're mad, you know that?" Elijah said with a smile. His work left him with little time to nurture male friendships, but over the years, he had formed a solid camaraderie with his brother-in-law. "I should be insulted you're saying this to my face, seeing as you're married to my sister, but I know she can be a handful."

"Nothing I'm not used to." Kunle then gave Elijah a knowing look. "But how are things between you and Tiwa?"

Elijah let out a deep sigh and gulped down some Guinness before responding. "To be honest with you, we're not in a good place. Ever since the doctor's diagnosis, she's become very distant, which is understandable, but it's lasting longer than I thought it would. I hoped the women's group she started going to would lift her spirits, but it hasn't. Kunle, I have prayed fervently, but this distance between us is widening every day. We're not like we used to be."

Kunle nodded as he stroked his moustache. "How did you used to be?"

"We used to have such an intense longing for each other. When we met in Paris, our first kiss, I felt like I had finally found the woman God had intended to be my wife." Elijah took another swig of his stout before continuing. "But now I feel as though she has switched off from herself and me. If that makes sense?"

Kunle did not answer immediately but continued stroking his facial hair. He studied Elijah. "We Christians believe that our marriage will always be on steady ground because God is at the centre of it. But do you want to know why that isn't true?"

"I'm all ears," Elijah said, reclining in his chair.

"Because being in a marriage is like being on a ship at sea where God is the captain. The mood of the sea ebbs and flows. Sometimes the current is calm and relaxed. But other times, the current is violent. The ship is rocking from side to side as the waves crash into it, and you feel it might sink at any moment. So you either have a choice to stay or abandon ship."

Elijah regarded Kunle for a moment and then leaned forward. "So, what are you saying?"

"I'm saying that marriage is a choice. Continuing to love someone is a choice. When your marriage is in rocky waters, you have the choice to abandon it or stay the course. But we do not abandon the ship."

"Because God is at the helm," Elijah said, nodding his head but still feeling uncertain.

Kunle finished the remnants of Guinness in his glass jug with one long swig and slammed it on the wooden table. "Trust in the Lord, *oga*. He will steer the ship out of the storm even when it feels like the waves are about to tear it apart."

"But what if I created a massive hole in the ship and now it's rapidly flooding with water?"

Kunle let out an unrestrained laugh. "In that case, you better hope you're a good swimmer."

Both Elijah and Kunle howled in laughter for an entire minute. Elijah caught his breath and let out small chuckles as he tried to compose himself. A loud chirruping noise sounded from his pocket and, wiping a tear from his eye, Elijah took out his Blackberry. Esther's name was flashing on the screen.

"Sorry, Kunle. I need to take this."

Esther was sitting on a bench in Brockwell Park, gazing at the oak tree and the lush foliage that covered its branches like a green mushroom cloud. It was comforting to Esther that, despite how much Brixton had changed, this oak tree, where she had created her most precious memories growing up, was still here.

When Ayesha told Esther that Dick Sheppard had been knocked down and replaced by private housing, Esther felt a deep sadness. It was like someone had ruthlessly wiped away so many memories of fights in the playground, teenage kisses and smoking cigarettes by the swimming pool building, overlooking the park. But at least the oak tree in Brockwell Park remained.

A slight breeze caressed Esther's skin as she looked at the London skyline in front of her, sparkling against a fading blue backdrop that was dotted with dim stars. Feeling oddly sentimental after visiting SOAS University of London, Esther had come to Brockwell Park to be with her thoughts, just as she did as a teenager. She had also called Elijah, asking him to meet her here. He had agreed without hesitation.

An hour ago, Professor Dankworth had called, asking Esther to meet him tomorrow at his house in Maida Vale. While the knowledge that she was as close as she had ever been to finding her father circled her mind, it was her feelings towards Elijah that currently occupied her thoughts. She did not yet know what she was going to do about the intense reignited attraction she had for him. Run from it or embrace it? Whatever Elijah meant to her now was tangled in intricate knots of desire, confusion and guilt. At some point, she would have to untangle the knots and come to a decision.

Almost as if she could sense him coming, Esther turned to her left and saw Elijah walking down the stony pathway towards her, his black overcoat flapping in the wind to reveal his office suit underneath. As he approached, he gave her an unsure smile, no doubt wrestling with his own emotions towards her.

"How are you doing?" Elijah said, taking a seat next to her on the bench.

Esther smiled. Already she could feel herself relax around him as if his very presence absorbed her tension and stress. "I'm fine, thanks. I managed to find the university where Professor Dankworth worked and I went to meet him today."

"That's great news. So he was the right person then?"

Esther nodded her head. "Yes, he was the one that came to your church with my father. He also confirmed that my father was alive, but we didn't get much chance to speak because he was starting a lecture. But I gave him my number, and he's already called me. He wants to meet me at 7 p.m. tomorrow at his home in Maida Vale."

"Good. It sounds like you're one step closer to finding your father…It's been quite a journey, hasn't it?"

"Yeah, definitely," Esther said, fixing her eyes on Elijah's face. "Would you have time to follow me tomorrow? After all your help, I think it's only fair you're there for the big reveal."

Elijah chuckled, and Esther found herself laughing too.

"Of course I'll be there with you."

For a few minutes, they sat in silence and watched London's skyline as the twilight reflected across the darkening sky. Esther looked up at the oak tree, thinking about how many times in their youth she had kissed Elijah underneath its branches and flurry of leaves, hidden away from everyone else.

A distant memory floated into Esther's mind like a leaf carried by the wind. She smiled to herself as she looked in the direction of Brockwell Lido. The public pool was a few minutes' walk from where they sat. "Do you remember, a lifetime ago now, when we sneaked into Brockwell Lido one night?" she said, turning to face Elijah.

Elijah nodded and let out a faint chuckle. "I do remember."

"And do you remember what we said to each other?"

"I do."

"It's funny when you think about it. After everything we said to each other that night and yet here we are."

Elijah turned away from the view and looked at Esther. "I can drive you home? I'd like to spend some time with you this evening if you're okay with that?"

Esther stared into Elijah's eyes, and she could see his raw desire for her; he was not even trying to conceal it. She placed her hands on his own, unintentionally brushing the cold metal of the wedding ring on his finger.

"Yes, I would like you to come back with me tonight."

CHAPTER 26

September 1985

A rage, scorching and fierce, like an uncontained wildfire, engulfed the collective mood of Brixton's black youth. But this revolt against authority was no longer exclusive to them. Now, Brixton's white youth burned with a passion of the political kind. Both blacks and whites were driven to rebellion by socialist ideas, a lack of job opportunities and disillusionment with those in power.

Esther sat in the passenger seat of Elijah's father's red Austin Maestro with Elijah behind the wheel, driving towards Brixton police station. An enraged mob of young people, mostly black but some white, had gathered outside, protesting the latest police injustice.

A few hours earlier, Esther had been at home in her bedroom with her Walkman in one hand and headphones in her ears, dancing to Evelyn King's 'Love Come Down'. She swung her hips in front of her mirror, mouthing the lyrics with an imaginary microphone. Her parents had gone to a Saturday church service, no longer asking her to come with them, which suited her fine.

Evelyn King's soaring vocals trailed away as her ballad came to an end, and Esther heard the telephone by her window ringing. When she held the telephone handle to her ear, Ayesha's excitable voice immediately started speaking at fifty miles per hour. Esther calmly asked her to slow down. Although Ayesha was not completely clear with the details over the phone, too overexcited to speak slowly, Esther understood the gist of what she had said.

A local black woman named Cherry Groce, who lived on Normandy Road, had been shot earlier that morning in what sounded like a botched police raid. According to Ayesha, the police had been searching for Cherry Groce's son. When they stormed into her house, believing he was there, they shot his mother instead. Although no one yet knew if Cherry Groce had died or not, a large group of incensed locals had gathered outside Cherry Groce's house, demanding answers. Ayesha had asked Esther to come with her and their other friends to protests outside Brixton's local police station.

After the phone call, the first thing Esther did was dial Elijah's house number on her telephone. She had been spending a lot more time with him now that they had restarted their friendship. When Elijah answered the phone, Esther repeated what Ayesha had told her. He had just finished returning from the same Saturday service her parents had attended and, not having much to do in the afternoon, he agreed to drive her to Brixton Road and join the protest.

"No way we're getting through that," Elijah said. He was looking at the herd of people a few metres away. "This is another riot waiting to happen."

Esther's heart leaped at the thought of a potential riot. She could smell rebellion in the air like sulphur. The Austin Maestro came to a forceful stop at Brixton Road, just underneath the overhead train bridge where the message *Welcome to Brixton* was written in large white letters. Crowds of black and white youths, and some older Brixton residents, sprawled across the street. The press and police had already descended upon them. Yet the police were not in their usual black custodian helmets and black police jackets. For the first time in her life, Esther was seeing police officers decked out in riot helmets, gripping riot shields and brandishing their truncheons, prepared for battle. Another war in Brixton.

"I'm getting out. Come on."

"Esther wait, shouldn't we…"

But Esther had already opened the door of the car before Elijah could complete his protest. In front of her, she could see an energised throng of people marching towards Brixton police station, some with bricks, bottles and wooden stakes in their hands. Esther scanned the sea of people, like a captain on the mast of a ship, trying to spot Ayesha or anyone else she recognised.

"I can't see her," Esther said, turning towards Elijah who had come to stand next to her. He could not keep his eyes still, looking in every direction as if a stray bullet might ricochet from anywhere and hit them. "I'm going closer to the police station."

"Is that a good idea?" Elijah said, in a tone that betrayed how very worried he was about the whole situation.

But Esther ignored him, adrenaline pulsing through her. "Come on."

Together, they followed the direction of the aggravated protestors heading towards the station. As they got closer to Brixton's police station, Esther realised there was an even greater mass of people than she had seen from the car. Protestors were shouting and swearing at the row of police officers standing in front of them, who held their riot shields firmly, truncheons ready for the slightest provocation.

It all happened without warning. In the same moment that Esther spotted Ayesha and a group of other black boys and girls she knew, someone from the crowd threw a Molotov cocktail at the police station.

Now under attack, the police charged at the crowd of youths, and a swarm of screaming people ran towards Esther, desperate to evade them. With no time to think, she dashed across the road to another street some yards away, losing sight not only of Ayesha but of Elijah as well.

Screaming. Shouting. Truncheons breaking bones. Esther's senses were in dizzying overdrive as her eyes frantically searched the mass of scattered people running all over Brixton Road for any sign of Elijah or Ayesha. Across the road from her, she witnessed a dozen young boys, black and white alike, smash the window of a local clothes shop her mother frequently visited. The looters ran inside like a swarm of locusts devastating a farm.

Before Esther could register her disgust, she felt a forceful push against her chest, knocking her off her feet, and she crashed headfirst into the pavement.

First, she felt the surge of throbbing pain in her head, followed immediately by a ringing sensation in her ears. Esther struggled to her feet, and even in her concussed daze, she could see the police officer above her, ready to smash her skull in with his truncheon.

Before he could deliver the blow, the officer was thrown onto the floor. Esther looked up, her vision still blurry, and could just make out the silhouette of a young black man. As clarity slowly returned to her eyesight, she realised it was Elijah now standing in front of her. His lip had been cut and a line of blood trickled from the wound down to his chin.

"We gotta get out of here. Now!"

Elijah grabbed Esther by her arm and forced her onto her feet.

"You're alright, yeah?"

"Yeah," Esther said, nodding and then wincing with pain as her head hammered in response.

With an urgent pace, like soldiers moving across a battlefield littered with mines, Esther and Elijah slid through the disorder and mayhem swirling around them. As Esther walked through Brixton Road, holding Elijah's hand so they wouldn't lose each other, her surroundings played out in quick flashes. Young men throwing bricks and bottles against the riot shields of the retreating police. Upturned cars burning into disfigured black metal. The smell of smoke filling her nostrils.

Through the kaleidoscope of violence flashing before her eyes, she saw young men and some women walking out of Frank Johnson Sports, arguably Brixton's most popular sports shop, with trainers and boxes in their hands. Did these youths even care about the mother who had been shot by the police? Did they even know? Esther suddenly felt ashamed for having been so thrilled about the idea of a riot. She could see, first-hand, that all it had done was bring destruction and violence.

Esther let out a sigh of great relief as the Austin Maestro came into view. The car was undamaged but that could change at any moment if they did not leave immediately. Hands shaking with adrenaline, Esther opened the passenger door and jumped into the vehicle with Elijah. He wasted no time at all. The ignition started and the car's engine rumbled into life.

Esther watched with a throbbing behind her eyes as Elijah quickly turned the steering wheel and sped down Brixton Road, away from the warzone of Brixton's second riot.

"Does that feel better?" Elijah asked, observing Esther as she sat on a chair beside the dining table in his parents' house, holding a frozen bag of peas to the back of her head.

"Yeah, it's helping. Thanks a lot."

Elijah smiled warmly at her and picked up his mother's mirror, examining the small cut at the bottom of his lip, a painful result of a police officer barging him to the ground. Residual adrenaline still lingered within Elijah even in the comfort of his home, miles away from the rioting. He had seen minor skirmishes between the police and black people before, but it paled in comparison to what he had just witnessed. Violence and wanton destruction had surrounded him, almost consuming him like a vacuum sucking up a piece of discarded rubbish. Only by God's grace had he and Esther escaped without severe injuries. Some raw instinct to survive had awakened within him as he dodged the police and rioters and saved Esther from being seriously wounded. Only by God's grace.

Satisfied that the cut on his lip had stopped bleeding, Elijah walked out of the kitchen and into the living room. Without giving it any thought, he switched on the television to BBC News. As he expected, the riot, the second in Brixton in the space of four years, was being reported. As the newswoman spoke, footage of wrecked, burning vehicles and smashed windows of ransacked shops played on the screen. Brixton had once again become a warzone – the black and white youths on one side and the police on the other. Elijah wondered if it would be this way forever between Britain's black community and the British police. Constantly at war with one another.

"Hey."

The voice snapped Elijah out of his thoughts, and he looked up to see Esther standing by the doorway of the living room. She was no longer holding the bag of frozen peas to the small bruise at the back of her head.

"I wanted to say sorry for being an idiot," she said, smiling weakly at Elijah. "I should have listened to you."

Elijah took Esther in for a moment. She was wearing a pink tank top and ripped jeans that emphasised the curve of her thighs. Not for the first time, Elijah's heart raced at the thought of kissing and undressing her.

"It's alright," he said, trying his best to ignore the erection that had swelled in his jeans at the idea of seeing Esther naked. "All that matters is God got us out of there safely."

"Yeah, I guess so," Esther said, giving Elijah a much brighter smile. She checked her watch. "It's nearly seven, and I ain't got no idea how I'm gonna get back to Loughborough Estate. Brixton Road's probably cornered off by now...I hope Ayesha's okay."

"Don't worry, it's Ayesha, she'll be fine. And it would be way too dangerous to try and get home now," Elijah said. "You know what? You can stay here until the morning. My family aren't coming back from Nigeria until Monday so you can sleep on the couch if you want?"

"Wicked. I owe you big time." Esther let out a heavy sigh and suddenly looked crestfallen. "It was sickening, you know. Seeing those people looting shops. Destroying businesses. Burning cars. It'll only make young black people look worse and that's what the police want. We're playing into their prejudice." Esther stared at Elijah with sadness in her eyes. "How can we be so stupid?"

"I can't fully blame them. Young black people are angry," Elijah said, a thoughtful look on his face. "Until this country stops treating us black people as second class, we'll always burn with rage. Britain is our home too."

Although the day's events had been exhausting, Esther was not eager to fall asleep straight away. Fortunately, neither was Elijah. Instead, he suggested they watch *Back to the Future*, which had not been released in the UK yet. He had bought a bootleg version of the movie on VHS at Brixton market a week ago.

It was coming to 8 p.m. as Elijah and Esther sat next to each other on the brown sofa in his living room. A packet of Butterkist was nestled between them, which they dipped their hands into occasionally to grab a handful of popcorn. They watched silently as Marty McFly and Doc Brown jumped into a DeLorean and travelled back in time to 1955. Elijah wondered what it would be like to go back to Brixton in 1955 and how different things might be. Would there still have been riots? He knew from speaking to his West Indian friends that many West Indian immigrants had come to England after the Second World War, arriving on a cruise ship called Empire Windrush. But what about Africans like himself? Had they been on the Empire

Windrush too? Why had he not been taught about the history of black people in Britain when he was at school?

Before Elijah could ponder this question further, Esther spoke.

"Can I ask you a question? It's personal though, so you don't have to tell me."

Elijah turned away from the TV screen and looked at Esther curiously. "Sure?"

"Are you a virgin?"

It was not a question Elijah had been expecting, and it caught him off guard. At seventeen years old, he was as pure a virgin as they came and had never seen a woman naked in real life. Of course, like most teenage boys, he had guiltily ogled at the exposed breasts of white women on page three of *The Sun* newspaper. On several occasions, Elijah had masturbated during the night while his parents and sister were asleep. The thought of sex had crossed his mind more times than he would openly admit, and there had been opportunities where he could have lost his virginity already had he pursued further. But instead he focused on his education and living up to his family's puritanical standards.

"Yeah, I'm a virgin," Elijah said, feeling embarrassed as if he were telling Esther he had a small penis. "Are you a virgin?" Even as Elijah asked the question, he already knew the answer.

"No," Esther said, her eyes burning into Elijah's. "I've had sex with boys and girls."

"Ayesha as well?"

Esther nodded her head. "Yeah, her as well.

"Oh, right."

"So are you waiting to get married before you have sex? The Christian way?"

Even though *Back to the Future* was still playing on the VCR, Elijah could no longer pay attention to the movie. Instead, his eyes kept moving from Esther's lips to the inside of her tank top. Now that she was leaning towards him, he could partly see her brown breasts concealed by a white bra. His erection was throbbing.

"I'm waiting for the right person," Elijah said, his voice tremulous and much quieter than he wanted it to be.

Then Esther grabbed his hand and placed it on her right breast. "I see the way you look at me, you know. I want you and I don't care you're a virgin. I just want you. Right now."

Elijah pushed the popcorn bag aside, its contents spilling onto the floor, and kissed Esther full on the lips. His heart hammered inside his chest as she pulled down his jeans while their mouths were still locked together.

Esther backed away and stood from the couch. Eyes fixed on Elijah, she slowly removed all her clothes. Elijah felt himself almost ejaculate just from staring at her full breasts with their dark, erect nipples. She gave him a reassuring smile. Still sitting on the couch, Elijah nervously pulled down his boxers, and Esther climbed on top of him.

"Relax, okay."

"I don't have a condom," Elijah suddenly said, panic pricking his arousal.

"Don't worry, okay. I'm on the pill."

"What's the pill?"

Esther giggled as she stroked his penis and guided it to the opening between her thighs. "It's a pill that stops me from getting pregnant. Now relax."

With those words, soothing to Elijah's ears, Esther sank onto him. As she began to move her hips rhythmically, Elijah let out a gasp of pleasure, feeling the warm wetness inside of her as his lust for her body, bottled inside, unleashed itself.

Esther lay on Elijah's naked chest as he played with strands of her curly afro. Both were breathing heavily, appreciating the cool of the hardwood living room floor against their flushed skin.

Since she had started having sex, Esther had never cuddled afterwards. She had only had sex with a grand total of six people. There was Ayesha, of course, and two Jamaican girls she had met at a reggae night in Vauxhall. Then there had been two black boys and one older white man, all of whom she had met at The Atlantic. But she had never felt anything other than physical pleasure with them, even Ayesha.

But with Elijah, it was different. Very different. She loved him, and it changed the way she experienced sex. There was an intensity that came from being able to lose herself to him entirely, without holding anything back. Now that she could finally admit to herself that she loved him, it felt incredible to express that love physically.

"Was I...was I good?" Elijah asked.

Esther turned her face towards him and kissed his lips. "You were great. I liked it. Did you?"

"Yeah. Yeah, I really did."

They were quiet for a moment, the sounds of police sirens and the voice of Marty McFly cutting through the silence. After another minute basking in each other's presence, Elijah spoke again.

"Esther, I don't just want to be another person you have sex with. I need it to be something more."

"I know you do," Esther replied. "I want it to be something more as well. You're the only person I want to be with...because I love you."

Elijah stroked her face and looked at her as if she were God's perfect creation. It made Esther feel like the most beautiful woman on the earth. "And I love you too, Esther."

Overcome with passion, Esther turned over and kissed him until they were both wrapped around each other again. Within minutes, they were having sex for the second time on the living room floor. As Brixton burned outside, they made love all night to the sound of police sirens.

CHAPTER 27

July 2008

Whatever salary the university was paying Professor Dankworth, it was a very generous one.

As Esther walked beside Elijah on a sultry Tuesday evening, she stared at the pristine, white Victorian townhouses in Maida Vale. Parked in front were the latest BMWs and Range Rovers. This part of London was so far removed from Brixton that it felt like another city entirely. For most of her American friends back in Chicago, this is what they pictured when they thought of London. They would probably be disappointed by the grittiness of Brixton's Electric Avenue, even though it represented the reality of most average Londoners.

"Since when could a university professor live in an area like this?" Elijah said. With his long, grey coat and crisp shirt and tie, he looked like someone who could live in an area like this himself. "I haven't seen one Ford Fiesta."

Esther let out a chuckle. "You know I was just thinking the same thing. But he's written dozens of books about Africa. So that should be a nice secondary income."

"Yeah, must be. You know, I should write a book myself."

"Yeah, about what?"

Elijah shrugged his shoulders, then smiled. "My memoir. 'The Last Prophet of Brixton: How One Man Brought the Good News to the People of Lambeth.'"

Esther shook her head and laughed. Even as she shared this joke with him, a part of Esther's conscious kept tugging at her, like an annoying child demanding attention.

Yesterday evening she had slept with Elijah again, and it had been just as physical and sensual as the last time. After sharing themselves intimately, they had lain side by side, naked and dripping with sweat as they stared at the white ceiling. Elijah had turned to her and said:

"I don't know what this is yet. But I enjoy spending time with you. Every moment, Esther. I've missed this with you more than I realised."

At that moment, Esther should have asked Elijah how he felt about betraying his wife with her. She should have told him that what they were doing together was rooted in selfishness even if their feelings towards each other were genuine. She should have stated that he was better than this. They both were.

But these thoughts remained locked in her head and she brushed them away like fluffs of dust under a bed. Soon after, Elijah had gotten dressed, said goodbye and left the flat. When he had gone, Esther lay in the bed where she had made forbidden love in complete silence for almost thirty minutes, consumed with the shame that she was no better than her unfaithful father.

And now here she was with Elijah again, turning a corner on a wealthy street as they walked towards Professor Dankworth's home. Despite the conflicting feelings towards him raging war on the battlefield of her principles, she was still glad that he was beside her in this significant moment.

They came to a halt in front of a cream-coloured, three-story Victorian townhouse with a marble front porch and arched windows. Esther pushed open the front gate and walked up to the door, pausing to admire its shiny black paint. She rang the doorbell and waited.

In less than a minute, the door opened, and Professor Dankworth stood behind it with an inviting smile. He looked more casual than when Esther had last seen him, wearing a blue Ralph Lauren polo, brown shorts and black sandals. It gave him the air of a man who was completely content with the elegant lifestyle he had afforded. Even if it was built on a career writing about the plight of Africa's people and its resources.

"Good evening, Esther. It is a pleasure to see you again," he said, beckoning her into the narrow hallway whose only decoration was a massive silver mirror hanging on the spotless white walls.

As Elijah followed her into the house, Esther noticed Professor Dankworth give Elijah a probing look. "Good afternoon, sir," he said, shaking Elijah's hand a bit too enthusiastically.

"Please excuse my forwardness, but I believe I know you from somewhere?" Professor Dankworth's eyes widened in recognition. "Ah, that's right, I came to your church with Kelechi when you were preaching. Mr Oduwole, I believe?"

"That's right. Nice to meet you, although I'd be lying if I said I recognised you," Elijah said, stepping into the hallway.

"Oh, I wouldn't have expected you to, Mr Oduwole. If I recall, the church hall was filled with a great number of people on that particular day. I grew up Catholic, but I have visited quite a few African Protestant churches in my time. And I must say, I have enjoyed them immensely. Forgive my presumptuousness, but I love the way Nigerians and Ghanaians go about the business of worshipping God. Full of joyous song and dance. It really brings the gospel to life."

Elijah nodded his head and smiled. Looking at him, Esther was not sure whether Elijah was smiling because he was flattered by Professor Dankworth's enthusiasm or embarrassed by it. Either way, it had been quite entertaining for Esther to witness the exchange.

"Anyway, that's enough from me. Gosh, I talk too much for my own good," Professor Dankworth said as he led them through the hallway. "Please follow me to the dining room, I'll introduce you to my wife. We are having grilled sea bass with fennel and dill. Of course, I am happy to order you both something else should you not fancy that?"

The food sounded as posh as the house looked. Esther knew sea bass was a type of fish, but she did not have the faintest clue as to what fennel and dill could be. Though she was not going to take advantage of Professor Dankworth's hospitality and ask for something else. She turned to look at Elijah for his answer, and he nodded his head in response.

"That's fine with both of us. Thank you for your hospitality," Esther said, following Professor Dankworth into his home with Elijah close behind.

The living room and the kitchen of the house connected in an open-plan design, and the whole decor of the place was spotless, oozing wealth and luxury. Elegant paintings inspired by African imagery decorated the walls. A golden chandelier hung from the ceiling, and expensive vases filled with vibrant flowers were dotted around the living room. The air was rich with the smell of lavender.

A woman in a yellow bodycon dress was standing in the middle of the state-of-the-art kitchen, cutting vegetables. As soon as they entered her vicinity, she looked up and gave them a radiant smile. Esther was taken aback by how stunning she was. The woman had light-brown skin and full lips, with a distinct cupid's bow, but the feature that made her most attractive to Esther was her completely shaved head. It brought out her high cheekbones.

"This magnificent woman here is my wife, Ashanti," Professor Dankworth said as if he were introducing a contestant on a television show.

"It is a pleasure to meet you both," Ashanti said in a South African dialect that was a little flatter than her husband's but more titillating coming from her. In another life and in an entirely different context, Ashanti was the type of woman Esther would immediately flirt with at a bar and, if sparks flew, take home for the night.

"You look so much like your father," Ashanti said, shaking Esther's hands. Her touch was delicate and refined, like her surroundings.

Once the introductions had been made, Elijah and Esther took a seat at the glass dining table situated with a view of the small but lush garden. Wearing a smile that seemed incapable of leaving her face, Ashanti poured everyone a glass of freshly squeezed orange juice and sauntered back to the kitchen. A minute later, she returned with plates of grilled sea bass, fennel and dill, which carried the alluring smell of grilled fish mixed with spices. Ashanti took a seat next to her husband, and the four of them ate silently for a few minutes.

"So, to the matter of your father," Professor Dankworth said, as he dabbed a napkin around his mouth. "As I told you, your father is indeed alive. What I didn't have time to tell you when you came to visit me at the university is that he is in hospital."

Esther swallowed a chunk of sea bass and dropped her cutlery on her plate with a clatter. "He's in hospital!?" Esther said, surprised by the magnitude of fear she felt upon hearing this. "What happened to him? How long has he been there for?"

"All very valid questions, Ms Nubari," Professor Dankworth said with a slightly nervous tone. He suddenly looked distraught and Ashanti squeezed his hand. "But I think it is best if I start from the beginning, so you have a full picture, if you understand?

"Yeah, sure. Please go on."

"I met Kelechi at a homeless shelter in Peckham, around late December."

Esther shook her head in disbelief. "A homeless shelter?"

"Yes, my wife and I often volunteer at the Southwark shelter in Peckham during Christmas time. I served your father a bowl of soup, and we quickly struck up a natural rapport. Forgive me if I come across as impolite, but I was pleasantly surprised at how well-spoken and educated your father was. It just goes to show that homeless people can come from any type of class and from any walk of life."

If Professor Dankworth was expecting some form of acknowledgement from Esther regarding his observations about homeless people, it was not forthcoming, so he continued.

"Your father told me that he had left a teaching position at a school in east London at the very end of 2006. A woman he had been in a nine-year relationship with had evicted him from her home when their relationship broke down. So your father moved to Peckham, where he managed to get another teaching position at the start of 2007, but then things took a turn for the worse."

"What happened?" Esther said, somewhat impatiently, as she was becoming irritated by Professor Dankworth's style of delivering information. Could he not get to the point quickly, or did he enjoy the sound of his own scholarly voice?

"Around six months into his teaching position, your father began to succumb to severe depression and developed a drinking problem." A solemn expression crossed Professor Dankworth's face, and he sighed heavily. "From what he told me, his drinking habits became very serious. It was to the point where, one day, he came to his classroom, reeking of alcohol, and proceeded to vomit in front of his students.

"My God," muttered Elijah.

"Because of his actions," Professor Dankworth continued with his eyes on Esther, "your father was banned from teaching indefinitely. This was around August last year. Without a stable salary and little support from the council, he eventually found himself homeless and teetering on the edge of complete destruction. It was in this condition that I met your father at the homeless shelter. Very much a broken man. I am terribly sorry, Ms Nubari, that you had to hear this account from me."

Esther's mind was so busy trying to make sense of this new information about her father's struggle with depression and alcoholism that she was unable to think clearly enough to string a sentence together. She closed her eyes and rubbed her head. The thought of him homeless, lost and alone made her deeply ashamed that she had abandoned him for eighteen years. Tears threatened to emerge from her eyes.

"Are you okay?" Elijah said. Esther felt him place his hand on her shoulder, and just his touch helped her compose herself.

"I'm okay. Just a lot to digest, you know." Esther looked at Professor Dankworth and nodded her head, indicating for him to continue.

"During our conservations at the homeless shelter, I was impressed by your father's love of literature," Professor Dankworth said, smiling at Esther. Surprisingly, this made her feel better. "I was also greatly interested in the details he shared about the troubles of his homeland, Ogoniland. He told me about fleeing Nigeria in 1996 and leaving his wife behind. There was a high risk he would be killed by the Nigerian government for his actions during the Niger Delta conflict. It just so happened that, at the time of meeting your father, I was commencing preliminary research for my forthcoming book examining that same conflict."

Professor Dankworth smiled at his wife and squeezed her hand. "My wife and I invited Kelechi to come and live with us. While we helped him get back on his feet, he assisted me in writing my book. It was all going well. Your father was making such a great recovery until he was involved in an accident."

"What accident?" Esther said, once again gripped by a fear that almost stopped her from breathing.

"He was involved in a terrible car collision at the start of March."

Esther felt like every tendon and muscle in her body had stiffened.

This time it was Ashanti who spoke, looking at Esther with sadness in her eyes. "He was in a taxi coming from the rehabilitation centre where he was receiving treatment for his alcohol addiction. On his way back to our home, the taxi collided with a bus."

Professor Dankworth finished the story. "The taxi driver was killed outright during the collision. Although your father survived the impact, he…" Professor Dankworth turned away from Esther and closed his eyes as a tear trickled down his face. "Your father's spinal cord was completely crushed, paralysing him from the waist down. I am so sorry, Ms Nubari. Your father is very much alive, but he is completely paralysed. He will never walk again."

Esther sat in the passenger seat of Elijah's BMW as he drove through Warwick Avenue, passing the Paddington Basin canal as they entered Little Venice. Her thoughts were twisting and curving through her mind, like the canals and rivers outside the window, carrying haunting images of her paralysed father with them.

Upon hearing that her father would never use his legs again, Esther had burst into inconsolable tears. Not even Elijah's tight embrace had quelled her grief. After everything he had been through, for all his faith in God, her father was now just a paralysed old man. And he was alone because his daughter had abandoned her parents, choosing to turn her back on them to follow a dream that, in the end, had only made her reckless and sad. Esther realised she had been crying not only for her father but also out of shame at herself.

Before they left, Professor Dankworth had told Esther that her father was currently receiving treatment at the Royal National Orthopaedic Hospital, in a ward that specialised in quadriplegic patients. He had agreed to take Esther there on Saturday. In the meantime, he would call the hospital and ask the staff to inform her father that his daughter was in London.

"I've failed my family," Esther said, feeling the threat of more tears as her voice trembled. "I abandoned them. I'm a terrible person, Elijah."

"No, don't do that to yourself," Elijah said, putting his free hand on her shoulder. "William Cowper, an English poet, once wrote that 'God works in mysterious ways. His wonders to perform; He plants His footsteps in the sea; And rides upon the storm'."

"Sounds incredibly beautiful, Pastor. But what does it mean?"

"What I'm saying is, your mother got in touch with you after eighteen years, asking you to find your father. You could have ignored her request, but you chose not to. Instead, you came to London to search for him, and you found him, Esther. You've found your father. Now you have another chance to rebuild your relationship and reunite your family. That is the work of God. None of us is perfect, but we can always be redeemed through our actions. God has given you a second chance with your family. Take comfort in that."

"Thank you for those words," Esther said, sniffing back tears as she smiled at him. She felt like she wanted to lean over and kiss him. "Really, thank you for everything you've done for me."

Out of nowhere, a flash of blinding blue light followed by the ear-piercing wail of a police siren filled the small space between them. Esther looked out the rear windshield. A police car was tailing Elijah's BMW.

Elijah sighed. "Really? I'm being stopped?"

With an air of annoyance, Elijah drove past Westbourne Park Station. He turned into Tavistock Road, where he pulled over into a vacant parking space opposite a pub. From the windshield, Esther could see the police car come to a halt behind them. A police officer stepped out of the vehicle and walked towards Elijah's car. Elijah had already begun to wind down his window.

"Good evening, mate," Elijah said, smiling at the pasty-faced officer. He looked like somebody who was permanently annoyed at everything. The police officer leaned forward so that he was at eye level with Elijah.

"Evening, sir. You were going over the speed limit on a pedestrian road." He spoke with a coarse cockney accent.

"Really? I didn't think I was."

The police officer gave Elijah a blank stare, his face an expression of indifference. "May I please see your driving licence?"

"Of course."

Elijah reached into his pocket and took out his brown leather wallet. He removed his driving licence and handed it to the police officer. Esther looked at the man's steely face, wondering to herself if this was even necessary. Elijah had not been speeding, Esther was sure of it.

The police officer inspected the driving licence as if he were trying to find some fault with it, flipping it from back to front. He then handed it back to Elijah. "Thank you, sir. Could you please step out of the vehicle for me?"

Esther watched, her anger beginning to bubble like boiling water, as Elijah opened the door and climbed out. The police officer, who was noticeably shorter than Elijah, stood beside the car. He removed a rectangular device from his duty belt.

"Sir, I am going to ask you to breathe into this breathalyser," the police officer said, taking a few steps towards Elijah with the device in his hand.

Elijah shook his head. "This isn't necessary, mate. I haven't been drinking."

"Failure to comply with the breathalyser test is an offence, sir," the police officer said in a flat tone as if he were reading lines from a manual.

Esther gritted her teeth, incensed. *Some things never change.*

Elijah exhaled into the breathalyser device. The police officer checked the reading and Esther saw a quick flash of disappointment on his face. With no other reason to disturb their journey, the police officer waved goodbye and walked back to his vehicle. Elijah opened the door of his BMW and sat back in the driver's seat.

"Well that was bullshit," Esther said as Elijah turned the key in the ignition and the engine began to hum. "I swear, the more things change, the more they stay the same. Whether it's London or Chicago, there will always be police officers who can't pass up an opportunity to embarrass black people."

Elijah shrugged his shoulders as he drove onto the main road. "Yeah, there will always be police officers like that. We've both lived through it. But I will never give them the satisfaction of thinking they're getting to me. I rise above their behaviour and continue my journey. If we react violently or retaliate, then we're just giving them what they want and confirming their own prejudices. I remember you telling me something similar a long time ago. You remember?"

Esther nodded her head. "I do."

A satisfied smile formed on Elijah's face. "I'll leave it to God to deal with them."

CHAPTER 28

July 2008

With the soothing tones of Bill Withers' 'Lean on Me' playing in her ear, Esther tapped her Oyster card on the ticket barrier and exited Edgeware station onto the high street.

It was a summery Saturday afternoon, and the warmth of the sun sank into Esther's skin and lifted her spirits, but her nervousness still made her feel uneasy. Today she would come face to face with her father for the first time in eighteen years.

Hands in the pockets of her denim jeans, Esther walked through the busy high street, the backpack containing her father's diary bouncing a little with each step. She took out her iPhone to check if she was heading in the right direction and opened the message Professor Dankworth had sent her yesterday, containing instructions to the Royal National Orthopaedic Hospital.

Five minutes later, Esther was sitting on the 107 bus, heading towards Stanmore. An old man wearing a tweed jacket and round glasses sat opposite her. When she turned to face him, the old man gave her an encouraging smile, as if he could sense Esther's apprehension and wanted to reassure her. Esther returned the smile, and then a thought occurred to her. Her father would be around the same age. While this man looked fit and healthy, her father was now a cripple, unable to walk, run or even embrace his daughter.

The bus reached Brockley Hill and Esther could see Professor Dankworth standing by the bus stop. She switched off her headphones and alighted from the bus.

A part of Esther had hoped Elijah would be here with her today. She had phoned him yesterday when he had left work to ask him if he would like to accompany her. But Elijah explained that he could not make it as he had prior arrangements with his wife. The mention of his wife irked Esther, coldly reminding her that she was not the only woman in Elijah's life. If anything, she was his mistress now. Esther was the other woman he kept hidden in his closet like a spare jacket he wore when he wanted a change from his usual one. At some point, sooner rather than later, Esther knew she would have to decide what she was going to do about her and Elijah's affair. Just how far did she want it to go? It was a question that was getting too loud to ignore but now was not the time to answer it.

"Good afternoon, Esther," Professor Dankworth said as Esther shook his hand. She removed her headphones from her ears and placed them around her neck. "What delightful weather we have today. How are you feeling?"

"I'm fine, thank you, Professor Dankworth," Esther said. "And thank you again for coming with me today. It means a lot. You've already done so much, taking care of my father and paying for his medical bills. I'm indebted to you."

"Please, Esther, call me Edward. No need to be so formal. And I am happy to help your father, I consider him a good friend. You owe me nothing." Edward beamed at Esther, and her icy demeanour towards him melted. "Anyway, shall we?"

Esther nodded her head. "Yeah, let's get going."

She walked alongside Edward down the concrete pathway towards the entrance of the hospital, feeling her heartbeat quicken with each step she took. They entered the reception, and a lady directed them to the quadriplegic hospital ward. This was where Kelechi Nubari was currently recuperating.

"Hello, Mr Dankworth," said the brunette nurse who had come to greet Esther and Edward as soon as they walked into the ward. This section of the hospital had dull white walls and grey flooring. It smelled strongly of cleaning detergent as if the whole area had been recently sterilised.

Ayleen was printed on the brunette nurse's name badge clipped to the breast pocket of her navy shirt. Ayleen had a welcoming smile, but it seemed affected, like she practised it every morning before she left for work.

"Mr Nubari has been noticeably quiet this afternoon. Not that he's much of a speaker usually," Ayleen said. She handed Edward a clipboard with a white form attached. "As always, you'll need to sign in."

Ayleen then shifted her attention to Esther, and her smile widened. "And you must be Mr Nubari's daughter. Just sign in after Mr Dankworth and go down this corridor, he's in the fourth room on your right."

Once Esther had written her name, the date and the time she had arrived on the paper form, she took a step towards the empty corridor. It was quiet and still. She felt the odd sensation that her legs were somehow no longer connected to her body and froze at the top of the hallway, unable to move. Edward placed his hands on her shoulders.

"Come now. Let's go."

With slow and deliberate steps, Esther walked down the corridor, her heart beating so forcefully, she felt it could shatter her rib cage. As they approached the fourth room, Esther exhaled loudly to calm her nerves. This was it. Esther stepped inside the room.

Her father was sitting by the window on a polished, black wheelchair with his legs against the elevated footrests, and his head settled on a headrest. A white gown covered his frail body, and his entire silhouette was bathed in the natural sunlight that flooded the room. It gave her father an ethereal, angelic quality. When Esther had last seen him, he had a few strands of grey in his receding hairline, but now the sparse hairs left on his head were completely white.

"Dad?" Esther said it with an uncertain tone as if she had forgotten how to say the word correctly.

At the sound of her voice, Esther's father slowly turned his head away from the window to face her. With a rasp that matched the brokenness of his body, he uttered, "Esther? It's really you?" His voice, quiet and sad, sounded so unfamiliar to Esther and yet somehow she recognised it.

Esther started to feel tears stinging her eyes. "Yes, it's me."

A smile slowly formed across her father's sunken, dark-brown face. When he spoke more clearly, Esther could still hear his Nigerian accent. "It's been so long. I never thought I would see you again. God is good. God is good." Tears ran down her father's wrinkled cheeks.

At that moment, Esther felt like a young girl who wanted nothing more than a hug from her father. She walked towards him, knelt in front of his wheelchair and flung her arms around his waist.

"Esther. My only child," her father almost whispered, stroking her hair. "I have so much to say, so much to amend and so much to apologise for."

Eyes still blinded with tears, Esther tightened her embrace around her father, feeling his bony forearms. "There will be plenty of time for that, Dad. I have so much to tell you as well. But first I need to give you something."

Her hands shaking, Esther took off her backpack, unzipped it and brought out her father's old journal. She watched her father's eyes widen in recognition as he took the diary from her.

"My journal," he said, staring at the battered book as he inspected it with his bony figures. "How did you come across this?"

Esther placed her hands on top of her father's and looked into his dark eyes. "I met the woman you were with when you were living in east London. She gave me this diary. Now I know your story, I'll tell you mine. We've both led colourful lives."

At this, Esther's father gave her a smile so full of joy and warmth that Esther felt, for the first time in her life, that she could finally let him in.

"Tell me everything about yourself," her father said. He placed his diary on top of the windowsill. "I want to know who you are."

"What will you do now?" Elijah asked.

Esther rested her head against Elijah's naked torso. They lay together, without clothes, on the bed in Ayesha's spare room.

She had stayed with her father for almost two hours, and afterwards Esther returned to the flat feeling like her entire body had been given a massage. She felt looser, freer and nimbler, not only physically but spiritually as well. As if he had known she was home, Elijah sent her a text to say that he was free and could come over, and against her better judgement, Esther had said yes.

Once Elijah arrived, she sat him down and told him about the reunion with her father. She recounted how she had returned her father's journal and how he had listened, without judgement, as she shared the story of her whirlwind life as a short-lived R&B star in the nineties.

When Esther finished, she let Elijah kiss her, and they silently moved to the spare room, undressed each other and made love. She had no fears about getting pregnant – she had been taking the pill for years since deciding that she did not want children anymore – all the same, she made Elijah wear a condom this time. Now, as Esther lay beside Elijah, she could see the torn condom wrapper out of the corner of her eye. It made her feel dirty.

"I'm going to phone my mother on Sunday morning," Esther said, looking away from the wrapper and concentrating on the white ceiling instead. "I'll let her know I've found my father." The thought of hearing her mother's cry of joy made Esther smile. Even though her father was now paralysed, he was alive. That's all she believed her mother would care about.

Esther turned away from the ceiling to face Elijah. She swept her fingers through her curly afro hair. "Ayesha comes back tomorrow, and then I'm flying back to Chicago on Friday. I guess I'll have to come back at some point and take my father to Nigeria. But I'll figure that out later. I'm still trying to digest all this."

She felt Elijah gently squeeze her left hand. "Do you have to go back to Chicago so soon?"

Esther pulled her hand away and stood up from the bed. Suddenly feeling conscious that she was naked in front of Elijah, she picked her black underwear up from the floor. "What do you mean?" Esther said, slipping them on. "Of course I have to go back, Elijah."

"I know," Elijah said as he stood, grabbing his boxers. He put them on and walked towards Esther, then wrapped his arms around her in a tight embrace and rested his naked chest against her exposed breasts. "I love you, Esther," he whispered into her ear.

Esther stood back from him in total shock. Those three words came at her like a fastball she was supposed to catch, but she had ducked instead. "Elijah, what am I supposed to say to that?"

"Do you love me as well?"

It was a question so big that it seemed to consume the whole room. Esther studied Elijah for a moment. She stared into his dark eyes, not hidden behind glasses today, then at his fulsome lips. Her gaze fell to the line of stubble accentuating his jawline. Then she forced herself to look deeper into him, beyond the physical. It had been Elijah who let her walk out of his life all those years ago. Now here he was again, willing to walk away from another woman in his life. And yet, even after recognising this weakness within Elijah, she still loved him. But love alone was no longer enough. Not at this stage in their lives.

Esther shook her head, frustrated by her feelings. "Elijah, even if I love you, you're married, and I have a life in Chicago. Where are we supposed to go from here?"

"I know, I know," Elijah said, locking his eyes onto Esther's and placing his hands on her shoulders. "But these past few weeks, every time I'm with you, I've been genuinely happy. I can be myself. There's so much life in you and so much passion. But most of all, I can just be Elijah when I'm with you because that's all you've ever wanted from me. And I've only ever wanted you to be Esther."

Esther shook her head again, conflicted between the love she had for Elijah and the truth of their reality. Since returning to Brixton, she had also enjoyed rekindling her romantic relationship with Elijah. Spending time with him, making love again; it had unlocked her heart to him as if she had never taken the key away.

But they were not young lovers anymore. Both had individual lives with responsibilities and commitments, built over the past eighteen years they had been separated. Would it be irresponsible to abandon all of that for feelings they had only just rediscovered?

As if he could detect the conflict tearing through her, Elijah took her hands and enclosed them in his own. "It's a lot to think about, I know. It is for me as well. You're flying back on Friday, right?"

Esther nodded her head weakly, suddenly feeling drained. "Yes."

"Okay, I'll come see you on Monday after work. We can go somewhere and talk about this."

Esther studied Elijah's eyes. Standing in front of her now, he did not look like a confident man, certain of what he wanted.

Instead, he looked flustered and unsure, like a man trapped in a maze, unable to decide which route to follow towards freedom.

Fifteen minutes later, Elijah had dressed and left the flat. Esther put on a long t-shirt and sat on the bed, staring at the walls. Without reason, she turned her attention to the torn condom wrapper lying beside the bin. She stood from the bed, walked over to it and picked it up between the tips of her fingers as if it was something repulsive. With a sigh, Esther threw the wrapper into the bin.

Instantly, she knew what choice to make. The conflict between her morals and her love for Elijah was over. A clear victor had emerged.

Esther had made up her mind.

CHAPTER 29

August 1986

Esther sat on the toilet seat in Ayesha's house in Herne Hill. Her right hand was shaking as she stared at the First Response pregnancy test she had purchased from the chemist in Brixton. Two distinct pink lines were looking back at her from the tiny oval window. She was pregnant.

Upstairs, Ayesha was blasting Billy Ocean's 'When the Going Gets Tough' on full volume. But Esther felt like someone had put her ears on mute. Everything around her seemed to have shrunk into nothingness, and only her, this test and the truth it had revealed felt real. Too real.

A few more minutes passed as Esther sat on the toilet seat in silence, her eyes fixed on the stick in her unsteady grip, staring at it as if it were some object from another planet. Then, her mind still in a haze, Esther stood, pulled up her white jeans and opened the bathroom door.

As she approached Ayesha's bedroom, the potent smell of marijuana engulfed her senses. Ayesha was dancing to Janet Jackson's 'What Have You Done for Me Lately' in pink shorts and a white vest with a joint held to her lips. As soon as she noticed Esther standing by the doorway, Ayesha removed the joint and exhaled a thin stream of smoke.

"Well?"

"It's positive."

The moment those words slipped from Esther's lips, Ayesha dashed to the stereo cassette player resting on the window ledge and switched it off. "Oh my God, you're not kidding? Fuck."

Esther shuffled into Ayesha's bedroom, closing the door behind her. "Pass the joint, I need one right now."

Ayesha took one more drag and passed it to Esther. With the joint nestled between two fingers, Esther walked over to Ayesha's bed and slumped against the cushions. She sighed heavily, beginning to digest this new truth in her life, and then took a deep drag of the joint. She felt lightheaded almost immediately.

"So what are you gonna do, girl?" Ayesha said, leaning against the windowsill, her eyes on Esther.

"I don't know, Ayesha. Like obviously, I gotta tell Elijah," Esther said. She pulled on the joint again to calm the nerves that were now threatening to break down her emotional stronghold and flood her eyes with tears.

Esther had only been dating Elijah again for almost a year, and it was going well so far, better than she could have imagined. For the past few months, their relationship had followed a regular but exciting routine. Every weekday, she met him outside South London College's main building in West Norwood after his lessons and they spent an hour or two listening to soul and funk music in Elijah's father's red Austin Maestro. During the evening, when it was quiet and not many people were around, Elijah would drive to Brockwell Park. They had discovered a secluded area deep within the woodlands of the park and, covered by thick brown grass, Elijah and Esther would have passionate sex. Sometimes for a few minutes, sometimes for a few hours. On a couple of occasions, if Brockwell Park Estate was quiet, they would have a quickie in the backseat of his car. Esther had been surprised by Elijah's sexual appetite and willingness to take risks, considering he was the son of south London's most well-known pastor.

But now she was pregnant with Elijah's child. Even worse, she and Elijah were only eighteen years old. No longer able to contain the swirl of emotions tearing through her, Esther began to sob. Ayesha came to sit beside Esther and placed her arms around her.

"It's okay, girl. You're gonna be alright," Ayesha said, massaging Esther's shoulders as Esther buried her face into her hands. "Elijah is a good guy, right? He's a church boy and all that, so he'll understand."

"But I've been taking the pill," Esther said, removing her face from her hands and sniffling. "I might have taken it a little late a few times, but it was by accident, and I forgot once, but I didn't—"

"Esther, you're gonna drive yourself mad trying to think about how this happened," Ayesha said, her hands still rubbing Esther's shoulders. "Listen, you're meeting Elijah later today after he's finished college, right? Just tell him. Don't wait."

"I know I have to tell him, Ayesha," Esther said, wiping the tears from her eyes with the sleeve of her denim jacket. "But do I like...do I keep it?" The question carried more significance than any words Esther had spoken up to this point in her life.

"Well that's up to you, not him, if you ask me," Ayesha said.

"But it's his baby as well."

Ayesha snorted. "Yeah, so what? It's your womb."

With his rucksack, filled with mathematics and accounting books, slung over his right shoulder, Elijah walked out of the towering red-brick building where he had just finished another gruelling few hours of statistics and analysing balance sheets. Walking beside him was his classmate, Emmanuel Okafor. Emmanuel was a Nigerian-born, lanky boy around the same age as Elijah, who had left Lagos to come and study in London.

South London College's campus was built on a slight hill in West Norwood, overlooking London's central business district with its towering skyscrapers. Elijah glanced at the buildings on the horizon. Very briefly, he wondered if a black boy from Brixton could one day put on a smart suit and tie and shiny black shoes to go and work in one of those buildings.

"Elijah, I see you are daydreaming about working in the city again," Emmanuel said in his jolly voice, thick with the inflections of their motherland, as he patted Elijah's shoulders. "One day, my friend, we will be making big, big money like the white man."

"Of course, by God's grace," Elijah said, turning away from the skyscrapers. Across the road, as expected, Elijah spotted Esther sitting by the bus stop and felt a surge of happiness. She was the epitome of sex appeal in white jeans and a denim jacket over her white belly top. Esther saw him and waved with an uncertain smile.

"Your girlfriend is calling you," Emmanuel said, playfully elbowing Elijah in the side. "I know she's a beautiful girl but be careful with her, O. She looks dangerous."

"You got no idea, trust me," Elijah said, smiling to himself. "I'll catch you later, Emmanuel."

Leaving his friend with those parting words, Elijah skipped down the steps of the building and crossed the road towards the bus stop. As soon as he reached Esther, Elijah flung his arms around her waist and pulled her into him. He kissed her lips as if it were his first time tasting them. But Esther returned his kisses with less enthusiasm than usual.

"You okay, babe?" Elijah leaned back and examined Esther's face. Her eyes looked slightly bloodshot, and he suddenly caught a strong whiff of marijuana. "You've been smoking with Ayesha, right?"

"I have, and that's all I've been doing with her, I promise," Esther said, resting her right hand on Elijah's wrist to reassure him. She understood that he still felt uneasy about her friendship with Ayesha.

As she spoke, Elijah noticed Esther sounded tired, but he was not sure if that was an effect of the weed, as he had never tried it himself. He could not afford to compromise the sharpness of his mind while studying for his A-Levels.

"I trust you with Ayesha. I'll always trust you. But what's up?"

Esther bit her lip and sniffed. It sounded like she was holding back tears. "Can we go to your car, babe. We need to talk."

The sense of urgency in her voice alarmed Elijah. The first thought that entered his mind was that she wanted to break up with him. At this, his heart began to beat faster, and he started to overthink. Was it something he had said to her? Did she want to be with a girl now, instead of a boy? These thoughts bashed into each other like bumper cars in Elijah's mind as he and Esther walked to his car at the end of the street. They did not say a word to each other, and the tension made Elijah's armpits sweaty.

Elijah almost dropped his keys as he took them out of his jeans pockets and fumbled with the lock, his nerves getting the better of him. Finally he got inside and pushed open the passenger door to let Esther in. She entered the car, closed the door shut and let out a deep sigh. Elijah gulped. The moment of truth.

"I'm pregnant."

Her words were clear and intelligible. Yet Elijah did not immediately understand them. It was like someone had slapped him before he had even seen the hand coming to his face. He shook his head and gaped at Esther, feeling blindsided by this revelation. "How do you know?"

Esther reached into her pocket and took out a white stick, waving it in front of Elijah. She did not need to explain any further: he understood all too well. As the truth began to sink into his mind, Elijah suddenly felt very tense, and he grabbed the steering wheel to help compose himself. For a minute, they both stared at the street ahead, without saying a single word. It was Esther who eventually shattered the silence.

"I've been nauseous all week, and a few mornings I threw up." As she spoke, she was not looking at Elijah but staring at the car's windshield as it helped her focus her words. "It's never happened to me before, so Ayesha said I should take a pregnancy test. Looks like she was right for once."

Elijah began to feel a prickle of annoyance. "But how could this happen, babe? You were on the pill. It's supposed to stop you from getting pregnant, right?"

Perhaps it was the tone of his voice, but Esther swung towards Elijah, her face filled with anger as she narrowed her eyes at him. "Well, I must have accidentally taken it late or something. You sound like you're just blaming me, but I didn't impregnate myself, did I now?"

"Babe, I'm not blaming anyone," Elijah said. He reached out his left hand and rested it on Esther's lap. "I'm sorry if that's how I sounded, alright?"

Esther gave Elijah a weak smile and let out another deep sigh. "So what now then? Do we keep it?"

Elijah snatched his hand back and stared at Esther as if she had just asked him to jump from a plane without a parachute. "We can't keep it, Esther."

"Well ain't it wrong to take a life?" Esther said, turning her head away from Elijah. "You shag me, and now you want us to get rid of the baby you put in me. You wouldn't win Christian of the year, that's for sure, Prophet." There was a naked repulsion in her tone.

Although her words scratched Elijah's conscience, he did not let them cut him deep. "This is a difficult situation, I know, babe. But how can we have a baby now? We're only eighteen. I'm still studying, and you're working part-time at The Atlantic. And how could I introduce you to my parents as my pregnant girlfriend? My dad's a Nigerian pastor! And what about your parents, your dad would kill you."

Esther looked at Elijah now. He could see her eyes begin to water. "You want to introduce me to your parents?" Her voice held a tender shyness that he had not heard before.

Elijah leaned forward, took Esther's hands and enclosed them around his own. "I love you so much, and I want you to meet my parents very soon. But not in a situation like this. We're too young to have a baby. Do you really think our love is strong enough to withstand all of that responsibility?"

Without responding to his question, Esther dropped her gaze to her feet. Elijah wished he could read her mind like Professor Xavier from the X-Men comics he sometimes read. A minute passed before Esther looked up from the floor and directly at Elijah. Tears were running down her cheeks.

"Promise me that you'll come to the abortion clinic with me," Esther said, her lips wobbling as she spoke between sobs. "You have to be there with me, babe."

Elijah gently wiped away the tears trickling down her cheeks with the stub of his fingers. "I would never let you experience that alone, babe. I will never leave your side, I promise."

CHAPTER 30

July 2008

The second Sunday of each month seemed to bring every Nigerian in Lambeth to the Pentecostal Church of Christ. No bench or chair was empty. Attendees had to arrive at least an hour early, no easy feat for Nigerians, if they wanted to get a seat. Everyone came dressed wearing their best clothes. The women aimed to outdo each other with elaborate and colourful head wraps as if they were attending a Nigerian version of Ascot. The single men made sure they had sharp haircuts and expensive cuffs, to communicate their financial wealth and, consequently, their worthiness as husbands.

Even Elijah, who, like his late father, was not one to dress ostentatiously, had worn a dark purple robe for this Sunday that hung from his shoulders down to his shins.

With a microphone in his hand, Elijah walked to the podium. In front of him, he could see at least a hundred or more black faces of different shades and from different walks of life. They were beaming at him, waiting with anticipation for him to deliver his sermon. Most of his immediate family sat in the front row of benches, apart from Jairus, who was on the far right of the stage with the church band. Tiwa was seated beside his mother, radiant in a yellow *ankara* dress with a matching head wrap.

Seeing how lovely his wife looked this Sunday, Elijah felt pained, like someone had pressed a hot rod against his skin to brandish him as the adulterer he was. A false prophet.

But Elijah fought back these negative thoughts, even if they carried the truth, into a locked cage in his mind. Now was not the time to think about how he had betrayed his wife and whether their marriage could survive. He closed his eyes, whispering a silent prayer to God to forgive him for his sin and give him the confidence to preach the gospel this Sunday.

Elijah shouted into his microphone. "Praise the Lord!"

Booming through the hall came the enthusiastic response: "Hallelujah!"

"I have to say that everyone is looking beautiful this morning. It is going to be hard to decide who wins the prize for the best head wrap of 2008."

A mixture of light laughter and outright chortling erupted from the congregation.

"But in all seriousness, we must give thanks to God Almighty that we are here today," Elijah said, once they had quietened down. "For many people in this church today, it has been a difficult month. It certainly has been for me. The middle point of the year is always a time where we reflect on the choices we have made and assess how far we have come in accomplishing our goals. Are we serving God better? Are we managing our finances more smartly? Have we reduced our waistline, or are we still eating too much pounded yam?"

Another short round of laugher rippled through the congregation before fading away to silence.

"I believe that this is an important time to not only reflect but give praise to God. And I say praise because we can thank God for what He has already given us at this point. So, before I begin my sermon this morning, I would like to start with some testimonies. Please raise your hand if you would like to give a testimony and my good friend, Kunle, will pass you the microphone."

About a dozen hands shot into the air. Elijah watched as Kunle walked through the rows of benches, looking like he was going to give the microphone to whoever seemed the most eager. He stopped somewhere in the middle of the congregation and passed it to a woman whose face was hidden by an oversized head wrap in front of her.

"May I ask you to please stand up," Elijah said.

At that moment, Elijah's eyes widened in shock.

Esther smiled at him as she stood in the middle of the church and spoke into the microphone.

It had been a long time since Esther had this many eyes focused on her. "Praise the Lord," she said into the microphone, hoping the uncertainty she felt was not infecting her voice.

"Hallelujah!" came the loud response from the church faithful.

"My name is Esther Nubari. From my accent, you'd probably think I'm from America, and you'd be half right. I've been living in Chicago for almost eighteen years. But before moving there, I grew up in Brixton and used to attend this church as a young girl singing in the choir. I even recognise a few faces."

From the corner of her eye, Esther could see Elijah's younger brother Jairus look at her with raised eyebrows and an expression of shock. Like his older brother, Jairus had aged well since the last time she had seen him, but he still had none of Elijah's softer features.

"I've never given a testimonial in my life. To be honest, my Christian faith is tentative at best. But I grew up in a Christian household. The religious expectations of my parents, particularly my father, caused a massive rift between us. I felt I could never be the daughter they wanted me to be." Esther paused and briefly looked around the hall. The congregation stared back at her with expectant faces. She chose not to look at Elijah as she continued speaking. "When my parents decided to return to Ogoniland, where they're from, I travelled to Chicago instead. I didn't speak to them for eighteen years after that. I forced myself to block them out until it became normal to me. Then two months ago, I received a call from my mother in Nigeria. She told me my father had left Nigeria years ago to return to London and she wanted me to find him. Even though I hadn't spoken to my mum in so long, I chose to come back to London to find my father. And I did find him, praise the Lord."

The congregation clapped and whistled for at least a minute. The support of these people, most of whom Esther did not know, made her feel hopeful, and her heart soared with gratitude. Perhaps this was the pull of the church that had eluded her for so long. Maybe the point of the church was not only to praise God but to collectively share your love for God and the great things he had done in your life without judgement. After the congregation settled down, Esther continued to speak.

"When I found my father, he had been paralysed from the neck down because of a car accident. As I hugged him from his wheelchair, I just thought to myself, if my mother hadn't called me, and if I'd ignored her, I would never have found my father. I would never have been able to forgive him and forgive myself for what happened between us. But most importantly, I would never have been able to reunite my family. I testify today because God gave me the strength to forgive. A friend once told me that the most important thing the Bible teaches us is love and, this month, God has reminded me of how true that is. Thank you all for listening."

A round of applause erupted across the church hall. Esther gave the microphone back to the man who had passed it to her and sat on the bench. Her mind went to Ms Evans, and she realised that by sharing her testimony, she, too, had removed the chains from her feet. More than any point in her life, Esther felt like she was finally at peace with who she was.

The rest of the church service lasted for two hours. Elijah gave his sermon on 1 Chronicles 16:23-13, where he talked about the power of worshipping the Lord and receiving blessings when all focus is on Him. Preaching from the podium, it took every ounce of resistance and discipline not to allow his thoughts to shift to Esther or to look in her direction.

After the church service ended, and the band began to play music while everyone noisily shuffled out of the church, Elijah manoeuvred through the crowd of people. His palms were sweaty nerves as he tried to locate Esther. Still reeling from her surprise appearance at the church, Elijah scanned the hall, ignoring the brown faces nodding and smiling at him for a glimpse of Esther. He was terrified at the prospect of her speaking to any of his family members. It was not in Esther's character to say anything about her personal life, especially to Elijah's family. Still, the meaning of her appearance was unclear to him and this made him wary of her motives.

In the corner of the church, Elijah spotted Esther speaking to Tiwa, his mother and Mary, and he made his way towards them with urgent strides.

"There you are," Tiwa said with a strained smile as Elijah came into view. He hoped he appeared calm and collected and that the trepidation consuming him inside was not influencing his body language.

"Esther was just telling me how much you helped with finding her father," Tiwa said. Her voice sounded friendly, but Elijah detected the faintest hint of malice.

"I did the bare minimum. I just drove her around London to different places her father had lived. She did all the detective work, with God's help, of course," Elijah said with a sheepish tone. He could feel the eyes of both his mother and sister burrowing into him like lasers. Elijah realised this was the first time the two of them had heard anything about Elijah spending time with his ex-girlfriend.

"We thank God." Esther smiled warmly at Tiwa. "It's been a pleasure to meet you finally." Elijah watched as Esther turned her attention to his mother, and the warmth in Esther's face dropped almost imperceptibly. "Good to see you again, Auntie, and you as well, Mary. You both look well."

"Thank you, Esther," Elijah's mother said. She had a calculating look on her wrinkled face as if she were trying to understand the machinations behind Esther's visit to the church the same way Elijah was. "It's a surprise to see you again, especially at a church. But I'm happy to hear you have reconciled with your father. A good Christian man like that having suffered so much." As she said this, there was an undertone of satisfaction in her voice, as if she felt Esther's father deserved his fate. One of these days, Elijah would need to sit down with his mother and ask her about the exact nature of her past relationship with Kelechi Nubari. It seemed personal.

Esther smiled through gritted teeth and curtsied towards Elijah's mother. "Thank you, Auntie." There was a moment of silence between all four of them, and Elijah wished that this conversation between Esther and his family would end.

As if she had heard Elijah's thoughts, Esther spoke up. "Well, I need to go. There's somewhere I need to be this evening. Take care of yourselves. Goodbye." Esther then looked at Elijah directly. "Goodbye, Elijah."

With those parting words, Esther walked away, and Elijah watched her make her way towards the church's entrance and leave without looking back.

CHAPTER 31

December 1989

"Put your hands together and welcome Big Daddy Kane!"

The DJ, flanked by two massive sound speakers with a chest-sized turntable in front of him, bellowed the arrival of the American rapper onto the stage. Elijah felt like his eardrums were about to explode as Brixton Academy's main hall erupted with thundering screams and whistles from the hundreds of young people packed together in the stalls.

Beside Elijah, Esther was jumping on the spot as though her white Reebok Workout trainers had springs underneath them. With a smile on her face, she gently squeezed Elijah's right hand, and he caressed her palms in return. He looked at her, in awe of the energy and passion that seemed to explode from inside her.

Elijah knew that Esther was in her element right now. She was wearing denim shorts, a waist-length matching jacket and a pink tank top. With all the attitude and confidence of a seasoned performer, Esther sang the lyrics to 'Ain't No Half-Steppin''.

"Yo, there's no half-steppin'," Esther said, her lips twisting into a mischievous grin as she turned to Elijah. "Show me what you got, babe."

Elijah did not need convincing and grabbed Esther by the waist, pulling her body to his. With the flashing lights spinning around them, Elijah began moving his pelvis to the rhythm of Esther's hips. Then Elijah brought her face closer to his, felt her curly afro hair and kissed her deeply. He closed his eyes so he could focus on the texture of her lips and the intense desire, both spiritual and physical, that they had for each other.

As Esther pulled away, she had a glow in her eyes. Elijah could see she was in a genuinely happy place in her life. She refocused her attention on Big Daddy Kane, who was hopping across the stage, rapping into his microphone, but Elijah kept his gaze on Esther. He was so lucky to still have her, after all they'd been through in the last four years. Esther having the abortion had been tough for them both but that had not been the most challenging part of their relationship. His mind travelled back to the first time he had introduced Esther to his parents. To Elijah, this marked a turning point in their relationship that had tested their commitment to each other.

It had been around October in 1986. After Esther had the abortion, he decided to introduce Esther to his parents on his nineteenth birthday, when they would be throwing a party at the house. At this point, he had not told anyone in his family about their relationship. However, his younger sister had coerced the secret out of him when she had overheard him saying, "I love you," to Esther over the telephone. Elijah had managed to keep Mary's mouth sealed by buying her the newly released Atari. This gesture had not been kind to his wallet, but he did not want his parents to learn about his relationship from the big mouth of his twelve-year-old sister.

Although Elijah's parents did not know about his romantic relationship with Esther, they knew who she was: Esther had once been part of the church choir and her parents were long-time attendees. But by 1986, Esther had not been going to church consistently for the past three years. Knowing his parents, Elijah anticipated that the fact Esther had stopped attending church and, even worse, stopped being a practising Christian would be a significant problem.

Not only that, but Elijah was also aware that Esther behaved like a "fast Jamo girl." This was a derogatory phrase his mother used to refer to Jamaican girls in Brixton who partied and slept around. Esther was not like the Nigerian girls in Osogbo that Elijah had seen when he sometimes travelled there with his parents to see his younger brother. The young girls in Osogbo showed respect to their parents by prostrating when greeting uncles or aunties. Their dress sense was modest, almost too modest for Elijah's taste. They helped their mothers cook stew, regularly attended church and read their Bibles diligently.

Esther Nubari, on the other hand, liked to wear tight jeans around her curvy hips, loose tank tops and big, gold earrings. She did not read her Bible, had told Elijah several times that she did not like her parents all that much, had a fast mouth and, to top it all off, she had slept with boys and girls. If Elijah's mother knew these things about her son's girlfriend, Elijah would not be surprised if she collapsed on the floor in shock. From his father: a swift chastising.

So Elijah had been nervous about introducing Esther to his parents, even though he loved her for who she was. Fortunately, Esther had read his mood. A week before his birthday party, while they lay naked next to each other on Esther's bed, Esther had kissed Elijah's chest before saying, "You know I can always tell when you're worried." She rested her head on his shoulders. "All you've been thinking about is what your parents will think of me. I know I'm not the God-fearing, Bible-reading saint they would want for their superstar son."

Elijah sighed and kissed her forehead, feeling her kinky hair against his neck. "I love you for who you are. Even your big mouth, believe it or not." Esther elbowed him lightly. "I don't want you to feel uncomfortable. I want you to be yourself."

Esther took Elijah's fingers into her own and squeezed them. "I know, babe. And I know how much your parents' respect means to you. Don't worry, okay?"

On the day that Esther finally met Elijah's parents, in a house full of uncles, aunties, friends and relatives, she had made herself look completely different. At the time, it had utterly shocked Elijah. Esther had not worn tight jeans, a loose tank top or even her signature big, gold earrings. Instead, she had tied her afro into one bun and she wore a long, navy-blue skirt and a white shirt. Elijah's jaw had almost disconnected from his head when

Esther had shown his parents the proper Yoruba respect and prostrated when greeting them. From that point on, his parents had embraced Esther, and Elijah felt relieved.

But this façade would not last for long. As Elijah's parents became familiar with Esther, traces of who she really was started to spill out, like poking holes into a carton of milk. At first, it had started with harmless probing from his parents when Esther would come to visit Elijah. One day, while Elijah studied for an exam in the kitchen, Esther was assisting his mother with the cooking, doing her best to marinate meat for the stew, when Elijah's mother turned to her and asked, "What church do you go to now?" As soon as his mother asked the question, Elijah stopped reading his textbook on *Accounting Basics*. He looked at his mother then at Esther, feeling nervous.

"Oh, a church in North London," Esther answered with a confident smile to hide her lie.

"Why do you not follow your parents to our church anymore?" his mother said, glancing briefly at Elijah.

"I just prefer the church I go to."

Later that same day, when Esther had sat next to Elijah at the dining table to eat with his family, Elijah's father asked, "Are you going to go to university?"

"Yes, I plan to eventually. I'll probably study music," Esther said.

"Music is fun. But what future is there in that? It's not a serious profession," Elijah's father said, tearing into the tough meat on his plate with a fork as his eyes remained on Esther. "Do you have another more serious subject in mind?"

"Maybe I'll go into teaching." Esther used the same confident smile again to convince them, but it had not fooled Elijah. He caught the tremor in her voice.

Over a year, this type of relentless questioning from Elijah's parents continued, and Esther did her best to act like the perfect young Nigerian lady.

Then it all unravelled in June 1987.

Neither Elijah nor Esther had expected it. After church service one Sunday, Elijah's parents had reached out to hers. They had spoken briefly before but never engaged in proper conversation. When they did, Esther's father had only awful things to say about his daughter, exposing Esther's web of lies and deceit. He had told Elijah's parents that Esther was a broken young girl, who no longer attended church, showed disinterest in her Nigerian heritage, and had become carried away by Western culture.

Esther's father's words were like an earthquake – they desolated Elijah's relationship with his parents and his relationship with Esther, causing cracks and fissures in every foundation. His parents demanded that he stopped dating Esther immediately and Elijah, much to his surprise, outright refused.

"She only lied because you're both so judgemental!" Elijah had shouted to his parents one evening during a fierce argument in the living room. "We're Christians, and yet we think that gives us the right to point the finger!" He received a swift slap from his father for that one.

The situation only got worse. Not long afterwards, Elijah had travelled to New Cross to meet up with Esther after she had gone to tour the Goldsmith's University music department. They agreed to go to Fordham Park and talk. But their talk soon turned into a war of words, fought with accusations that were laced with anger and hurt.

"Your parents think they are better than everyone else!" Esther screeched. "Because they lead a church, they think they have a right to look down on me."

"You don't talk about my parents like that!" Elijah shouted back, with equal rage. "They're not perfect, but they're still my parents, Esther. For once, show some respect!"

After their clash, Elijah and Esther had not spoken to each other for two weeks. By then, Elijah missed her presence, her kisses and the sound of her laughter. And Esther must have felt the same because one afternoon she appeared outside the Polytechnic of North London campus where he had just finished a lecture. Upon seeing Elijah, she threw her arms around him and made him promise that they would never fight again.

They resumed their relationship much to the barely concealed disapproval of Elijah's parents. Esther would visit Elijah's house infrequently and never stayed for long. When she did come over, she would say, "Good evening, Uncle and Auntie, how are you?" to his parents, but all she had got in return was a mumbled, "We are fine," followed by the sucking of teeth. Elijah suspected it was only because he was doing well academically that his father had not ejected him from the family home for continuing to date Esther. It was an act of rebellion that most Nigerian parents would not tolerate.

Elijah shook off the memories, watching Esther throw her arms in the air as Big Daddy Kane broke into his next song. As Elijah looked at her, he knew he was reaching a pivotal moment in his life. He was still unsure if God approved of his relationship with Esther, no matter how many times he had prayed about it. There was a choice he would need to make, and Elijah was surprised to find that he wasn't sure which he wanted more – a life with Esther or to live up to his parents' expectations?

"Man, I don't know why I let you talk me into these things," Elijah said. He was currently in a squatting position, giving Esther a boost with his cupped hands as she attempted to climb over Brockwell Lido's brick walls. "This is crazy."

After they had left Brixton Academy at around 11 p.m., Elijah and Esther quickly realised how tipsy and horny they were as they walked towards Brixton Station. So Esther had somehow convinced Elijah that they should head to Brockwell Park and make love behind one of the bushes. Common sense taking a back seat to the alcohol in his bloodstream, Elijah had agreed. Once they reached Brockwell Park, instead of finding their usual spot, Esther decided it would be fun to sneak into Brockwell Lido.

With a push from Elijah, Esther managed to successfully climb the lido's walls, and she stretched her arms out triumphantly as she sat on top of the ledge. "I can see the pool from here," Esther said. "You've gotta get up here."

After some considerable difficulty and with Esther's help, Elijah hauled himself up beside her and, using the wall's ledge as support, they both jumped down into the pool enclosure.

It was around 11.30 p.m. and the night carried in a cold breeze that coalesced into thick patches of fog, hanging in the air like spectres. Elijah put on his gloves and buried his hands inside his green and black ski jacket as they walked by the pool. Moonlight shone across the water, giving it a glassy quality, and the reflected lights coming from the low and high-rise buildings in Herne Hill rippled on the surface. Elijah and Esther removed their trainers and socks then sat by the edge.

"That's cold," Elijah said as he dipped his feet into the pool. "If my mother saw me now, she would be shouting at me in Yoruba. *Olodo!*"

Esther laughed and kicked her feet gently in the water. "Why does Yoruba always sound so harsh?"

"Hey! At least I can speak and understand Yoruba. Do you even know what language Ogoni people speak?"

A sadness crossed Esther's face, and she turned away from Elijah to look at the pool. Usually, Esther would laugh whenever Elijah made fun of her because she couldn't speak her native language. But this evening, he sensed his remarks had pricked a sensitive nerve.

"Babe, I was only playing…"

"I know, it's not you," Esther said, staring at the pool with the look of someone who was contemplating something that had been troubling them for a long time. "I haven't told you yet, but my father and mother are going back to Nigeria next year. Back to Ogoniland. My father keeps talking about the struggle of his people and how he can no longer stay in London and just watch what's happening in Ogoni. He's always rambling about Nigeria."

"You're not going with them, are you?" Elijah said, a slight panic in his voice.

"No way, of course not," Esther said, with a tone that suggested to Elijah that he should have already known the answer to the question he had asked.

"Nigeria is not my home, babe. Yeah, I was born there, but I left Ogoniland when I was five years old, I barely remember anything about that place. It might as well be Russia to me. I don't speak any of the native languages, I don't have any friends over there, and I talk with a bloody British accent. How can my parents just expect me to start my life again? My father never considers me."

Elijah nodded his head, and although he sympathised with Esther, he could not exactly relate to her feelings. In some ways, Elijah did feel more British than he did Nigerian. His British accent, the types of music he listened to and the fact he was less conservative than his parents marked him as British. But unlike Esther, he had been to Nigeria several times in his life so far. His parents had encouraged him and his sister to speak Yoruba at home and eat Nigerian food. Elijah was not disconnected from his Nigerian heritage the same way Esther was.

"I've been thinking," Esther finally said after a few minutes of silence had passed, "that I'm going to move to Chicago next year."

"Chicago? Next year? But you just started your course at Goldsmiths."

Esther turned her head away from the pool and looked at Elijah directly, her eyes level with his own. "Yeah, I know, and I'm gonna quit the course. I don't want to be studying and dissecting music as if I'm in a science class. I want to play music and sing it in front of people. Seeing Big Daddy Kane perform tonight reminded me of why I want to be a performer. I don't want to waste my time studying anymore."

Elijah considered Esther's ambitions, his mind now thrown into a state of confusion as though someone had shaken him. If Esther travelled to Chicago, then where did that leave their relationship?

As if she had access to his internal thoughts, Esther slotted her fingers between Elijah's and smiled at him. "I was hoping, since you graduate next year, that you could come with me to Chicago. Leave Brixton together. Leave all this drama with our parents behind and start our lives somewhere else. I love you, babe, but it's your choice."

Your choice. If there was one thing that Elijah struggled with, it was making choices when the right decision was not clear to him. He had always been gifted academically, so it was a clear choice to go to university. His family were Christians, so it was a clear choice that he would also be a Christian and study the Bible. Have a baby at eighteen? It was a clear choice that he could not do that. But choosing to follow Esther to Chicago and start a life there? That was not such a clear choice, and was it one that was worth the risk? There was no time for more questions, she was looking at him, waiting for an answer. He decided it was.

Elijah smiled back at Esther and squeezed her fingers. "I love you too, Esther. We're both still young anyway, so let's start a life in Chicago and see how it goes. So long as I have you by my side, getting me into mischief. I promised I would never leave you, remember?" When Elijah stopped, he suddenly was not sure if it was the alcohol or his heart that had shaped his words.

Esther leaned towards Elijah and kissed him on the lips. It felt like the longest and deepest kiss she had ever given him. As their mouths slid against each other, Elijah could feel the air dip in temperature and the fog begin to dampen his jacket.

"We better get out of here before this fog gets any worse," Esther said, disconnecting her lips from Elijah's. She stood up from the edge of the pool. "We'll find our way back much easier if we can actually see where we're going."

CHAPTER 32

June 1990

The first thing Esther noticed about Elijah's younger brother was his dark complexion compared to Elijah, who was already quite a dark shade of brown. Although he resembled his older brother – they both had the same potato-shaped head – Jairus's facial features were rougher. As Esther laid down the plates and cutlery on the dining table in Elijah's home in Denmark Hill, she glanced at Jairus. He was sitting quietly beside his father, who was focused on watching ITN news. Without warning, Jairus's gaze pounced in her direction and he stared at her with a look of silent disapproval. His eyes reminded Esther of a snake's.

There was something about Jairus that gave him this sense of otherness. Even though he was dressed in a white Nike t-shirt and denim jeans, Esther could tell he grew up in Nigeria and not in London. He had a rigidness and formality to him that exceeded his age. It was hard to believe he was two years younger than Elijah. When Jairus had greeted her, she noticed that he spoke slowly and deliberately, with a heavy Nigerian accent colouring his vowels and syllables. Although she had just met Jairus, Esther already knew that they were not going to be best friends.

After helping Elijah's mother set the table, Esther sat down next to Elijah. He turned to look at her and smiled, squeezing her left hand underneath the table. The rest of the Oduwole family took their seats, and after a short prayer, Elijah's mother began to serve everyone a plate of jollof rice, fried plantain and meat.

It had come as a surprise to Esther when, a week ago, Elijah had invited her to his family's house for a big dinner to celebrate Jairus's arrival in England. Elijah's younger brother would now be permanently living with the family in London. But Elijah had not brought Esther to his house just to meet his brother. This evening, he would finally reveal to his family that, after his graduation, he would be moving to Chicago with Esther.

Esther was overjoyed and somewhat relieved to hear this. Since they had decided to take their lives in this direction, Esther and Elijah had done a lot of research into how they would travel to the USA and find work there. They had a full-proof plan, but for the last few months she had been fighting the fear that Elijah might change his mind.

"So Jairus, I know you've only been here a couple of days but how are you finding London so far?" Esther asked as she cut a fried plantain in half and put it in her mouth, relishing the salty but sweet taste.

"In Osogbo everything is brown and in London everything is grey," Jairus said, without looking at her. He took a sip of water from his glass and then glanced at Esther with narrowed eyes. "You are from Nigeria?"

"Yeah, my parents are from Ogoniland. I was born there and came to London when I was five."

"So you are from the Rivers State?"

"Erm, I think so, yes," Esther said in a sheepish tone.

"You think so?" Jairus said, his eyebrows raised. "How can you think so?"

Elijah's mother sucked her teeth loudly, and his father shook his head as he stuck a piece of plantain into his mouth. This was not the first time that Esther had been subject to indirect belittling and insults from Elijah's family, mainly from his mother. Instead of telling Esther to her face that she did not approve of her relationship with her eldest son, Elijah's mother would make faces or suck her teeth whenever Esther was in her vicinity. Elijah's father was less overt in his displeasure. Instead, he simply gave her the type of look you would give a poor person you passed on the street every day on your way to work.

Before Esther could open her mouth and respond to Jairus's jibe with a rude retort of her own – something about the shape of his head – Elijah interjected.

"Everyone. I have an announcement to make this evening," Elijah announced, with a touch of theatricality.

Mary, who was sitting next to him, grinned widely. "You're going to get married to Esther, aren't you?"

"What? No, shut up," Elijah said, giving Mary an annoyed sidelong glance.

"Daddy, Elijah told me to shut up."

"Yes, because you did not let your big brother finish," Elijah's father said, glaring at his daughter. "Now me, your father, is telling you to also shut up and you better shut up, O."

Mary folded her arms and sulked as Elijah's father gestured for him to go on. "Continue, son," he said. "What is your announcement?

Elijah looked at Esther, and she smiled encouragingly at him. With a deep breath, Elijah faced his parents. "Esther and I have decided that we are moving to Chicago at the end of the month after I graduate."

All at once, Mary gasped, Jairus jerked his head back in shock, Elijah's father dropped his fork on his plate and his mother shrieked.

"Ah-ah now, Elijah!" Elijah's mother said with a high-pitched voice. "Please tell me you are joking, O. What are you thinking?"

"Mum, listen—"

But Elijah's mother had gone into a state of hysteria, and Esther watched her with shock as she threw her arms in the air. "My son wants to leave his family for America!" She pointed her finger at Esther as if it were a loaded gun. "You have let this wayward girl take over your brain. Have you lost your sense? Tell me, my son, have you?"

"Dinah, calm down," Elijah's father said, putting a hand on his wife's shoulder. Esther was surprised at how measured his tone was. He turned his attention to Elijah, and Esther could tell his focus was on his son and no one else at that moment. Knowing that opening her mouth would only make things worse, Esther sealed her lips and looked down at her plate. She could feel the heated glare coming from Elijah's mother.

"Elijah, this is a surprise to your family," Elijah's father said. "Have you thought this through?"

Esther heard Elijah gulp down some saliva before he responded.

"Yes, I have. I mean, we have, Dad," Elijah said as he took Esther's hands in his and smiled at her again. "In January, we both visited the US Embassy and took out visa applications. It took us three days to fill them out because they're so complicated. We didn't know if they would grant it to us because it's hard to get a visa to work in America but, God being so good, we got them. I should have told you earlier and I apologise for that, Mum and Dad."

The whole room became deathly silent. Elijah's mother was shaking her head, Jairus' eyes flicked from Esther's to Elijah's with a nonplussed expression on his face and Mary was looking at Elijah, wide-eyed. It was only Elijah's father who seemed unfazed, but Esther could tell he was quietly contemplating this revelation.

"Are you sure this is what you want?" Elijah's father said, emphasising each word, as if he wanted to make sure Elijah understood the magnitude of this decision.

"We love each other. And we both feel this is the best for both of our lives," Elijah said, and for just a moment, Esther thought she detected the faintest hint of uncertainty in his voice.

It was eight in the evening by the time Esther left the house, and the hopeful mood that Elijah had carried with him all day seemed to leave with her. Elijah sat on the couch in the living room beside his brother, while Mary retreated to her room upstairs to do some homework. Elijah's mother was taking the plates from the dining table and adding them to the stack balanced on her raised forearm, muttering angrily to herself and shaking her head.

Elijah had seen his mother annoyed before, but he could not remember the last time she had looked so upset. Seconds after Esther's departure, his mother had torn off all her self-restraint and hurled a tirade of disapproval at Elijah. His father had to calm her down while Elijah just sat in his chair at the dining table, feeling mystified and hurt. The last thing he had wanted was to bring his mother this much pain.

Fifteen minutes later, he was sitting on the long couch in the living room beside Jairus. In front of them, their father lay back in the reclining leather chair that he'd claimed as his. A king's throne. He stroked his rough beard, eyes pointed at the television screen. But Elijah had seen this ruminative look on his father's face many times before. He was not really watching television but was meditating on the developments of the evening. After several minutes of silence, his father finally spoke.

"You know, I was a little bit older than you when I came to London," his father said in his measured tone. "I came to live with my younger brother, your late uncle, may his soul rest in perfect peace. Our parents thought we were too young and begged us to stay in Nigeria, but we had our hearts set on England. And in hindsight, although I am doing well now in this country, it was one of the most difficult experiences of my life. Do you want to know why I am telling you this, Elijah?"

It was a rhetorical question, but Elijah nodded his head anyway.

"Because you remind me so much of my brother, your uncle Samuel," Elijah's father said. "He passed away when you were still an infant. He was a young man when he died. Gone before his time. And let me tell you, he had so much potential, my son. He would have been a great pastor, just like I see in you."

"You see me as a great pastor one day?" Elijah said, sitting upright and reclining his head back in shock. His father had never said this to him before.

"Yes, I do. I have watched you evangelise at church, and your knowledge of the gospel is better than my own when I was your age. You are academically brilliant, and you have made me a proud father, Elijah. It is you, my first son, that I would like to lead the church I have built when I am too old, with your younger brother by your side. Do you understand?"

"I understand, Dad," Elijah said, feeling his father's words wash over him like a cool shower. Jairus shuffled beside him, as if the cushions were making him uncomfortable.

Not till this moment had Elijah considered the prospect that he might one day lead his family's church as the senior pastor. Yet when his father said this to him now, almost as if it were a prophecy, it made complete sense to Elijah.

"You are a young man, and I can see with my own eyes that Esther is a very beautiful girl," Elijah's father said. His eyes were now focused on Elijah, using them to help drill the message into his son. "I was a young man once as well, and I know how a beautiful woman can lead a man astray. I don't want it to happen to you. I am no fool, my son, I know you are sleeping with her. Do not try to deny it."

This remark caught Elijah off guard, and he felt the embarrassment slap him right in the face. If he had white skin, he would have been as red as a Routemaster bus.

"But whatever you have been doing with her is neither here nor there. You can always repent for your sins, but what you cannot do is take back the choices you make, Elijah. If you travel to Chicago with her, I feel you will waste your potential. She may be pretty, but she is not a Christian, and she is lost, my son. I see it in her. You are unequally yoked with an unbeliever that could destroy your future. And you have too much potential. It would be a shame if you squandered it because of her."

Elijah sighed heavily and sank back into the sofa. He looked at a framed picture of himself hanging on the wall; he was wearing his school uniform, twelve years old and only in his first year at Dick Sheppard. A part of him longed to be at that age again when life consisted of easy choices. Do your homework or be punished? Watch *Transformers* or *G.I. Joe*? *Transformers*, obviously. Be like most of the black boys at school who fought at Brockwell Park or concentrate on your studies? These were clear and easy choices for Elijah. Now that he was entering adulthood, life was presenting him with much harder decisions.

After hearing his father's words this evening, Elijah was no longer sure that going to Chicago with Esther was the best choice. He loved Esther, but was love enough? He would need to start over in Chicago. Even if it would be a new adventure, in London, everything was already set for him: his father had just promised him the church. What higher calling was there than being in ministry?

Elijah sat up straight and smiled at his father. "Thank you, Dad, for your advice and wisdom. I see now that maybe I was about to make the wrong choice."

"It's okay. You are young, and this is an important moment in your life." Elijah's father stood up from his leather chair, and Elijah got to his feet too. Jairus watched from the couch as they embraced each other.

Still locked in a tight embrace with his father, Elijah heard him speak into his ear. "Seek God for guidance, and he will show you the right path to take. Trust in Him always, my son."

CHAPTER 33

July 2008

Why isn't she picking up her phone? As Elijah drove through Coldharbour Lane, taking the quickest route to Pullman Court, his mind kept replaying the events of the morning's church service.

It was not the fact that Esther had turned up that aggravated him. It was that she had turned up unannounced. No phone call or text message to let him know she would be coming to his church on the busiest Sunday of the month. Knowing full well what was going on between them and with the understanding that Elijah's family attended the church, Esther's actions had been insensitive and even degrading. He was not excusing himself; he knew very well that he was equally responsible for their affair, but Esther had no right parading it in his face like that. Not in front of his wife.

As if she was deliberately trying to make a fool of him further, Esther was not even answering her phone. Elijah had called her almost twenty times, and though it had been ringing before cutting off, now his calls were going straight to her voicemail. Desperate and angry, Elijah had sent her dozens of texts, each one shorter and blunter than the last, but still there was no response.

Elijah parked his BMW outside Pullman Court's white apartment blocks. After the church's board meeting had finished, Elijah had lied to Tiwa, saying that he had to rush to his office in Canary Wharf as his boss needed a report on the company's taxes first thing in the morning. Tiwa had not questioned him but had given him a mournful look. Perhaps his wife understood that they were now far apart and there was a possibility that they could no longer reach each other again.

With his BlackBerry pressed to his right ear, Elijah kept trying to reach Esther as he walked through the lush communal courtyard towards Ayesha's flat. "What's going on, Esther?" Elijah muttered to himself as he walked up the steps and onto the second floor of the apartment block. Unable to get through to her again, Elijah stuffed his phone into trousers with more force than necessary. When he reached the front door of the flat, Elijah rang the doorbell and waited. Right now, anger tainted his feelings towards Esther, and although he tried to calm himself by controlling his breathing, he was not sure what words would come from his mouth when Esther opened the door.

What he did not expect was for Ayesha to open the door. Elijah almost stumbled back in shock, not only at the surprise of seeing Ayesha, whom he had not seen or spoken to in years, but the waxiness of her skin. It was not until he regained his composure that he realised Ayesha had covered her face with a light-brown face mask. She was wearing a fluffy, white bathrobe with a towel wrapped around her head, and Elijah was astounded that she would answer the door in such a state until he quickly remembered Ayesha's personality. Evidently, it had not changed much since their formative years.

"Fuck off, is that you, Elijah?" Ayesha said with a thick south London accent. "Oh my God, Esther did not mention how fine you look these days."

"It's nice to see you again, Ayesha," Elijah said, already feeling his impatience rising. It was not that Elijah disliked Ayesha, but he had always found her difficult to tolerate for more than a minute or two. He could never fathom how Esther was able to put up with Ayesha's personality for so long.

Ayesha put one hand on her hip. "You do know I came back this morning, right?"

"What? Oh yes," Elijah said, suddenly recalling that Esther had mentioned on Saturday evening that Ayesha would be back from her trip to Jamaica today. "I've been trying to call her, but she's not picking up her phone. Is she inside?"

"Elijah, babe, she's flying back this evening."

"What!?" Elijah said, the shock hitting him so squarely in the chest that he almost felt winded. "No, she told me her flight back to Chicago was on Friday."

Ayesha shook her head, and for a moment, Elijah could have sworn she had looked at him with pitiful eyes, like she was a teenage girl telling him that her best friend does not date losers. "She changed her flight yesterday evening, babe."

Elijah put his right hand on his forehead and closed his eyes. Why would she change her flight and not tell him but then show up at his church? The finality in her tone when she had said goodbye to him suddenly made sense, and he felt a sinking feeling in his stomach.

"Her flight is at 7 p.m.," Ayesha said as if she had sensed Elijah's bitter disappointment. "She left in a taxi to Heathrow Airport about thirty minutes ago so you might be able to catch her still."

For a split second, Elijah thought he might hug Ayesha, until he remembered that she was in a bathrobe and wearing a face mask. "Thank you, Ayesha." He smiled at her and turned, hurrying towards the stairs. Just as Elijah was about to make his way down, Ayesha called his name.

"Hey, Elijah."

Elijah turned back and looked at her. She had an uneasy expression on her face, as if she were not sure if she should speak. "Obviously, this ain't none of my business really, but Esther told me everything about you and her, so it kinda is, and you also did have sex in my flat so..."

"Ayesha, please get to the point," Elijah snapped, having exhausted all the patience he had with her.

"You've missed the window with her, babe. Do the right thing and let her go. You did it before."

Elijah considered Ayesha. Her face mask had started to harden on her skin.

"It was nice seeing you again, Ayesha," Elijah said, and he walked down the steps.

As Elijah dashed through the courtyard back to his BMW, he checked his watch. It was coming to 5.15 p.m., and it would take him at least 45 minutes to get from Brixton to Heathrow Airport if traffic were light on the M4.

Once Elijah was inside his car, he started the engine but did not drive onto the main road immediately. Instead, he looked at his eyes in the rear-view mirror. Was he going to drive to Heathrow Airport? *Do the right thing and let her go.* Ayesha's last words echoed in his mind. Elijah removed the handbrake, pressed his foot on the accelerator and turned his BMW onto Brixton Hill Road.

Consumed with the fear that he might not make it in time before Esther's flight, the logical and objective part of Elijah's brain had momentarily switched off. As a result, he had forgotten just how difficult it was to find a parking space in Heathrow Airport. There was a car park for each terminal and an endless number of cars but not nearly enough available parking spaces. It took Elijah almost twenty infuriating minutes to find a space as he drove around rows of parked vehicles, searching for a vacant spot like a lurking predator waiting for its prey to emerge.

Once Elijah managed to find a free parking space, he wasted no time making his way to an information desk where rows and rows of outbound and inbound flights flashed across the electronic display board. He checked his watch. It was nearing 6.50 p.m.; Esther would have already checked-in and would soon start heading to the security gate. Once she did, that was it. Elijah scanned the board, waiting for Esther's flight to come up. Then he saw it:

Heathrow Airport (LHR) - Terminal 5 - O'Hare International Airport (ORD) - Terminal 1
DEP: 20:00

Elijah jumped in an elevator to Terminal 5. When the doors opened, he stepped out into the terminal, along with five other people who were dragging wheelie suitcases, and for a few seconds, he felt like he had walked into the interior of a spaceship. Terminal 5 had only opened three months ago, to much fanfare, and still had a gloss to it.

All around him, Elijah could see swarms of people: families chattering away as they held their luggage, their over-excited kids running around them, airport staff giving directions to holidaymakers and people in suits, clearly travelling for business. He stepped back to avoid a man dragging his suitcase behind him as his bushy dog raced in front, attached to a lead. Among all this commotion, he saw no sign of Esther.

Elijah checked his watch once more. It was 7 p.m., and Esther would be making her way to the departure gate. He yanked his phone out of his pocket in desperation: no signal. He was too late.

Just as Elijah was about to accept the painfully disappointing truth that there was nothing more he could do; he caught a familiar flash of red out of the corner of his eye.

Esther was walking towards the security gate, headphones in her ears and wearing a denim jacket, black jeans, boots, and her signature red bandanna, with her wheelie suitcase in tow.

Without a second thought, Elijah hurried towards her, calling her name.

CHAPTER 34

July 2008

Esther took her American passport from the agent at the check-in gate after it had been scanned and verified. Dragging her suitcase and listening to Bobby Caldwell's 'What You Won't Do for Love', she smiled at the thought of returning to Chicago and then calling her mother in Nigeria to tell her that she had found her father in London.

At some point this year, Esther would come back to London and take her father to Ogoniland to be reunited with her mother. And she would be with them. A once broken family now reconciled. Perhaps she would spend a few months in Nigeria and finally learn about her heritage and her culture, with her mother and father there to teach her.

Just as Esther reached the security gate, she swore she heard Elijah's voice calling her name over the sound of Bobby Caldwell's silky vocals. For a moment, she thought she imagined it.

"Esther, wait."

Esther turned around and widened her eyes in surprise as she saw Elijah hurrying towards her, looking like a dishevelled man running for the last train that was about to depart. She removed her headphones.

Elijah came to a halt in front of her, panting. "What are you doing?" he said in between gasps of air as he caught his breath. His tone of voice was a combination of sharp annoyance and grateful relief.

"I'm going back to Chicago, Elijah," Esther replied, making sure she sounded as matter of fact and distant as possible. She had made up her mind, and she was not going to change it. "What are you doing here? How did you even know I was at the airport?"

"You weren't answering your phone or your messages, so I went to Ayesha's flat to see if you were there. She told me you changed your flight to Chicago from next Friday to today…I drove here to get an explanation of why you came to the church today." All the time he had been talking, Elijah's gaze had fixed on Esther's eyes as if the meaning behind her actions was buried in them. "Why are you behaving like this?"

"I didn't want to speak to you when you were calling and texting me. I was going to contact you when I landed in Chicago because I felt it was better that way. And what do you mean by '*behaving like this*'?" Esther said, hands on her hips now. "How do you expect me to *behave*, Elijah?"

"I don't know. Well first, maybe by not coming to my church to embarrass me."

"Elijah, you know me. Do you think I would come to your church to embarrass you? I came to give my testimony, as you saw, and to look into your wife's eyes, so I knew I was doing the right thing."

"The right thing?" Elijah's face scrunched with the painful realisation of what she meant.

"Yes, the right thing. Which is to continue with my own life and let you continue with yours. Separately."

"Don't you love me, then?" His words rang with a desperation that Esther found sad rather than romantic.

"Maybe I love you, Elijah," Esther said, keeping her voice firm because she knew Elijah needed to hear this. It was her turn to help him now. "But it doesn't matter. Not anymore. There was a moment when we could have had a life together. But it's too late for that. Choices were made, remember? Now we'd only be kidding ourselves. Are you going to leave your wife, your position in the church, your job, for me? Would you irresponsibly throw that all away for a love that might not be strong enough to withstand it?"

Not for the first time, Elijah looked lost. He shied away from her eyes, staring towards the terminal's curved ceiling. Elijah shook his head. "I don't know," he finally said, in a hushed voice.

"Let me ask you this then. Your wife, do you still love her?"

At this, Elijah jerked his head towards her and seemed taken aback. Esther could tell it was a question that Elijah had been fighting with internally.

After a few seconds of silence, Elijah said, "To be honest, I'm not sure."

Esther stepped forward so that she was close to Elijah's face. She closed her hands around his. "Look at your wife, Elijah. I mean really look at her. She's beautiful, and I think that maybe you still do love her. But you need to be honest with her about everything. You can't run away from the difficulties in your marriage and your life, and I won't allow myself to be your false remedy. I know you love to leave things in God's hands, but you have a responsibility as well. I mean, God can't help you get off your ass if you're not willing to get off your ass, right? I'm sure that's in the Bible somewhere."

"Not in those exact words, but yes, I understand what you're saying," Elijah said with a weak chuckle.

"Don't leave it to the last minute, like you did with me. Don't break that promise you made to your wife when you married her. Speak to her, Elijah. Speak to her before it's too late."

For a few minutes, they stood in silence, their hands still interlocked. Esther knew this was the last time they would be together, and she felt Elijah understood it too.

Elijah breathed in and exhaled, letting out a long sigh. He squeezed Esther's hand. "If I had a time machine, I would go back and get on that plane eighteen years ago. I would have kept that promise I once made to you."

"I know you would," Esther said with a regretful sigh of her own. "But we don't have a DeLorean."

They both laughed at this shared joke, enjoying the last moment of each other's presence and the history that would connect them forever.

Elijah gulped, and his voice sounded dry. "So this is it, then?"

Esther leaned in and kissed Elijah lightly on the cheek. When she reclined her head back, she looked directly into Elijah's eyes. "Goodbye, Prophet."

Elijah nodded his head, and his mouth formed into a pained smile – one of sadness but also of gratitude. "Goodbye, Esther Nubari."

With nothing more to be said to each other, Esther let go of Elijah's hand. She grabbed the extended handle of her suitcase and walked towards the security gate. Before disappearing through the barrier, she turned back to look at Elijah one last time. He was standing with his hands in his trouser pockets, a pensive look on his face.

Knowing Elijah would be alright, Esther gave him a final encouraging wave. She then raised her headphones to her ears and walked through the gate, smiling to herself as she pondered the future ahead of her.

CHAPTER 35

July 2008

The sky was streaked with flaming orange and deep purple as the afternoon began its descent and evening emerged to end the day. After an hour of driving back from Heathrow Airport, Elijah was now in Denmark Hill, making his way to his mother's house for family dinner.

Elijah had watched Esther walk through the departure gate until he could no longer see her, then returned to his BMW and cried in the driver's seat. Stinging, blinding tears of shame and regret. Sitting inside his expensive car, he had opened the door to his soul. What he discovered behind the door made him weep. The only way to redeem himself was to clean out the grime and soot in his spirit.

So for almost thirty minutes, Elijah had prayed to God. For the first time in a long time, Elijah did not pray to Him with deliberate falseness to his words. No, he prayed to God with the door to his rotten heart wide open and with raw and unflinching truth. *How do I save my marriage? Am I a worthy pastor?* These were the questions he had asked Him. And God had responded as a voice invited into his head, telling him what he must do. At first, Elijah was afraid because the actions God had told him to take would be painful, but he knew in his heart that they were necessary.

Now, driving through the street in Denmark Hill, Elijah quickly glanced at his Blackberry, resting on the passenger seat. The text his wife had sent him a few minutes ago was still open. Tiwa had said that she had a lot of schoolwork to mark tonight, so she would not be able to attend dinner. Although he had not texted her back yet, Elijah intended to tell Tiwa that he was heading to his mother's house but would not be staying for long. As per God's instructions, there were some announcements he needed to make to his family first.

Just a few minutes after 9 p.m., Elijah arrived at this mother's house. He parked his BMW outside Ruskin Park and prayed to God one final time, asking him to give him the strength to face his family, before he exited his car. As he walked down the quiet street towards his mother's house, Elijah had the overwhelming feeling that he was about to take a difficult maths test and was unsure of what the outcome would be, even though he knew the equations.

Mary answered the door after Elijah rang the bell.

"Well, where have you been, sir?" Mary said with a cheeky smile on her face. "It's not like you to follow African time, especially when it comes to food."

Elijah forced himself to chuckle and patted his sister's shoulder as he stepped into the hallway. "I had to take care of something."

When Elijah entered the living room with Mary by his side, he was met with the familiar scene of his family members eating and socialising, and his stomach twisted. Jairus sat next to Kunle with a bottle of Supermalt in his hand, a can of Guinness in Kunle's. Both were engaged in an animated discussion. His mother had taken her position as the matriarch, sitting at the end of the dining table where she could oversee the family.

"Elijah," his mother said in her sharp Nigerian accent as she lit up at the sight of her eldest son. "How are you?"

"I'm fine, Mother," Elijah said. Mary had gone to take her seat next to Kunle, but Elijah hovered by the living room door. "Sorry for being late, I had to take care of something."

"You look tired, my son. Come. Sit down and eat," Elijah's mother said, waving her hand across the pots filled with jollof rice, pounded yam, *egusi* soup, and fried meat. "It is a shame Tiwa cannot join us, but please take some food for her when you leave."

Any other evening, Elijah's mother would not even have to ask Elijah to sit down and eat. But this was not any other evening. Elijah could feel everyone's eyes fall on him as he remained standing in front of them. Jairus was already giving him a questioning look.

"I have something to say that will be very difficult for you all to hear…I've been having an affair." The words flew out from Elijah's mouth like a gust of wind.

A range of incredulous and shocked expressions struck the faces of his family members. Kunle and Mary's jaws hung, their eyes bulging. Even Jairus looked taken aback, staring at Elijah as if he had just announced that he had committed murder.

His mother scrunched her face in confusion, shaking her head as though she had imagined the words that came from Elijah's mouth. "An affair? What are you talking about?" Elijah could hear the simmering pain in his mother's voice.

"It's been going on for almost a month." Elijah was not even thinking as he spoke; his mouth moved of its own accord.

A deathly quiet descended on the room as Elijah's confession sunk into everyone's minds and hearts. Looking at the stunned expressions of his family, Elijah knew they were forming their judgement on him, trying to make sense of how Elijah, the golden child of the Oduwole family, could commit such an act. It was Jairus's sharp voice that slashed the thick silence first.

"It is with Esther, isn't it?" he said, watching Elijah's face with narrowed eyes. "The woman who gave a testimony at our church today about finding her missing father? Your ex-girlfriend from Brixton."

"No! Esther!?" Mary gasped, equally surprised and appalled.

Elijah cast his eyes down, no longer able to face his sister or anyone else in the room. "Yes, it was with Esther," he said, his words struggling out of his mouth.

"Shame on you. How could you do that to Tiwa?" Jairus's tone swam with damnation. "I warned you when I saw the two of you together. Shame on you, brother."

When God had told Elijah to confess his extramarital affair to his family, Elijah had known it would be difficult. Still, the judgement and disappointment he was receiving from them felt like lashes against his pride. God was punishing him, and he must accept it.

Elijah's mother had closed her eyes, and Elijah knew she was thinking deeply. Over the years, he had noticed that his mother, having gained a deeper maturity that comes to women in their later years, had become less reactionary to harmful or unwanted events in her life. When she opened her eyes, she gazed at Elijah with a calm, unflinching look, just like Elijah's father used to.

"There is an African proverb that says: 'to get lost is to learn the way,'" his mother said, her tone even. "My eldest son, you have no doubt lost your way, but by confessing your affair today, you have also learned your lesson. Even the prophet Moses faced challenges in the desert." His mother closed her eyes again in thought. Everyone in the room remained silent, anticipating her next words. She opened her eyes once more.

"This confession does not need to leave these four walls, my eldest son. Do you understand? We do not need the judgement from outsiders. We do not need people questioning your position as senior pastor of the church or insulting our family name. I wish you had kept this to yourself, Elijah. You must not tell Tiwa, and everyone else present should keep this quiet. Her reaction could tear apart the family and our credibility in the church and the community. Pray for God's forgiveness and repent, my eldest son. That is enough."

"No, Mother, I won't do that," Elijah said, looking directly into his mother's eyes, appalled by her suggestion. "Firstly, I cannot ask everyone in this room to keep such a secret from Tiwa. She must know what I've done, otherwise how can I truly receive God's forgiveness? And secondly, I'm quitting my position in the church as the senior pastor."

Everyone in the room gasped. Jairus cocked his head back in shock, staring at Elijah with his mouth slightly open.

"Elijah, that's a very drastic step to take," Kunle said. "You're going to give up your position so soon after your father passing away?"

"I prayed to God before I made this decision." Elijah looked at Kunle and then back at his mother. "And this is the only way I can set my path straight and concentrate on saving my marriage. I will always serve God but not from the position of a senior pastor. That role I now give to you, Jairus."

For the first time in Elijah's recent memory, Jairus appeared dumbstruck, like someone who had finally been given the keys to a house they had coveted for so long, only to realise the house was much bigger than expected.

"It is no secret to any of us that you feel you can lead the church better than I can, so I'm giving you a chance. Now I have to go." Elijah felt drained from pouring the contents of his heart out for his family to see and judge. His body ached as though it just had been through an intense workout.

"Elijah, O. My son, please wait," Elijah's mother said, desperation in her voice.

Although Elijah heard his mother, he walked out of the living room. He opened the front door of the house and stepped into the dimly lit street, his thoughts on Tiwa and what would become of his marriage when he told her of his betrayal.

Elijah closed the door of his house behind him. He could see the light was on in the living room, so he knew Tiwa was sitting there, no doubt marking her school papers.

Suddenly, Elijah could not move. He felt like his legs were frozen. Throughout the drive home, he had been telling himself that God was with him and this was the best way to move forward, the first difficult step in hopefully repairing his marriage. But the daunting reality of finally admitting to an affair with Esther was all too real. A sense of dread overwhelmed him. How could he look Tiwa in the eyes and tell her he had slept with another woman, lied to her face and broken their marriage vows? Not only that, but Elijah was still uncertain if he genuinely loved her.

"Elijah?" Tiwa's voice came from the living room.

"Yes, it's me. I'm just hanging my coat up."

Elijah removed his long coat and hung it on the rack attached to the wall. With a sigh, his heart beating noticeably faster, he strolled into the living room with considerable will power.

When Tiwa looked up from her scattered exam papers on the dining table to smile at him, Elijah almost felt like he was looking at her for the first time. It was as if he had been seeing her through a veil for so long and was only now lifting it as he had on their wedding day. Everything about her seemed sharper and more beautiful. Her braided brown hair falling down the sides of her face. Her full, heart-shaped lips. Her light-brown skin, the warm colour of an African desert. He remembered the care she had for other people, the kindness she showed everyone, which brightened her surroundings as if she were a radiant star. Admiring his wife, Elijah suddenly knew there was no doubt in his mind as to whether he loved her.

Elijah inhaled a deep breath, mentally steeling himself for the challenging conversation they were about to have. As he took a step towards the dining table to sit next to her, he immediately stopped.

Tiwa had begun to sob. Her face was buried in her hands and her whole body shook uncontrollably.

At this point, Elijah could feel his hands trembling. Did Tiwa already know about the affair? Who had told her? If anyone had rung her this evening and spoken to her, it would have been Jairus. A swell of rage rose in Elijah, but he quickly managed to stifle it. Now was not the time to give in to anger.

"Tiwa, let me sit down and explain," Elijah said, unconsciously reaching his left hand out to her as he took another step towards the dining table. "I don't know who told you—"

Tiwa cut Elijah off before he could finish his sentence.

"Elijah," she said in a voice that carried a depth of joy Elijah had not expected. Tiwa removed her hands from her face and beamed at him, tears now running down her cheeks. It had been a long time since he had seen so much life in her expression.

"God is so good."

Elijah stared at her blankly and uselessly said, "What?"

"Elijah, I'm pregnant."

The story continues in

The Wife of a Prophet
COMING SOON

Sign up for updates at www.lekeapenawriting.com

ACKNOWLEDGEMENTS

As my first attempt to write a half-decent novel that someone might read, writing *A Prophet who loved Her* has been a rewarding experience. That isn't to say it wasn't challenging. After all, half the book is set in London during the 80s. I was not even an idea in my father's head during this period. Therefore, this novel would never have seen the light of day without the following people.

Firstly, my younger sister, Tinuke. Her feedback was invaluable, especially when it came to writing Esther. Having lived as a man all my life, I was not exactly in the best position to be writing about Esther: a young black woman struggling with her sexual identity and her place in the world as a woman of colour. My sister provided me with a lot of vital feedback to ensure that Esther felt like an authentic, real and layered black heroine.

Trying to capture the experience of living as a black Briton during the 1980s was incredibly challenging but truly fulfilling exercise. I would like to thank my mother and my father for their encouragement but also for sharing small anecdotes about their experience living in London during the 80s, some of which inspired a few scenes in this novel. I would also like to extend my gratitude to Delroy Headman. He attended Dick Sheppard in the mid-80s and provided some valuable insight into how school life was back then.

With no traditional publisher backing me, I had to pay for the editing, the jacket design, marketing and printing costs of this book. Therefore, it's only right I thank my younger brother, Seun, for not chasing me on some of the money he has borrowed me. If you're reading this, I promise I'll pay you back. Perhaps with interest but don't hold me to that last part.

I would like to thank my editor, Lottie Clemens. This was my first time working with an editor and she really tightened the prose. With her sharp eye and her constructive criticism, she made me understand why writers should never edit their own work. Thank you for your honest feedback and spotting those plot inconsistencies. You were worth every penny.

Lastly, I would like to thank all my English teachers over the years who always praised my writing. If not for you, I might never have bothered to keep writing as I foolishly thought it was too geeky and not something that would impress the ladies. But through writing, I have learnt to better understand the world around me and myself. I will never stop creating stories.

Lightning Source UK Ltd.
Milton Keynes UK
UKHW010458300820
368903UK00009B/3